AUTUMN

DAVID MOODY

INFECTED BOOKS
www.infectedbooks.co.uk

AUTUMN

Published by INFECTED BOOKS
www.infectedbooks.co.uk

This edition published 2005
Copyright David Moody 2002

A catalogue record for the paperback edition of
this book is available from the British Library

Paperback ISBN 0-9550051-0-8

2-L1-0505-1

Prologue

Billions died in less than twenty-four hours.
William Price was one of the first.

Price had been out of bed for less than ten minutes when it began. He had been standing in the kitchen when he'd felt the first pains. By the time he'd reached his wife in the living room he was almost dead.

The virus caused the lining of his throat to dry and then to swell at a remarkable rate. Less than forty seconds after initial infection the swelling had blocked his windpipe. As he fought for air the swellings began to split and bleed. He began to choke on the blood running down the inside of his trachea.

Price's wife tried to help him, but all she could do was catch him when he fell to the ground. For a fraction of a second she was aware of his body beginning to spasm but by that point she had also been infected. By that point the volume of oxygen reaching her lungs had reduced to less than ten per cent of her normal oxygen requirement.

Less than four minutes after Price's initial infection he was dead. Thirty seconds later and his wife was dead too. A further minute and the entire street was silent.

1
Carl Henshawe

I was almost home by the time I knew that it had happened.

It was still early - about half-eight I think - and I'd been out of the house since just after four. Looking back I was glad I hadn't been home. It was bad enough seeing Sarah and Gemma lying there after it had happened to them. Christ, I wouldn't have coped seeing it get them both. I just couldn't have stood seeing them both suffer like that. I couldn't have done anything for either of them. It hurts too much to even think about it. Better that they were gone and it was over by the time I got home.

I'd been out on a maintenance call at Carter and Jameson's factory five miles north of Billhampton. I usually ended up going there once or twice a month, and usually in the middle of the night. The bastard that was in charge of the place was too tight to pay for new machinery and too bloody smart to get his own men repairing the system when he knew that he could call us out. Didn't matter what went wrong or when, he always got us out. He knew the maintenance contract better than I did.

I was six miles short of Northwich when I first realised that something was wrong. I'd stopped at the services to get a cup of coffee and something to eat and I was just coming off the motorway when the radio started playing up. Nothing unusual about that - the electric's in the van had a mind of their own - but this was different. One minute there was the usual music and talking, the next nothing but silence. Not even static. Just silence. I tried to tune in to a couple of other stations but I couldn't get anything.

Like an idiot I kept driving and trying to sort out the radio at the same time. I only had one eye on the road, and the sun kept flashing through the tops of the trees. The sky was clear and blue and the morning sun was huge and blinding. I wanted to get back home so I kept my foot down. I didn't see the bend in the road until I was half way round and I didn't see the other car until it was almost too late.

I slammed my foot on the brake when I saw it. It was a small mustard-yellow coloured car and its driver was obviously as distracted as I was. He was coming straight at me, and I had to yank the steering wheel hard to the right to avoid hitting him. I must have missed him by only a couple of feet.

There was something about the way the car was moving that didn't seem right. I slowed down and watched it in my rear view mirror. Instead of following the bend that I had just come round, it just kept going forward in a straight line, still going at the same speed. It left the road and smashed up the kerb. The passenger-side door scraped against the trunk of a heavy oak tree and then the car stopped dead when the centre of the bonnet wrapped itself around another tree trunk.

There was no-one else about. I stopped and then turned the van around in the road and drove back towards the crash. All I could think was the driver was going to blame the way I was driving and it would be his word against mine and Christ, if he took me to court he'd probably have a good case. I kept thinking that I was going to lose my job and that I'd have to explain what had happened to the boss and...and bloody hell, I didn't even stop to think that the other driver might be hurt until I saw him slumped over his steering wheel.

I stopped my car a few feet behind the crash and got out to help. My legs felt heavy - I didn't want to look but I knew that I had to. As I got closer I could see the full extent of the damage to the car. It had hit the tree at such a bloody speed that the bonnet was almost wrapped right around it.

I opened the driver's door (it was jammed shut and it took me a while to get it open). The driver looked about thirty-five years old, and I didn't need to touch him to know that he was dead. His face had been slammed hard against the steering wheel, crushing his nose. His dead eyes gazed up at me, giving me a cold stare which made me feel as if he was blaming me for what had just happened. Blood was pouring from what was left of his nose and from his mouth which hung wide open. It wasn't dripping; for the best part of a minute the thick crimson blood was literally pouring from the body and pooling on the floor around the dead man's feet.

I didn't have a fucking clue what to do. For a few seconds I just stood there like a bloody fool, first looking up and down the silent road and then staring at the jet of steam which was shooting up from the battered car's radiator and into the cold morning air. I felt sick to my stomach, and when the hissing eventually stopped all I could hear was the drip, drip, drip of blood. It had only been a couple of minutes since I'd eaten. I looked back at the body again and felt myself lose control of my stomach. I dropped down to my knees and threw up in the grass at the side of the road.

Once the nausea had passed I dragged myself up onto my feet and walked back to the van. I reached inside for the phone, realising that although there was nothing I could do for the poor bastard in the car, I had to do something. In a strange way it was easier knowing that he was dead. I could just tell the police that I'd been driving along and I'd found the car crashed into the tree. No-one needed to know that I'd been around when the accident took place.

The bloody phone wasn't working.

There I was, out in the countryside just outside a major town and I couldn't get a signal. I shook the phone, waved it in the air and even banged it against the side of the fucking van but I couldn't get rid of the 'No Service' message on the display. I wasn't thinking straight. I tried dialling 999 three or four times but I couldn't get anything. It didn't even ring out. The phone just kept bleeping 'unobtainable' in my ear.

So if no-one needed to know that I'd seen the crash, I found myself thinking, no-one needed to know that I'd been the one who found it. It sickens me now when I think back and remember that the next thing I did was climb back into the van with the intention of driving home. I decided that I'd call the police or someone from there and tell them that I'd seen an abandoned car at the side of the road. I didn't even need to tell them about the body. I guess that it must have been the effects of shock. I'm not usually such a spineless bastard.

I was in a daze, almost a trance. I climbed back into the van, started the engine and began to drive back towards town. I stared at the crashed car in the rear view mirror until it was out of sight, then I put my foot down on the accelerator.

There were a couple more bends in the road before it straightened and stretched out for a clear half mile ahead of me. I caught sight of another car in the near distance, and seeing that car made me give way to my mounting guilt and change my plans. I decided that I'd stop and tell the driver about what I'd seen. There's safety in numbers, I thought. I'd get them to come back with me to the crash and we'd report it to the police together. Everything would be okay.

I was wrong. As I got closer to the car I realised that it had stopped. I slowed down and pulled up alongside. The driver's seat was empty. There were three other people in the car and they were all dead - a mother in the front and her two dead children in the back. Their faces were screwed up with expressions of agony and panic. Their skin was pale grey and I could see on the body of the child nearest to me that there was a trickle of blood running from between its lips and down the side of its lifeless face. I kept the van moving slowly forward and saw that a couple of metres further down the road the body of the missing driver lay sprawled across the tarmac. I had to drive up onto the grass verge to avoid driving over him.

I was so fucking scared. I cried like a baby as I drove back towards home.

I can't be sure, but I must have seen another forty or fifty bodies by the time I'd made it back to Northwich. The streets were littered with the dead. It was bizarre - people just seemed to have fallen where they'd been standing. Whatever they'd been doing, wherever they'd been going, they'd just dropped.

The situation was so unexpected and inexplicable that it was only at that point that I thought about the safety of my family. I put my foot down flat on the accelerator and was outside my house in seconds. I jumped out of the van and ran to the door. My hands were shaking and I couldn't get the key in the lock. Eventually I opened it and immediately wished that I hadn't. The house was silent.

I ran up to the bedroom and that's where I found them both. Sarah and our beautiful little girl both dead. Gemma's face was frozen in the middle of a silent scream and there was blood all around her mouth and on Sarah's white night dress and the sheets. They were both still warm and I shook them and screamed at them to wake up and talk to me. Sarah looked terrified. I tried to close her frightened eyes to make believe she was just sleeping but I couldn't. They wouldn't stay shut.

I couldn't stand to leave them but I couldn't stand to stay there either. I had to get out. I put Gemma into bed with her mum, kissed them both goodbye and pulled the sheets up over their heads. I left the house, locked the door behind me and then walked.

I spent hours stepping through the bodies just shouting out for help.

2
Michael Collins

So there I was, standing at the front of a class of thirty-three sixteen year olds, tongue-tied and terrified. The boss had volunteered me for one of those 'Industry into Schools' days. One of those days where instead of sitting listening to their teacher drone on for hours, children were made to listen to sacrificial lambs like me telling them how wonderful the job they really despised was. I hated it. I hated speaking in public. I hated compromising myself and not being honest. I hated knowing that if I didn't do this and I didn't do it well, my end of month bonus would be reduced. My boss believed that his middle-managers were the figureheads of his company. In reality we were just there for him to hide behind.

My talk didn't last long.

I'd made some notes which I held in front of me like a shield. I felt quite calm inside, but the way that the end of my papers shook seemed to give the class the impression that I was paralysed with nerves. The sadistic sixteen year olds quickly seized on my apparent weakness. When I coughed and tripped on a word I was history.

'The work we do at Caradine Computers is extremely varied and interesting,' I began, lying through my teeth. 'We're responsible for...'

'Sir,' a lad said from the middle of the room. He was waving his hand in the air.

'What?'

'Why don't you just give up now,' he sighed. 'We're not interested.'

That stopped me dead. I'd never have dared speak out like that at school. I looked to the teacher at the back of the class for support but as soon as we'd made eye contact she turned to look out of the window.

'As I was saying,' I continued, 'we look after a wide range of clients, from small one-man firms to multinational corporations. We advise them on the software to use, the systems to buy and...'

Another interruption, this time more physical. A fight was breaking out in the corner of the room. One boy had another in a headlock.

'James Clyde,' the teacher yelled across the classroom, 'cut it out. Anyone would think you didn't want to listen to Mr Collins.'

As if the behaviour of the students wasn't bad enough, now even the teacher was being sarcastic. I didn't know whether she'd meant her words to sound that way, but that was definitely how the rest of the class had taken them. Suddenly there was stifled laughter coming from all sides, hidden by hands over mouths and pierced by the occasional splutter from those who couldn't keep their hilarity in check. Within seconds the whole room was out of control.

I was about to give up and walk out when it happened. A girl in the far right corner of the room was coughing. Far more than any ordinary splutter, this was a foul, rasping and hacking scream of a cough which sounded as if it was tearing the very insides of her throat apart with each painful convulsion. I took a few steps towards the girl and then stopped. Other than her painful choking the rest of the room had become silent. I watched as her head dropped down and thick sticky strings of blood and spit dripped and trailed into her cupped hands and over her desk. For a second she looked up at me with huge terrified eyes. She couldn't breath. She was suffocating.

I looked towards the teacher again. This time she stared straight back at me, fear and confusion written clearly across her face.

On the other side of the room a boy began to cough. He too was suddenly gripped with unexpected terror and excruciating pain. He too could no longer breathe.

A girl just behind and to the right of me began to cry and then to cough. The teacher tried to stand up and walk towards me but then stopped as she also began to cough and splutter. Within no more than a minute of the first girl's agony beginning, every single person in the room was tearing at their throats and fighting to breathe. Every single person, that was, except me.

I didn't know what to do or where to go to get help. Numb with shock, I staggered back towards the classroom door. I stumbled and tripped over a school bag and grabbed hold of the nearest desk to steady myself. A girl's hand slammed down on mine. I stared into her face. She was deathly white save for a crimson trickle of blood which spilled down her chin and onto the books on her desk. Her head kept lurching back on her shoulders as she tried desperately to breathe in precious molecules of oxygen. Each uncontrolled spasm of her body forced much more air out of her lungs than was allowed in.

I wrenched my hand away and threw the door open. The noise inside the room was appalling. A deafening, echoing cacophony of desperate cries which pierced right through me, but even out in the hallway there was no escape. The pitiful noises which came from my classroom were only a small fraction of the screaming confusion which rang through the entire school. From places as remote as assembly halls, gymnasiums, workshops, kitchens and offices, the cold morning air was filled with the terrified screams of hundreds of desperate children and adults, all of them suffocating and choking to death.

By the time I'd reached the end of the corridor it was over. The school was silent.

I instinctively walked down the stairs towards the main entrance doors. Sprawled on the ground at the foot of the staircase was the body of a boy. He must have been only eleven or twelve. I crouched down next to him and cautiously reached out to touch him. I pulled my hand away as soon as it made contact with his dead flesh. It felt cold, clammy and unnatural, almost like wet leather. Forcing myself to try and take control of my fear and disgust, I pushed his shoulder and rolled him over onto his back. Like the others I had seen his face was ghostly white and was smeared with blood and spittle. I leant down as close as I dare and put my ear next to his mouth. I held my breath and waited to hear even the slightest sounds of breathing. I wished that the suddenly silent world would become quieter still so that I could hear something. It was hopeless. There was nothing.

I walked out into the cool September sunlight and crossed the empty playground. Just one glance at the devastated scene outside the school gates was enough for me to realise that whatever it was that had happened inside the building had happened outside too. Random bodies littered the streets for as far as I could see.

In seven hours since it happened I've seen no-one else.

My house is cold and secure but it doesn't feel safe. I can't stay there. I have to keep looking. I can't be the only one left.

The phones aren't working.

There's no electricity.

There's nothing but static on the radio.

I've never been so fucking frightened.

3
Emma Mitchell

Sick, cold and tired.

I felt bad. I decided to skip my lecture and stay at home. I had one of those fevers where I was too hot to stay in bed and too cold to get up. I felt too sick to do anything but too guilty to sit still and do nothing. I had tried to do some studying for a while. I gave up when I realised that I'd had five attempts at reading the same paragraph but had never made it past the middle of the third line.

Kayleigh, my flat mate, hadn't been home for almost two days. She'd phoned so she knew I felt bad and she'd promised to pick up some milk and a loaf of bread. I cursed her as I searched through the kitchen cupboards for something to eat. They were empty, and I was forced to accept that I'd have to pull myself together and go shopping.

Wrapped up in my thickest coat I tripped and sniffed to the shop at the end of Maple Street feeling drained, pathetic and thoroughly sorry for myself.

There were three customers (including me) in Mr Rashid's shop. I didn't pay any of them any attention at first. I was stood there haggling with myself, trying to justify spending a few pence more on my favourite brand of spaghetti sauce, when an old bloke lurched at me. For the fraction of a second before he touched me I was half-aware that he was coming. He reached out and grabbed hold of my arm. He was fighting for breath. It looked like he was having an asthma attack or something. I was only five terms into my five years of medical study and I didn't have a clue what was happening to him.

His face was ashen white and the grip he had on my sleeve tightened. I started to try and squirm away from him but I couldn't get free. I dropped my shopping basket and tried to prise his bony fingers off my arm.

There was a sudden noise behind me and I looked back over my shoulder to see that the other shopper had collapsed into a display rack, sending jars, tins and packets of food crashing to the ground. He lay on his back amongst them, coughing, holding his throat and writhing around in agony.

I felt the grip on my arm loosen and I turned back to look at the old man. Tears of inexplicable pain and fear ran freely down his weathered cheeks as he fought to catch his breath. His throat was obviously blocked, but I couldn't tell by what. My brain slowly began to click into gear and I started thinking about loosening his collar and laying him down. Before I could do anything he opened his wide, toothless mouth and I saw that there was blood inside. The thick crimson blood trickled down his chin and began to drip on the floor in front of me. He dropped to the ground at my feet and I watched helplessly as his body convulsed and shook.

I turned back to look at the other man who also lay on the marble floor, thrashing his arms and legs desperately around him.

I ran to the back of the shop to try and find Mr Rashid. The shop led directly into their home. By the time I found him and his wife they were both dead. Mrs Rashid had fallen in the kitchen and lay next to an upturned chair. The tap was still running. The sink had overfilled and water was spilling down the units and collecting in a pool around the dead lady's legs. Mr Rashid lay in the middle of the living room carpet. His face was screwed up in agony. He looked terrified.

I ran back through to the front of the shop. Both of the men I'd left fighting for breath were dead.

I walked back outside. The sun was incredibly bright and I had to shield my eyes. There were bodies everywhere - even through the brightness the dark shapes on the ground were unmistakable. Hundreds of people seemed to have died. I looked at the few closest to me. Whatever it was that had killed the people inside the shop had killed everyone outside too. They had all suffocated. Every face I looked into was ashen white and the mouth of every body was bloodied and red.

I looked up towards the junction of Maple Street and High Street. Three cars had crashed in the middle of the box junction. No-one was moving. Everything was still. The only thing that changed was the colour of the traffic lights as they steadily worked their way through red, amber and green.

There were hundreds, maybe even thousands of bodies around me. I was numb, cold and sick and I walked home, picking my way through the corpses as if they were just litter that had been dropped on the streets. I didn't allow myself to think about what had happened. I guess I knew that I wouldn't be able to find any answers. I didn't want to know what had killed the rest of the world around me and I didn't want to know why I was the only one left.

I let myself into the flat and locked the door behind me. I went into my room, drew the curtains and climbed back into bed. I lay there, curled up as tightly as I could, until it was dark.

4

By eleven o'clock on a cold, bright and otherwise ordinary Tuesday morning in September over ninety-five percent of the population were dead.

Stuart Jeffries had been on his way home from a conference when it had begun. He'd left the hotel on the Scottish borders at first light with the intention of being home by mid-afternoon. He had the next three days off and had been looking forward to sitting on his backside doing as little as possible for as long as he could.

Driving virtually the full length of the country meant stopping to fill up the car with petrol on more than one occasion. Having passed several service stations on the motorway he decided that he would wait until he reached the next town to get fuel. A smart man, Jeffries knew that the cheaper he could buy his petrol, the more profit he'd make when it came to claiming his expenses back when he returned to work on Friday. Northwich was the nearest town, and it was there that a relatively normal morning became extraordinary in seconds. The busy but fairly well ordered lines of traffic were thrown into chaos and disarray as the infection tore through the cool air. Desperate to avoid being hit, as the first few cars around him had lost control he had taken the nearest turning he could find off the main road and had then taken an immediate right into an empty car park. He had stopped his car, got out and ran up the side of a muddy bank. Through metal railings he had helplessly watched the world around him fall apart in the space of a few minutes. He saw countless people drop to the ground without warning and die the most hideous choking death imaginable.

Jeffries spent the next three hours sitting terrified in his hire car with the doors locked and the windows wound up tight. The car had only been delivered to his hotel late the previous evening but in the sudden disorientation it immediately became the safest place in the world.

The car radio was dead and his phone was useless. He was two hundred and fifty miles away from home with an empty petrol tank and he was completely alone. Paralysed with fear and uncertainty, in those first few hours he'd been more scared than at any other point in the forty-two years of his life so far. What had happened around him was so unexpected and inexplicable that he couldn't even begin to accept the horrors that he'd seen, never mind try and comprehend any of it.

After three hours cooped up in the car the physical pressure on him gradually matched and then overtook the mental stress. He stumbled out into the car park and was immediately struck by the bitter cold of the late September day. Almost as if he was subconsciously trying to convince himself of what he'd seen earlier, he silently walked back towards the main road and surveyed the devastation in front of him. Nothing was moving. The remains of wrecked and twisted cars were strewn all around. The dirty grey pavements were littered with cold, lifeless bodies and the only sound came from the biting autumn wind as it ripped through the trees and chilled him to the bone. Other than the corpses that were trapped in what was left of their cars there didn't seem any immediately obvious reason for any of the deaths. The closest body to Jeffries was that of an elderly woman. She had simply dropped to the ground where she'd been standing. She still had the handle of her shopping trolley gripped tightly in one of her gloved hands.

He thought about shouting out for help. He raised his hands up to his mouth but then stopped. The world was so icily silent and he felt so exposed and out of place that he didn't dare make a sound. In the back of his mind was the very real fear that, if he was to call out, his voice might draw attention to his location. Although there didn't seem to be anyone else left to hear him, in his vulnerable and increasingly nervous state he began to convince himself that making a noise might bring whatever it was that had destroyed the rest of the population back to destroy him. Paranoid perhaps, but what had happened was so illogical and unexpected that he just wasn't prepared to take any chances. Frustrated and afraid, he turned around and walked back towards the car.

At the far end of the car park, hidden from view at first by overhanging trees, stood the Whitchurch Community Hall. Named after a long forgotten local dignitary it was a dull, dilapidated building which had been built (and, it seemed, last maintained) in the late 1950's. Jeffries cautiously walked up to the front of the hall and peered in through a half-open door. Nervously he pushed the door fully open and took a few tentative steps inside. This time he did call out, quietly and warily at first, but there was no reply.

The cold and draughty building took only a minute or two to explore because it consisted of only a few rooms, most of which led off a main hall. There was a very basic kitchen, two storerooms (one at either end of the building) and male and female toilets. At the far end of the main hall was a second, much smaller hall, off which led the second storeroom. This room had obviously been added as an extension to the original building. Its paint work and decoration, although still faded and peeling, was slightly less faded and peeling than that of the rest of the rooms.

Other than two bodies in the main hall the building was empty. Jeffries found it surprisingly easy to move the two corpses and to drag them outside. In the hand of a grey-haired man who looked to have been in his early sixties he found a bunch of keys which, he discovered, fitted the building locks. This, he decided, must have been the caretaker. And the equally grey-haired lady who had died next to him was probably a prospective tenant, looking to hire the hall for a Women's Institute meeting or something similar. He heaved the stiff and awkward bodies through the doorway and placed them carefully in the undergrowth at the side of the building.

It was while he was outside that he decided he would shelter in the hall until morning. It seemed to be as safe a place as any in which to hide. It was isolated and although not in the best of repair, it looked strong enough and seemed warmer than the car. Jeffries decided that there didn't seem to be any point in trying to get anywhere else. The only place he wanted to be was back home, but that was a few hours drive away. He quickly convinced himself that it would be safer to stay put for now and then to try and get petrol in the morning. He'd siphon it from one of the wrecked cars outside.

As the light began to fade he discovered that there was no electricity in the hall. A quick run to the end of the car park revealed that it wasn't just the hall that was without power. The entire city for as far as he could see was rapidly darkening. Other than a few flickering fires he couldn't see any light - not even a single street lamp - and as he watched it seemed that the world around him was being steadily consumed by the thick shroud of night.

Being a hire car, there was nothing to help inside Stuart's vehicle. He cursed the irony of the situation - he kept a blanket, a shovel, a toolbox, a first-aid kit and a torch in the back of his own car. If he'd only made the journey in his own car then he would at least have had some light. All that he had now was the hire car itself. He toyed with the idea of leaving the front door of the hall open and shining the headlamps into the room but he quickly decided against it. Although he seemed to be the last person alive in the city, shutting the door made him feel marginally safer and less exposed. With the door shut and locked he could at least pretend for a while that nothing had happened.

Just before nine o'clock Jeffries' solitary confinement was ended. He was sat on a cold plastic chair in the kitchen of the hall listening to the silence of the dead world and trying hard to think of anything other than what had happened today and what might happen to him tomorrow. A sudden crash from outside caused him to jump to his feet and run to the front door. He waited for a second or two, almost too afraid to see what it was that had made the noise. Sensing that help and explanations might be at hand he took a deep breath, opened the door and ran out into the car park. To his left he could see movement. Someone was walking along the main road. Desperate not to let them go, he sprinted up the bank to the railings and yelled out. The shadowy figure stopped, turned around and ran back to where Jeffries stood. Jeffries reached out and grabbed hold of Jack Baynham - a thirty-six year old bricklayer. Neither man said a word.

The arrival of the second survivor brought a sudden hope and energy to Jeffries. Between them they could find no answers as to what had happened earlier, but for the first time they did at least begin to consider what they should do next. If there were two survivors it followed that there could be a hundred and two, or even a thousand and two. They had to let other people know where they were.

Using rubbish from three dustbins at the side of the hall and the remains of a smashed up wooden bench they built a bonfire in the centre of the car park, well away from the hall, the hire car and any overhanging trees. Petrol from the mangled wreck of a sports car was used as fuel. Baynham set the fire burning by flicking a smouldering cigarette butt through the cold night air. Within seconds the car park was filled with welcome light and warmth. Jeffries found a compact disc in another car and put it into the player in his. He turned the key in the ignition and started the disc. Soon the air was filled with classical music. Sweeping, soaring strings shattered the ominous silence that had been so prevalent all day.

The fire had been burning and the music playing for just under an hour when the third and fourth survivors arrived at the hall. By four o'clock the following morning the population of the

Whitchurch Community Hall stood at more than twenty dazed and confused individuals.

Emma Mitchell had spent almost the entire day curled up in the corner of her bed. She'd first heard the music shortly after ten o'clock but for a while had convinced herself that she was hearing things. It was only when she finally plucked up the courage to get out of bed and opened her bedroom window that it became clear that someone really was playing music. Desperate to see and to speak to someone else, she threw a few belongings into a rucksack and locked and left her home. She ran along the silent streets using the feeble illumination from a dying torch to guide her safely through the bloody mass of fallen bodies, terrified that the music might stop and leave her stranded before she could reach its source.

Thirty-five minutes later she arrived at the Community Hall.

Carl Henshawe was the twenty-fourth survivor to arrive.

Having left the bodies of his family behind, he had spent most of the day hiding in the back of a builder's van. After a few hours he had decided to try and find help. He'd driven the van around aimlessly until it had run out of fuel and spluttered and died. Rather than try and refuel the van he decided to simply take another vehicle. It was while he was changing cars that he heard the music.

Having quickly disposed of its dead driver, Carl arrived at the hall at day break in a luxury company car.

Michael Collins had just about given up. Too afraid to go back home or indeed to go anywhere that he recognised, he was sat in the freezing cold in the middle of a park. He had decided that it was easier to be alone and deny what had happened than face returning to familiar surroundings and risk seeing the bodies of people he'd known. He lay on his back on the wet grass and listened to the gentle babbling of a nearby brook. He was cold, wet, uncomfortable and terrified, but the noise of the running water disguised the deathly silence of the rest of the world and made it fractionally easier to forget for a while.

The wind blew across the field where he lay, rustling through the grass and bushes and causing the tops of trees to thrash about almost constantly. Soaked through and shivering, Michael eventually clambered to his feet and stretched. Without any real plan or direction, he slowly walked further away from the stream and towards the edge of the park. As the sound of running water faded into the distance, so the unexpected strains of the music from the car park drifted towards him. Marginally interested, but too cold, numb and afraid to really care, he began to follow the sound.

Michael was the final survivor to reach the hall.

5

Michael Collins was the last to arrive at the hall but the first to get his head together. More than his head, perhaps, it was his stomach that forced him into action. Just before midday, after a long, slow and painful morning, he decided it was time to eat. In the main storeroom he found tables, chairs and a collection of camping equipment labelled up as belonging to the 4th Whitchurch Scout Group. In a large metal chest he found two gas burners and, next to the chest itself, four half-full gas bottles. In minutes he'd set the burners up on a table and was keeping himself busy by heating up a catering-size can of vegetable soup and a similar sized can of baked beans which he'd found. Obviously left over from camps held in the summer just gone, the food was an unexpected and welcome discovery. More than that, preparing the food was a distraction. Something to take his mind off what had happened outside the flimsy walls of the Whitchurch Community Hall.

The rest of the survivors sat in silence in the main hall. Some lay flat on the cold brown linoleum floor while others sat on chairs with their heads held in their hands. No-one spoke. Other than Michael no-one moved. No-one even dared to make eye contact with anyone else. Twenty-six people who may as well have been in twenty-six different rooms. Twenty-six people who couldn't believe what had happened to the world around them and who couldn't bear to think about what might happen next. In the last day each one of them had experienced more pain, confusion and loss than they would normally have expected to suffer in their entire lifetime. What made these emotions even more unbearable today, however, was the complete lack of explanation. The lack of reason. Coupled with that was the fact

21

that everything had happened so suddenly and without warning. And now that it had happened, there was no-one they could look to for answers. Each cold, lonely and frightened person knew as little as the cold, lonely and frightened person next to them.

Michael sensed that he was being watched. Out of the corner of his eye he could see that a girl sitting nearby was staring at him. She was rocking on a blue plastic chair and watching him intently. It made him feel uncomfortable. Much as he wanted someone to break the silence and talk to him, deep down he didn't really want to say anything. He had a million questions to ask, but he didn't know where to start and it seemed that the most sensible option was to stay silent.

The girl got up out of her chair and tentatively walked towards him. She stood there for a moment, about a metre and a half away, before taking a final step closer and clearing her throat.

'I'm Emma,' she said quietly, 'Emma Mitchell.'

He looked up, managed half a smile, and then looked down again.

'Is there anything I can do?' she asked. 'Do you want any help?'

Michael shook his head and stared into the soup he was stirring. He watched the chunks of vegetable spinning around and wished that she'd go away. He didn't want to talk. He didn't want to start a conversation because a conversation would inevitably lead to talking about what had happened to the rest of the world outside and at that moment in time that was the last thing he wanted to think about. Problem was, it was all that he could think about.

'Shall I try and find some mugs?' Emma mumbled. She was damn sure that he was going to talk. He was the only person in the room who had done anything all morning and her logic and reason dictated that he was the person it would be most worth starting a conversation with. Emma found the silence and the lack of communication stifling, so much so that a short while ago she'd almost got up and left the hall.

Sensing that she wasn't going to go away, Michael looked up again.

'I found some mugs in the stores,' he muttered. 'Thanks anyway.'

'No problem,' she replied.

After another few seconds of silence, Michael spoke again.

'I'm Michael,' he said. 'Look, I'm sorry but...'

He stopped speaking because he didn't really know what it was he trying to say. Emma understood, nodded dejectedly and was about to turn and walk away. The thought of the stunted conversation ending before it had really started was enough to force Michael to make an effort. He began trying to think of things to say that would keep her at the table with him. It was involuntary at first, but within seconds he'd realised that he really didn't want her to go.

'I'm sorry,' he said again. 'It's just with everything that's... I mean I don't know why I...'

'I hate soup,' Emma grunted, deliberately interrupting and steering the conversation into safer, neutral waters. 'Especially vegetable. Christ, I can't stand bloody vegetable soup.'

'Nor me,' Michael admitted. 'Hope someone likes it though. There's four tins of it in there.'

As quickly as it had began the brief dialogue ended. There just wasn't anything to say. Small talk seemed unnecessary and inappropriate. Neither of them wanted to talk about what had happened but both knew that they couldn't avoid it. Emma took a deep breath and tried again.

'Were you far from here when it...'

Michael shook his head.

'A couple of miles. I spent most of yesterday wandering around. I've been all over town but my house is only twenty minutes walk away.' He stirred the soup again and then felt obliged to ask her the same question back.

'My place is just the other side of the park.' She replied. 'I spent yesterday in bed.'

'In bed?'

She nodded and leant against the nearest wall.

'Didn't seem to be much else to do. I just put my head under the covers and pretended that nothing had happened. Until I heard the music, that was.'

'Bloody masterstroke playing that music.'

Michael ladled a generous serving of beans into a dish and handed it to Emma. She picked up a plastic spoon from the table and poked at the hot food for a couple of seconds before tentatively tasting a mouthful. She didn't want to eat but she was starving. She hadn't even thought about food since her aborted shopping trip yesterday morning.

A couple of the other survivors were looking their way. Michael didn't know whether it was the food that was attracting their attention or the fact that he and Emma were talking. Before she'd come across he'd said less than twenty words all morning. It seemed that the two of them communicating had acted like a release valve of sorts. As he watched more and more of the shell-like survivors began to show signs of life.

Half an hour later and the food had been eaten. There were now two or three conversations taking place around the hall. Small groups of survivors huddled together while others remained alone. Some people talked (and the relief on their faces was obvious) while others cried. The sound of sobbing could clearly be heard over the muted discussions.

Emma and Michael had stayed together. They had talked sporadically and had learnt a little about each other. Michael had learnt that Emma was a medical student and Emma learnt that Michael worked with computers. Michael, she discovered, lived alone. His parents had recently moved to Edinburgh with his two younger brothers. She had told him that she'd chosen to study in Northwich and that her family lived in a small village on the east coast. Neither of them could bring themselves to talk much about their families in any detail as neither knew if the people they loved were still alive.

'What did this?' Michael asked. He'd tried to ask the question a couple of times before but hadn't quite managed to force the words out. He knew that Emma couldn't answer, but it helped just to have asked.

She shrugged her shoulders.

'Don't know, some kind of virus perhaps?'

'But how could it have killed so many people? And so quickly?'

'Don't know,' she said again.

'Christ, I watched thirty kids die in just a couple of minutes, how on earth could anything...'

She was staring at him. He stopped talking.

'Sorry,' he mumbled.

'It's okay,' she sighed.

Another awkward, pregnant pause followed.

'You warm enough?' Michael eventually asked.

Emma nodded.

'I'm okay.'

'I'm freezing. I tell you there are holes in the walls of this place. I stood in one corner this morning and I could push the bloody walls apart! It wouldn't take much to bring this place down.'

'That's reassuring, thanks.'

Michael shut up quickly, regretting his clumsy words. The last thing anyone wanted to hear was how vulnerable they were in the hall. Shabby, ramshackle and draughty it might be, but today it was all they had. There were countless stronger and safer buildings outside, but no-one wanted to take a single step outside the front door for fear of what they might find there.

Michael watched as Stuart Jeffries and another man (whose name he thought was Carl) sat in deep conversation in the far corner of the room with a third figure who was hidden from view by Jeffries' back. Jeffries had been the first one to arrive at the hall, and he'd made a point of telling everyone who'd arrived subsequently that he'd been the one who had found their shelter as if they should be grateful. In a world where position and stature now counted for nothing, he seemed to be clinging on desperately to his self-perceived 'status'. Perhaps it made him feel important. Perhaps it made him feel like he had a reason to survive.

The conversation in the corner continued and Michael began to watch intently. He could sense that frustrations were beginning to boil to the surface by the increasing volume of the voices. Less than five minutes earlier they had been mumbling quietly and privately. Now every survivor could hear every word of what was being said.

'No way, I'm not going outside,' Jeffries snapped, his voice strained and tired. 'What's the point? What's outside?'

The man hidden in the shadows replied.

'So what else should we do then? How long can we stay here? It's cold and uncomfortable in here. We've got no food and no supplies and we've got to go out if we're going to survive. Besides, we need to know what's happening out there. For all we know we could be shut away in here with help just around the corner...'

'We're not going to get any help,' Jeffries argued.

'How do you know?' Carl asked. His voice was calm but there was obvious irritation and frustration in his tone. 'How the hell do you know there's no-one to help us? We won't know until we get out there.'

'I'm not going out.'

'Yes, we've already established that,' the hidden man sighed. 'You're going to stay in here until you fucking starve to death...'

'Don't get smart,' Jeffries spat. 'Don't get fucking smart with me.'

Michael sensed that the friction in the corner might be about to turn into violence. He didn't know whether to get involved or just stay out of the way.

'I know what you're saying, Stuart,' Carl said cautiously, 'but we need to do something. We can't just sit here and wait indefinitely.'

Jeffries looked as if he was trying desperately to think of something to say. Maybe he was having trouble trying to reason the argument. How could you apply any logic and order to such a bleak and inexplicable situation? Unable to find the words to express how he was feeling he began to cry, and the fact that he was unable to contain his emotions seemed to make him even angrier. He wiped away his tears with the back of his hand, hoping that the others hadn't noticed, but knowing full well that everyone had.

'I just don't want to go out there,' he cried, finally being honest and forcing his words out between gasps and sobs. 'I just don't want to see it all again. I want to stay here.'

With that he got up and left the room, shoving his chair back across the floor. It clattered against the radiator and the sudden noise caused everyone to look up. Seconds later the ominous silence was shattered again as the toilet door slammed shut. Carl looked at the man in the corner for a second before shrugging his shoulders and getting up and walking away in the opposite direction.

'The whole bloody world is falling apart,' Michael said under his breath as he watched.

'What do you mean falling apart?' Emma asked quietly. 'It's already happened, mate. There's nothing left. This is it.'

He looked up and around at his cold grey surroundings and glanced at each one of the empty shells of people scattered about the place. She was right. She was painfully right.

6

Dead inside.

Henshawe sat alone in a dark corner of a storeroom with his head in his hands, weeping for the wife and daughter he'd lost.

Where was the sense in going on? Why bother? Those two had been the very reason he existed. He'd gone to work to earn money to keep them and provide for them. He'd come home every night to be with them. He'd been devoted to them in a way he thought he'd never be with anyone before he and Sarah had got together. And now, without any reason, warning or explanation, they were gone. Taken from him in the blinking of an eye. And he hadn't even been able to help them or hold them. He hadn't been there when they'd died. When they'd needed him most he had been miles away.

Outside in the main hall he could hear the moans and cries of other people who had lost everything. He could smell and taste the anger, frustration and complete bewilderment of the other survivors which hung like the stench of rotting flesh in the cold, grey air. He could hear fighting, arguing and screaming. He could hear raw pain tearing each one of the twenty or so disparate, desperate people apart.

When the noise became too much to bear he dragged himself up onto his feet with the intention of leaving. He was about to get up and walk and leave the hall and the rest of the survivors behind when his mind was quickly filled with images of millions of lifeless bodies lying in the streets around him and he knew that he couldn't go. The light outside was beginning to fade. The day was almost over. The thought of being out in the open was horrific enough, but to be out there in the dark - lost, alone and wandering aimlessly - was too much to even consider.

He leant against the storeroom door and peered into the main hall. The brilliant orange sunlight of dusk poured into the building from above his head, illuminating everything with vibrant, almost fluorescent colour. Curious as to the source of the light, he took a few steps out of the room and turned back around. In the sloping ceiling just above the door was a narrow skylight. The storeroom he had hidden in had been added as an extension to the original building and when he had arrived he had noticed that it had a flat roof. Sensing that his escape was at hand, Henshawe climbed onto a wooden table, stretched up and forced the skylight open. He dragged himself through and scrambled out onto the asphalt roof.

The coldest wind he had ever felt buffeted and blew him as he stood exposed on the ten foot square area of roof. From the furthest edge he could see out over the main road into Northwich and into the dead city beyond. By moving only his eyes he followed the route of the road as it splintered away to the left and headed off in the general direction of Hadley, the small suburb where he had lived. The small suburb where the bodies of his partner and child lay together in bed. In his mind he could still picture them both, frozen still and lifeless, their perfect bodies stained with dark, drying blood, and suddenly the icy wind seemed to blow even colder. For a while he considered driving back to them. The very least they deserved was a proper burial and some dignity. The pain he felt inside was unbearable and he dropped to his knees and held his head in his hands.

From his vantage point he could see countless bodies, and it struck him as strange and unnerving to think that he was already used to seeing the corpses. Before all this had happened he'd only ever seen one dead body, and at that time it had seemed an unusual and alien thing. He had been at his mother's side when she'd died. As the life had drained away from her he had watched her change. He'd seen the colour blanch from her face and her expression freeze and had watched the last breath of air be exhaled from her fading body. He'd seen her old and frail frame become heavy and useless. She'd had little strength

29

towards the end, but even then it had taken just a single nurse to help her get around. When she died it took two male porters to lift her from her bed and take her away.

Parts of the city in the distance were burning. Huge thick palls of dirty black smoke stretched up into the orange evening sky from unchecked fires. As he watched the smoke climb relentlessly his wandering mind came up with countless explanations as to how the fires could have started - a fractured gas main perhaps? Or a crashed petrol tanker? A body lying too close to a gas fire? He knew that it was pointless even trying to think about reasons why, but he had nothing else to do. And at least thinking like that helped him to forget about Gemma and Sarah for a while.

He was about to go back inside when one of the bodies in the road caught his eye. He didn't know why, because the body was unremarkable in the midst of the confusion and carnage. The corpse was that of a teenage boy who had fallen and smashed his head against a kerb stone. His neck was twisted awkwardly so that whilst he was lying on his side, his glazed eyes were looking up into the sky. It was as if he was searching for explanations. Carl felt almost as if he was looking to him to tell him what had happened and why it had happened to him. The poor kid looked so frightened and alone. Carl couldn't stand to look into his pained face for more than a couple of seconds.

He went back inside, and the cold and uncomfortable community hall suddenly seemed the safest and warmest place in the world.

7

Carl eventually returned to the other survivors and found them sitting in a rough circular group in one corner of the dark main hall. Some sat on chairs and benches whilst others were crouched down on the hard linoleum floor. The group was gathered around a single dull gas lamp and a quick count of the heads he could see revealed that he seemed to be the only absentee. A few of the poor bewildered souls glanced up at him as he approached.

Feeling suddenly self-conscious (but knowing that he had no reason to care) he sat down at the nearest edge of the group. He sat down between two women. He'd been trapped in the same building as them for the best part of a day and yet he didn't even know their names. He knew very little about anyone and they knew very little about him. As much as he needed their closeness and contact, he found the distance between the individual survivors still strangely welcome.

A man called Ralph was trying to address the group. From his manner and the precise, thoughtful way that he spoke Carl assumed he'd been a barrister or, at the very least, a solicitor until the world had been turned upside down yesterday morning.

'What we must do,' Ralph said, clearly, carefully and slowly and with almost ponderous consideration, 'is get ourselves into some sort of order here before we even think about exploring outside.'

'Why?' someone asked from the other side of the group. 'What do we need to get in order?'

'We need to know who and what we've got here. We need food and water, we need bedding and clothes and we should be able to find most of that in here. We also need to know what we haven't got and we should start thinking about where to get it.'

'Why?' the voice interrupted again. 'We know we'll find everything we need outside. We shouldn't waste our time in here, we should just get out and get on with it.'

Ralph's confidence was clearly a professional facade and, at the first sign of any resistance, he squirmed. He pushed his heavy-rimmed glasses back up the bridge of his nose with the tip of his finger and took a deep breath.

'That's not a good idea. Look, I think we've got to make our personal safety and security our prime concern and then...'

'I agree,' the voice interrupted again. 'But why stop here? There are a thousand and one better places to go, why stay here? What makes you any safer here than if you were lying on the dotted white line in the middle of the Stanhope Road?'

Carl shuffled around so that he could see through the mass of heads and bodies and identify the speaker. It was Michael, the bloke who had cooked the soup earlier.

'We don't know what's outside...' Ralph began.

'But we've got to go out there eventually, you accept that?'

He stammered and fiddled with his glasses again.

'Yes, but...'

'Look, Ralph, I'm not trying to make this any more difficult than it already is. We've got to leave here to get the supplies we need. All I'm saying is why bother delaying it and why bother coming back? Why not go somewhere else?'

Ralph couldn't answer. It was obvious to Carl and, probably, to pretty much everyone else, that the reason Ralph didn't want to go outside was the same reason Stuart Jeffries had admitted to wanting to stay trapped in the hall earlier. They were both scared.

'We could try and find somewhere else,' he began, hesitantly, 'but we've got a shelter here which is secure and...'

'And cold and dirty and uncomfortable,' Carl said quickly.

'Okay, it's not ideal but...'

'But what?' pressed Michael. 'It seems to me that we can pretty much have our pick of everywhere and everything at the moment.'

The room fell silent for a few seconds. Ralph suddenly sat up straight and pushed his glasses back up his nose again. He seemed to have found a reason to justify staying put.

'But what about the music and the fire?' he said, much more animated. 'Stuart and Jack managed to bring us all here by lighting the fire and playing music. If we did it again we might find more survivors. There might already be people on their way to us.'

'I don't think so,' said Michael. 'No-one's arrived here since me. If anyone else had heard the music they'd have been here by now. I agree with what you're saying, but again, why here? Why not find somewhere better to stop, get ourselves organised there and light a bloody big bonfire right in the middle of the road outside?'

Carl agreed.

'He's right. We should get a beacon or something sorted, but let's get ourselves safe and secure first.'

'A new beacon somewhere else is going to be seen by more people, isn't it?' asked Sandra Goodwin, a fifty year-old housewife. 'And isn't that what we want?'

'Bottom line here,' Michael said, changing his tone and raising his voice slightly so that everyone suddenly turned and gave him their full attention, 'is that we've got to look after ourselves first of all and then start to think about anyone else who might possibly still be alive.'

'But shouldn't we start looking for other survivors now?' someone else asked.

'I don't think we should,' he replied, 'I agree that we should get a beacon or something going, but there's no point in wasting time actively looking for other people yet. If there are others then they'll have more chance of finding us than we'll have finding them.'

'Why do you say that?' Sandra asked.

'Stands to reason,' he grunted. 'Does anyone know how many people used to live in this city?'

A couple of seconds silence followed before someone answered.

'About a quarter of a million people. Two hundred thousand or something like that.'

'And there are twenty-six of us in here.'

'So?' pressed an uncomfortable looking Ralph, trying desperately to find a way back into the conversation.

'So what does that say to you?'

Ralph shrugged his shoulders.

'It says to me,' Michael continued, 'that looking for anyone else would be like looking for a needle in a haystack.'

Carl nodded in agreement and picked up where Michael had left off.

'What's outside?' he asked quietly.

No response.

He looked from left to right at the faces gathered around him. He glanced across the room and made eye contact with Michael.

'I'll tell you,' he said quietly, 'there's nothing. The only people I've seen moving since all of this began are sitting in this hall. But we don't know if it's over. We don't know if we're going to wake up tomorrow. We don't know if what happened to the rest of them will happen to us.'

Ralph interrupted.

'Come on,' he protested, 'stop talking like that. You're not doing anyone any good talking like that...'

'I'm trying to make a point...'

Michael spoke again.

'Since this all started have any of you heard a plane or helicopter pass overhead?'

Again, no response.

'The airport's five miles south of here, if there were any planes flying we'd have heard them. There's a train station that links the city to the airport and the track runs along the other side of the Stanhope Road. Anyone heard a train?'

Silence.

34

'So how many people do you think this has affected?' Carl asked cautiously.

'If this was the only region affected,' Michael answered, 'logic says that help would have arrived by now.'

'What are you saying?' a man called Tim asked quietly.

Michael shrugged his shoulders.

'I guess I'm saying that this is a national disaster at the very least. The lack of air traffic makes me think that it could be worse than that.'

An awkward murmur of stark realisation rippled across the group.

'Michael's right,' Emma said. 'This thing spread so quickly that there's no way of knowing what kind of area's been affected. It was so fast that I doubt whether anything could have been done to prevent it spreading before it was too late.'

'But this area might be too infected to travel to,' Tim said, his voice strained and frightened. 'They might have sealed Northwich off.'

'They might have,' Michael agreed. 'But I don't think that's very likely, do you?'

Tim said nothing.

'So what do we do?' an unsure female voice asked from the middle of the group.

'I think we should get away from here,' Michael said. 'Look, if I'm completely honest I'm just thinking about myself here and the rest of you should make your own minds up. It's just that I'm not prepared to sit here and wait for help when I'm pretty sure that it's never going to arrive. I don't want to sit trapped in here surrounded by thousands of bloody bodies. I want out of the city. I want to get away from here, find somewhere safe, make myself comfortable and then just sit and wait and see what happens next.'

8

Michael spent the first five and a half hours of the following morning trying to find somewhere comfortable to sleep. When he finally managed to lose consciousness he only slept for forty-five minutes before waking up feeling worse than ever. He'd been lying on the cold hard floor and every bone in his tired body ached. He wished he hadn't bothered.

The main hall was freezing cold. He was fully clothed and had a thick winter jacket wrapped around him but it was still bitter. He hated everything at the moment, but he quickly decided that he hated this time of day most of all. It was dark and in the early morning shadows he thought he could see a thousand shuffling shapes where there were none. Much as he tried he couldn't think about anything other than what had happened to the world outside because absolutely everything had been affected. He couldn't bear to think about his family because he didn't know if they were still alive. He couldn't think about his work and career because they didn't exist anymore. He couldn't think about going out with his friends at the weekend because those friends were most probably dead too, lying face down on a street corner somewhere. He couldn't think about his favourite television programme because there were no television channels broadcasting and no electricity. He couldn't even hum the tune to his favourite songs because it made him remember. It hurt too much to think about memories and emotions that, although only gone for a few days, now seemed to be lost forever. In desperation he simply stared into the darkness and tried hard to concentrate on listening to the silence. He thought that by deliberately filling his head with nothing the pain would go away. It didn't work. It didn't matter which direction he stared in, all that he could see were the faces of other equally desperate survivors staring back at him through the darkness. He was not alone with his painful insomnia.

The first few orange rays of the morning sun were beginning to edge cautiously into the room. The light trickled in slowly through a series of small rectangular windows which were positioned at equal distances along the longest wall of the main hall. Each one of the windows was protected on the outside by a layer of heavy-duty wire mesh and each window had also been covered in random layers of spray paint by countless vandals through the years. Michael found it strange and unnerving to think that every single one of those vandals was almost certainly dead now.

He didn't want to move, but he knew that he had to. He was desperate to use the toilet but had to summon up the courage to actually get up and go there. It was too cold and he didn't want to wake any of the lucky few survivors who were actually managing to sleep. Problem was the hall was so quiet that no matter how careful he was in his heavy boots every single footstep he took would probably be heard by everyone. And when he got there it wouldn't be much better. The toilets didn't flush anymore because the water supply had dried up. The group had started to use a small chemical toilet which someone had found in the Scout's supplies. Even though it had been in use for less than a day it already stank. A noxious combination of strong chemical detergent and stagnating human waste.

He couldn't put it off any longer, he had to go. He tried unsuccessfully to make the short journey seem a little easier by convincing himself that the sooner he was up the sooner it would be done and he would be back. Strange that in the face of the enormity of the disaster outside, even the easiest everyday task suddenly seemed an impossible mountain to climb.

Grabbing hold of a nearby wooden bench with his outstretched right hand, he hauled himself up onto his unsteady feet. For a few seconds he did nothing except stand still and try to get his balance. He shivered in the cold and then took a few tentative stumbling steps through the half-light towards the toilets. He would be twenty-nine in three weeks time. This morning he felt at least eighty-nine.

Outside the toilet he paused and took a deep breath before opening the door. He glanced to his right and, through a small square window to the side of the main entrance door, he was sure that he could see something outside.

For a moment he froze.

He could definitely see movement.

Ignoring the nagging pain in his bladder, Michael pressed his face hard against the dirty glass and peered out through the layers of spray paint and mesh. He squinted into the light.

There it was again.

Instantly forgetting about the temperature, his aching bones and his full bladder, he unlocked the door and wrenched it open. He burst out into the cold morning and sprinted the length of the car park, stopping at the edge of the road. There, on the other side of the street, he saw a man walking slowly away from the community centre.

'What's the matter?' a voice asked suddenly, startling Michael. It was Stuart Jeffries. He and another three survivors had heard Michael open the door and, naturally concerned, had followed him outside.

'Over there,' Michael replied, pointing towards the figure in the near distance and taking a few slow steps forward. 'Hey,' he shouted, hoping to attract his attention before he disappeared from view. 'Hey you!'

No response.

Michael glanced at the other four survivors before turning back and running after the unknown man. Within a few seconds he had caught up as the solitary figure was moving at a very slow and deliberate pace.

'Hey, mate,' he shouted cheerfully, 'didn't you hear me?'

Still no response.

The man continued walking away.

'Hey,' Michael said again, this time a little louder, 'are you alright? I saw you walking past and...'

As he spoke he reached out and grabbed hold of the man's arm. As soon as he applied any force the figure stopped walking instantly. Other than that it didn't move. It simply stopped and stood still, seeming to not even be aware that Michael was there. Perhaps the lack of any response was as a result of shock. Maybe what had happened to the rest of the world had been too much for this poor soul to take.

'Leave him,' shouted one of the other survivors. 'Get back inside.'

Michael wasn't listening. Instead he slowly turned the man around until he was looking directly into his face.

'Fuck...' was all he could say as he stared deep into the cold, glazed eyes of a corpse. It defied all logic, but there was absolutely no doubt in his suddenly terrified mind that the man standing in front of him was dead. His skin was taut and yellowed and, like all the others, he had traces of dark, dried blood around his mouth, chin and throat.

Repulsed and in shock, Michael let go of the man's arm and stumbled backwards. He tripped and fell and then watched from the gutter as the figure staggered off again, still moving desperately slowly as if it had lead in its shoes.

'Michael,' Jeffries yelled from the entrance to the car park. 'Get back inside now, we're closing the door.'

Michael dragged himself back up to his feet and sprinted towards the others. As he approached he could see more figures moving in the distance. It was obvious by their slow, forced movements that, like the first man he'd seen, these people weren't survivors either.

By the time he reached the car park the others had already disappeared back into the community hall. He was vaguely aware of them yelling at him to come inside but in his disbelief, confusion and bewilderment their fear and panic failed to register. He stood staring out towards the main road, preoccupied by the impossible sight he now saw in front of him.

About a third of the bodies were moving. Roughly one in three of the corpses that had littered the streets around the community centre had become mobile again. Had they not been dead to start with? Had they just been in a coma or something similar? A thousand unanswerable questions began flooding into his mind.

'For Christ's sake, get inside!' yelled another one of the survivors from the hall, their voice hoarse with fear.

As if to prove a point, the corpse on the ground nearest to Michael began to move. Beginning at the outermost tip of the fingers on one outstretched hand, the body started to stretch and to tremble. As he stared in silent incredulity, the fingers began to claw at the ground and then, seconds later, the entire hand was moving. The movement spread steadily along one arm and then, with an almighty shudder, the body lifted itself up from the ground. It tripped and stumbled as it raised itself up onto its unsteady feet. Once upright it simply staggered away, passing within a metre of where Michael stood. The bloody thing didn't even seem to realise that he was there.

Terrified, he turned and ran back inside.

It took less than thirty seconds for the news to spread to all the survivors. Carl Henshawe, refusing to believe what he'd heard, clambered out onto the area of flat roof that he'd stood on last night.

It was true. As incredible as it seemed, some of the bodies were moving.

Carl stood and surveyed the same desperate scene he'd witnessed less than twelve hours earlier and saw that many of the cold and twisted corpses he'd seen had disappeared. He looked down at the place on the cold ground where the boy with the broken neck had died.

There was nothing. He had gone.

9

Almost an hour passed before anyone dared to move.

The survivors, already shell-shocked and beaten by all that they had been through, stood together in terror and disbelief and tried to come to terms with the morning's events. Surprisingly it was Ralph, the solicitor who had seemed so authoritative and keen to take control last night, who appeared to be having the most trouble accepting what he had seen and heard today. He stood in the centre of the room alongside Paul Garner (an overweight and middle-aged estate agent), struggling to persuade Emma, Carl, Michael and Kate James (a thirty-nine year old primary school teacher) not to open the door and go back outside.

'But we have to go out, Ralph,' Emma said, calmly and quietly. 'We've got to try and find out what's going on.'

'I'm not interested,' the flustered and frightened man snapped. 'I don't care what's happening. There's no way I'm going to go out there and risk...'

'Risk what?' Michael interrupted. 'No-one's asking you to go outside, are they?'

'Opening that door is enough of a bloody risk in itself,' Garner muttered anxiously. He chewed on the fingers of his left hand as he spoke. 'Keep it shut and keep them out.'

'We can't take any chances by exposing ourselves to those things...' Ralph protested.

'Things?' Emma repeated, her tone suddenly venomous and agitated. 'Those things are people you selfish shit. Bloody hell, your friends and family could be out there...'

'Those bodies have been lying dead on the ground for days!' he yelled, his face suddenly just inches from hers.

'How do you know they were dead?' Michael asked, perfectly seriously and calmly. 'Did you check them all? Did you check any of them for a pulse before you shut yourself away in here?'

'You know as well as I do that...'

'Did you?' he asked again. Ralph shook his head. 'And have you ever seen a dead body walk before?'

This time Ralph didn't answer. He turned away and leant against the nearest wall.

'Jesus Christ,' Garner cursed, 'of course we've never seen fucking dead bodies walking, but...'

'But what?'

'But I've never seen anyone drop to the ground and not get up for two days either. Face it Michael, they were all dead.'

'Look, Paul,' he sighed, 'let's be straight with each other for a second. None of us have got the first bloody clue what's happening here. The only thing I know for sure is that I'm interested in looking after myself and the rest of the people in this hall and...'

'If you're only interested in the people in here why do you want to go out there and...'

'I'm interested in looking after myself,' Michael repeated, still somehow remaining calm, 'but I need to go out there and see if I can find out what's happening and to see if any of those bodies pose a threat to us. I'm not interested in helping them, I just want to know what's going on.'

'And how are you going to find out what's happening?' Ralph demanded, turning around to face the rest of the group again. 'Who's going to tell you?'

For a moment Michael struggled to answer.

'Emma's studied medicine,' he replied, thinking quickly and looking across at her. 'You'll be able to tell us what's wrong with them, won't you?'

Emma shifted her weight uncomfortably from foot to foot and shrugged her shoulders.

'I'll try,' she mumbled. 'I can try and tell you whether they're dead or not but after that I...'

'But can't you see what you're doing?' Ralph protested, taking off his glasses and rubbing his eyes. 'You're putting us all at risk. If you'd just wait for a while and...'

'Wait for what?' Carl interrupted. 'Seems to me that we're at risk whatever we do. We're sat here in a hall that we could knock down with our bare hands if we tried hard enough, and we're surrounded by thousands of dead bodies, some of which have decided to get up and start walking around. Staying here seems pretty risky to me.'

Sensing that the conversation was about to stray into familiar waters with yet another pointless debate about whether to go outside or not, Michael made his feelings and intentions clear.

'I'm going outside,' he said. His voice was quiet and yet carried with it an undeniable force. 'Stay in here and hide if you want, but I'm going out and I'm going out now.'

'For Christ's sake,' Ralph pleaded, 'think about it before you do anything that might...'

Michael didn't stop to hear the end of his sentence. Instead he simply turned his back on the others and walked up to the main door out of the community centre. He paused for a second and glanced back over his shoulder towards Carl, Emma and Kate. The rest of the survivors were silent.

'Ready?' he asked.

After a second's thought Carl nodded and made his way to stand next to Michael, closely followed by Emma and Kate. Michael took a deep breath, pushed the door open and stepped out into the bright September sunlight.

It was surprisingly warm. Carl (the only one who had been outside for any length of time recently) noticed that last night's bitter wind had dropped. He shielded his eyes from the light and watched as Michael cautiously retraced the steps that he had taken earlier, walking away from the dilapidated wooden building and towards the road. When the first moving body staggered into view he instinctively stopped and turned back to face the others.

'What's the matter?' asked Emma, immediately concerned.

'Nothing,' he mumbled, feeling nervous and unsure.

The three other survivors walked towards him and stood close. Carl noticed that a crowd had gathered to watch them in the shadows of the doorway of the community hall.

'So what are we going to do now?' Kate James wondered. She was a quiet, short and round woman with a usually flushed red face which had suddenly lost much of its colour.

Michael looked around for inspiration.

'Don't know,' he admitted. 'Anyone got any ideas?'

Three faces returned three blank expressions. A few seconds later Emma cleared her throat and spoke.

'We need to have a good look at one of them,' she whispered.

'What do you mean?' Kate asked, her voice also quiet. 'What are we supposed to be looking at?'

'Let's try and see how responsive they are. We should see if they can tell us anything.'

While she had been speaking Michael had taken a few steps further forward.

'What about her?' he asked, pointing at one of the nearest moving bodies. 'What about that one there?'

The group stood together in silence and watched the painful progress of the pitiful creature. The woman's movements were tired and stilted. Her arms hung listlessly at her sides. She seemed almost to be dragging her feet behind her.

'What are we going to do with her?' Kate wondered nervously.

'Do you want to get closer and just have a look?' Carl asked.

Michael shook his head.

'No,' he said, 'let's get her inside.'

'What, back in there?' he gasped, gesturing at the building behind them.

'Yes, in there,' Michael replied. His voice still remained calm and unflustered and it was beginning to annoy Carl who silently

44

hoped that the others shared his mounting fear and unease because he certainly wasn't as together and as sure as Michael appeared. 'Is that a problem?'

'Not to me,' said Emma. 'Try convincing the others though.'

He obviously wasn't concerned.

'I think we should get her indoors and try and make her comfortable. We'll get more out of her if we can get her to relax.'

'Are you sure about this?' muttered Kate. Her nerves were obviously beginning to fray.

Michael thought for a moment before nodding his head.

'I'm sure,' he said, sounding confident. 'What about the rest of you?'

Silence.

After a few awkward seconds had passed Carl spoke.

'Bloody hell, let's just do it. We're never going to achieve anything just standing out here like this, are we?'

That was all that Michael needed to hear. With that he strode up behind the woman, reached out and rested his hands on her shoulders. She stopped moving instantly.

Emma jogged the last few steps and moved round to stand in front of the body. She looked up into her glazed eyes and saw that they seemed unfocussed and vacant. Her skin was pale and taut, as if it had been stretched tight across her skull. Although she was sure that the body couldn't see her (she didn't even seem to know she was there) Emma respectfully tried to hide her mounting revulsion. There was a deep gash on the woman's right temple. Dark blood had been flowing freely from the wound for some time and had drenched her once smart white blouse and grey business suit.

'We want to help you,' she said softly.

Still no reaction.

Michael gripped the woman's shoulders a little tighter and shuffled closer.

'Come on,' he whispered, 'let's get you inside.'

Carl and Kate watched the others with a morbid fascination.

'What the hell is happening?' Kate asked, her voice gradually becoming noticeably weaker and more unsteady each time she spoke.

'No idea,' Carl admitted. 'Bloody hell, I wish I knew.'

He surveyed the desperate scene around them. Not all of the bodies had moved. The majority still lay where they had fallen.

'Carl,' Michael shouted.

'What?' he mumbled nervously, turning back to face the others.

'Give us a hand, mate. Could you get hold of her legs?'

Carl nodded and walked over towards Emma and Michael. He crouched down and grabbed the woman's bony ankles, one in each hand, and, as Michael pulled back on her shoulders, he lifted her feet. She was surprisingly light. There was no weight to her at all and she didn't react to being moved.

The two men scuttled back to the community hall, closely followed by Emma and Kate. As they approached the doorway the survivors (who had continued watching intently throughout) quickly realised what was happening. They scattered like a shoal of frightened fish that had just been invaded by the deadliest predator shark.

'What the bloody hell are you doing?' Ralph stammered as Carl and Michael barged past him. 'What the hell are you doing bringing that in here?'

Michael didn't answer. He was too busy directing the others.

'Group yourselves around her,' he said authoritatively. 'Try and cage her in.'

Obediently Kate and Emma drew closer, as did another two survivors whose names Michael did not know. Carl gently lowered the sick woman's feet to the ground so that she was standing upright again and then took a couple of steps back so that he was level with the others. Once something resembling a circle had been formed and he was happy, Michael let go.

For a second the body did nothing. Then, without warning, it lurched towards Kate who screwed up her face in nervous trepidation and stretched her arms out in front of her to prevent the woman from getting too close. As soon as she made contact with Kate's outstretched hands the woman turned and staggered away in the opposite direction towards another survivor. This continued every time the edge of the circle was reached.

As the woman stumbled towards Michael he allowed himself for the first time to look deep into her face. For a dangerous few seconds he found himself transfixed, looking at the pitiful creature in front of him and wondering how she might have looked just a week earlier. A few days ago he might have found her attractive but, today, her emotionless gaze and drawn, almost translucent skin immediately dissipated any beauty or serenity that her face had previously known. There was an unnatural sheen to her exposed flesh. Michael noticed that her skin had a grey, almost light green tone and a greasy shine and it was tightly stretched over the bones of her skull. What had at first glance appeared to be dark bags under her frozen eyes were, in fact, the prominent ridges of her eye sockets. Her mouth hung open - a huge, dark hole - and a thick string of gelatinous saliva trickled continually down the side of her chin. He pushed her away.

The woman turned and began to stagger towards Carl. Clearly unable to control or co-ordinate her own movements, she tripped over her own clumsy feet and half-fell, half-lurched towards him. He recoiled and pushed her down to the ground, feeling a cold sweat prickle his brow as the pathetic and diseased creature scrambled back up onto its feet.

'Can she hear us?' Kate wondered. She hadn't really meant to ask the question, she'd just been thinking out loud.

'Don't know,' Michael answered.

'She probably can,' Emma said.

'Why do you say that?'

She shrugged her shoulders.

'It's something about the way she reacts.'

Ralph, who had until then been watching nervously from a corner of the room, found himself being drawn closer and closer to the circle of survivors.

'But she doesn't react,' he stammered, his voice uncharacteristically light and shaky.

'I know,' Emma continued. 'That's what I mean. She's walking and moving around, but I don't think she knows why or how.'

'It's instinctive,' Carl muttered.

'That's what I'm starting to think,' Emma agreed. 'She probably can hear us, but she doesn't know what the noises we make mean anymore. I bet she's still capable of speaking, she just can't remember how to.'

'But she reacts when you touch her,' Paul Garner jabbered anxiously.

'No she doesn't. She doesn't react at all. She turns away because she physically can't keep moving in a certain direction. I bet she'd just keep walking in a straight line forever if there wasn't anything in her way.'

'Christ, look at her,' Kate mumbled. 'Just look at the poor cow. How many millions of people like this are wandering around out there?'

'Did you check her pulse?' Michael whispered to Emma who was standing next to him.

'Sort of,' she replied, her voice equally low.

'What's that supposed to mean?' he hissed, annoyed by her vagueness.

'I couldn't find one,' she answered bluntly.

'So what are you saying?'

'I'm not saying anything.'

'So what are you thinking?'

Emma glanced across at him and shrugged her shoulders.

'Don't know,' she admitted.

'Get it out of here,' Garner hissed nervously from his vantage point in a doorway a safe distance away.

Michael looked around the circle and noticed that the others were suddenly either looking at the ground or looking at him. Sensing that it was up to him to make the next move he took a step forward and grabbed hold of the diseased woman's arm. He pulled her gently out of the hall and back towards the door which he opened with his free hand. He pushed her out into the sunlight and watched as she staggered away from the building and back across the car park.

10

The isolation and desperation of the situation affected all of the survivors, some much more than others. Carl spent most of the afternoon trying (unsuccessfully) to catch up on missed sleep and (also unsuccessfully) to forget everything that was happening outside. Time was dragging at an unbearable and painfully slow rate. An hour now felt like five and five hours more like fifty. As the sun began to sink back below the horizon he clambered out of the community hall once more and stood alone on the small area of flat roof he'd discovered the previous evening.

For a moment the air was pure and refreshing and he swallowed several deep, calming breaths before the now familiar smells of death and of burning buildings quickly returned, blown towards him on a cool and gusting wind. There was a sudden unexpected noise behind him and he span around to see Michael struggling to climb through the tiny skylight.

'Did I make you jump?' he asked as he dragged himself out onto the roof. 'Sorry, mate, I didn't mean to. I was looking for you and I saw you disappear up here and...'

Carl shook his head and looked away, disappointed that his little sanctuary had been discovered. In the community centre private space was at a premium and they had all been limited to just a few square feet each. Almost every move that every person made indoors could be seen by everyone else. Carl hated it and he'd been looking forward to getting out onto the roof and spending some time alone. The small square roof had been the only place so far where he'd been able to stretch, scratch, stamp, scream, punch and cry without feeling that he had to hold back on how he truly felt because of the effect it might have on the others. Stupid that almost everyone else was dead and yet he still instinctively found himself considering what the few remaining people might think of him rather than just being honest and true to himself. The effects of years and years of conditioning by society were going to take more than a few days to fade away.

'You're okay,' he sighed as the other man approached. 'I just came out here to get away for a while.'

'Do you want me to go back inside?' Michael asked anxiously, sensing that he was in the way. 'If you want me to go then I'll...'

Carl slowly shook his head again.

'No, it's okay.'

Glad to hear that he wasn't intruding (although not entirely convinced that he really was welcome) Michael walked across to stand next to Carl at the edge of the roof.

'What the bloody hell is happening?' he asked, his voice so low that Carl could hardly hear what he'd said.

'Don't know,' he mumbled in reply, equally quietly.

'Christ, it's just the speed of it all,' Michael mumbled. 'A few days ago everything was normal, but now...'

'I know,' Carl sighed. 'I know.'

The two men stood in silence for a while and surveyed the devastation around them. No matter how long and how hard either of them stared for, they still couldn't accept the sight of countless bodies lying face down on the cold ground. Even more difficult to accept were those pitiful corpses that were now moving. How could any of this nightmare be happening?

'Almost makes you envy them, doesn't it?' Carl muttered.

'Who?'

'The bodies still lying on the ground. The ones that haven't moved. I can't help thinking how much easier it would have been to be...'

'That's a fucking stupid way to talk, isn't it?' Michael spat.

'Is it?' he snapped back angrily.

In the heavy silence that followed Carl thought about his words. Bloody hell, how low and defeatist he suddenly sounded.

But why not, he thought? Why shouldn't he be? His life had been turned upside down and inside out and he'd lost everything. Not just his possessions and his property, he'd lost absolutely everything. And when he thought about poor Sarah and Gemma, lying there together in their bed at home, the pain he felt became immeasurably worse. But were they still there? Had they been affected by this new change? The thought of his beautiful little girl walking aimlessly through the dark streets alone was too much to bear. He tried unsuccessfully to hide the tears which streamed freely down his tired face.

'Come on,' Michael whispered, attempting to reassure him (although he already knew that there was no way he could).

'I'm okay,' Carl sniffed. It was patently obvious that he was not.

'Sure?' the other man pressed.

Carl looked into his face and forced himself to smile for a fraction of a second. He was about to reply with the standard 'yes, I'm alright,' when he stopped. There was no point in hiding the truth anymore.

'No,' he admitted. 'No, mate, I'm not alright...'

Suddenly unable to say another word, he found himself sobbing helplessly.

'Me neither,' Michael admitted, wiping tears of desperation and pain from his own eyes.

The two men sat down on the edge of the roof, their feet dangling freely over the side of the building. Michael stretched, yawned, and then ran his fingers through his matted hair. He felt dirty. He'd have paid any price to have been able to relax in a hot bath or shower and follow it up with a night spent in a comfortable bed. Or even an uncomfortable bed. Just something better than a hard wooden bench in a cold wooden building.

'You know what we need?' he asked.

'I can think of about a million things that I need,' Carl answered.

'Forget about all the practical stuff for a minute, and all the things that we should have like warmth, safety, security, answers to a million questions and the like, do you know what I need more than anything?'

Carl shrugged his shoulders.

'No, what?'

Michael paused, lay back on the asphalt and put his hands behind his head.

'I need to get absolutely fucking plastered. I need to drink so much fucking beer that I can't remember my own name, never mind anything else.'

'There's an off-licence over there,' Carl said, half-smiling and pointing across the main road. 'Fancy a walk?'

He glanced down at Michael who was shaking his head furiously.

'No,' he replied abruptly.

Another long silence followed.

'Christ, look at him would you,' Carl said, minutes later. Michael sat up.

'Who?' he asked.

'That one over there,' he said, nodding at a solitary figure in the distance which tripped and stumbled along the edge of the main road. The shadowy shell had once been a man, perhaps six foot tall and probably aged between twenty-five and thirty. It was walking awkwardly with one foot on the kerb and the other dragging behind in the gutter.

'What about him?'

Carl shrugged his shoulders.

'Don't know,' he sighed. 'Just look at the state of him. That could be you or me, that could.'

'Yes but it isn't,' Michael yawned, about to lie back down again.

'And there's another. See that one in the newsagents?'

Michael squinted into the distance.

'Where?'

'The newsagents with the red sign. Between the pub and the garage...'

'Oh yeah, I can see it.'

The two men stared at the body in the building. It was trapped in the entrance to the shop. A display rack had fallen behind it, blocking any movement backwards, and a crashed car prevented the door from opening outwards. The body moved incessantly, edging forward and then stumbling back, edging forward and then back.

'It just hasn't got a clue what's happening, has it?' Carl muttered. 'You'd think it would give up, wouldn't you?'

'It's just moving for the sake of it. It doesn't know how or why or what to do. It just needs to move.'

'And how long will they keep moving? Bloody hell, when will they stop?'

'They won't. There isn't any reason to stop is there? Nothing registers with them anymore. Look, watch this.'

Michael stood up and looked around. He walked over to where the slanted roof of the main part of the building met the flat roof they were standing on and pulled away a single slate. Carl watched bemused as he walked back to the edge of the roof.

'What the bloody hell are you doing?' he smirked.

'Watch,' Michael said quietly.

He waited for a few seconds until one of the wandering bodies came into range. Then, after taking careful aim, he threw the tile at the staggering corpse. He was surprisingly accurate and the tile hit the body in the small of the back. The body tripped and stumbled momentarily but carried on regardless.

'Why did you do that?' Carl asked, still bemused.

Michael shrugged.

'Just proving a point I suppose.'

'What point?'

'That they don't react. That they don't live like you and me, they just exist.'

Carl shook his head with despair and disbelief. Michael walked away again. In a strange way he regretted throwing the slate at the body. No matter what it was today, it had been a living, breathing human being just a few days ago. He felt like a mugger, preying on an innocent victim.

'Do you think it was a virus that did this?' Carl asked. 'Emma seems to think it was. Or do you think it was...'

'Don't know and I don't care,' Michael replied.

'What do you mean, you don't care?'

'What difference does it make? What's happened has happened. It's the old cliché, isn't it? If you get knocked down by a car, does it matter what colour it is?'

'So what are you saying?'

'I'm saying that it doesn't matter what did all of this. Okay, it matters in as far as I don't want it to happen to me, but what's done is done, isn't it?'

'Suppose so.'

'Look, I've lost friends and family just like the rest of them. I might sound like an uncaring bastard but I'm not really. I just can't see the point in wasting any time coming up with bullshit theories and explanations when none of it will make the slightest bit of difference. The only thing that any of us have any influence and control over now is what we do tomorrow.'

'So what are we going to do tomorrow?'

'Haven't got a fucking clue!' Michael laughed.

It started to rain. A few isolated spots at first which, in just a few seconds, turned into a downpour of almost monsoon proportions. Carl and Michael quickly squeezed back through the skylight and lowered themselves into the ominously silent hall.

'Does you good to get out now and then, doesn't it?' Carl mumbled sarcastically.

'There's a lot of truth in that,' Michael replied, fighting to make himself heard over the noise of the rain lashing down.

'What?'

'You're right. I think it would do us good to get out. Have you stopped to think about the bodies yet?'

'Christ I haven't thought about much else...'

Michael shook his head.

'No, have you stopped to think about what's going to happen when they start to rot? Jesus, the air's going to be filled with all kinds of germs and crap.'

'There's not a lot we can do about that, is there?'

'There's fuck all we can do about it,' he replied bluntly. 'But we could get away.'

'Get away? Where to? It's going to be like this everywhere, isn't it?'

'I don't know.'

'So what good will leaving here do?'

It became immediately apparent to Carl that Michael had been doing more logical thinking than the rest of the survivors put together.

'Think about it. We're on the edge of a city here. There are hundreds of thousands of bodies around.'

'And...'

'And I think we should head for the countryside. Fewer bodies has got to mean less chance of disease. We're not going to be completely safe anywhere but I think we should just try and give ourselves the best possible chance. We should pack up and leave here as soon as we can.'

'You really thinking of going?'

'I'd go tonight if we were ready.'

11

Despite the fact that each one of the survivors had reached new levels of emotional and mental exhaustion, not one of them could even contemplate trying to sleep. This lack of sleep meant that the disparate body of frightened and desperate people were becoming even more frightened and desperate with each passing minute. The hall was lit only by a few dim gas lamps and the odd torch, and this lack of light seemed to compound the disorientation and fear felt by all of them. By midnight the tensions and frustrations felt by even the most placid members of the group had risen to dangerously high levels.

Jenny Hall, who had held her three month old baby boy in her arms as he died on Tuesday morning, had dared to complain about the food she'd been given earlier in the evening. Although she'd meant nothing by her innocent comments, the cook - the usually quiet and reserved Stuart Jeffries - had taken it personally.

'You stupid fucking bitch,' he screamed, his face literally millimeters from hers. 'What gives you the right to criticise? Fucking hell, you're not the only one who's had it tough. Christ, we're all in the same fucking boat here...'

Jenny wiped streaming tears from her face with shaking hands. She was convulsing with fear and could hardly co-ordinate her movements.

'I didn't mean to...' she stammered. 'I was only trying to...'

'Shut your mouth!' Stuart shouted, grabbing hold of her arms and pinning her against the wall. 'Just shut your fucking mouth!'

For a second Michael just stood and watched, stunned and numbed and unable to quite comprehend what he was seeing. He quickly managed to snap himself out of his disbelieving trance and actually do something to help. He grabbed hold of Stuart and yanked him away from Jenny, leaving her to slide down the wall and collapse in a sobbing heap on the dirty brown floor.

'Bastard,' she spat, looking up at him. 'You fucking bastard.'

Michael manhandled Stuart across the room and pushed him down into a chair.

'What the hell is going on?' he demanded.

Stuart didn't respond. He sat staring at the floor. His face was flushed red. His fists were clenched tight and his body shook with anger.

'What's the problem?' Michael asked again.

Stuart still didn't move.

'Not good enough for her, are we?' he eventually muttered.

'What?'

'That little bitch,' he seethed. 'Thinks she's something special, doesn't she? Thinks she's a cut above the rest of us.' He looked up and stared and pointed at Jenny. 'Thinks she's the only one who's lost everything.'

'You're not making any sense,' Michael said, sitting down on a bench close to Stuart. 'What are you talking about?'

Stuart couldn't - or wouldn't - answer. Tears of frustration welled in his tired eyes. Rather than let Michael see the extent of his fraught emotion he got up and stormed out of the room, slamming the door shut behind him.

'What was all that about?' Emma asked as she walked past Michael and made her way over to where Jenny lay on the ground. She crouched down and put her arm around her shoulders. 'Come on,' she whispered, gently kissing the top of her head. 'It's alright.'

'Alright?' she sobbed. 'How can you say it's alright? After everything that's happened, how can you say it's alright?'

Kate James sat down next to them. Cradling Jenny in her arms, Emma turned to face Kate.

'Did you see what happened?' she quietly asked.

'Not really,' Kate replied. 'They were just talking. I only realised that something was wrong when Stuart started shouting.

He was fine one minute - you know, calm and talking normally - and then he just exploded at her.'

'Why?'

Kate shrugged her shoulders.

'Apparently she told him that she didn't like the soup.'

'What?' asked Emma incredulously.

'She didn't like the soup he'd made,' Kate repeated. 'I'm sure that's all it was.'

'Bloody hell,' she sighed, shaking her head in resignation.

Carl walked into the room with Jack Baynham. He'd taken no more than two or three steps when he stopped, quickly sensing that something was wrong.

'What's the matter?' he asked cautiously, almost too afraid to listen to the answer. The atmosphere in the room was so heavy that he was convinced something terrible had happened.

Michael shook his head.

'It's nothing,' he said. 'It's sorted now.'

Carl looked down at Emma on the floor and Jenny curled up in her arms. Something obviously had happened but, as whatever it was seemed to have been confined to inside the hall and resolved, he decided not to ask any more questions. He just didn't want to get involved. Selfish and insensitive of him it may have been, but he didn't want to know. He had enough problems of his own without getting himself wrapped up in other people's.

Michael felt much the same, but he found it impossible to be as private and insular as Carl. When he heard more crying coming from another dark corner of the room he instinctively went to investigate. He found that the tears were coming from Annie Nelson and Jessica Short, two of the eldest survivors. The two ladies were wrapped under a single blanket, holding each other tightly and doing their best to stop sobbing and stop drawing attention to themselves. Michael sat down next to them.

'You two okay? he asked. A pointless question, but he couldn't think of anything else to say.

Annie smiled for the briefest of moments and nodded, trying hard to put on a brave face. She nonchalantly wiped away a single tear which trickled quickly down her wrinkled cheek.

'We're alright, thank you,' she replied, her voice light and fragile.

'Can I get you anything?'

Annie shook her head.

'No, we're fine,' she said. 'I think we'll try and get some sleep now.'

Michael smiled and rested his hand on hers. He tried not to let his worry show, but her hand felt disconcertingly cold and fragile. He really did feel so sorry for these two. He had noticed that they had been inseparable since arriving at the hall. Jessica, he had learned from Emma, was a well-to-do widow who had lived in a large house in one of the most exclusive suburbs of Northwich. Annie, on the other hand, had told him yesterday that she'd lived in the same two bedroom Victorian terraced house all her life. She'd been born there and, as she'd wasted no time in telling him, she intended to see out the rest of her days there too. When things settled down again, she'd explained naively, she was going to go straight back home. She had even invited Jessica over for tea one afternoon.

Michael patted the old lady's hand again and stood up and walked away. He glanced back over his shoulder and watched as the two pensioners huddled closer together and talked in frightened, hushed whispers. Clearly from opposite ends of the social spectrum, they seemed to be drawn to each other for no other reason than their similar ages. Money, position, possessions, friends and connections didn't count for anything anymore.

Emma was still sitting on the floor two hours later. As half-past two approached she cursed herself for being so bloody selfless. There she was, cold and uncomfortable, still cradling Jenny Hall in her arms. What made matters worse was the Jenny had herself been asleep for the best part of an hour. Why am I always the one who ends up doing this, she thought? Christ, no-one ever bothers to hold me and rock me to sleep. Why am I always the one giving out? Emma didn't really need any help or support, but it pissed her off that no-one ever seemed to offer.

The hall was silent but for a muffled conversation taking place in one of the dark rooms off the main hall. Emma carefully eased herself out from underneath Jenny and lay her down on the floor and covered her with a sheet. In the still silence every sound she made, no matter how slight, seemed deafening. As she moved Jenny's body she listened carefully and tried to locate the precise source of the conversation. She was desperate for some calm and rational adult company.

The voices seemed to be coming from a little room that she hadn't been into before. Cautiously she pushed the door open and peered inside. It was pitch black, and the voices stopped immediately.

'Who's that?' a man asked.

'Emma,' she whispered. 'Emma Mitchell.'

As her eyes slowly became accustomed to the darkness of the room (which was, surprisingly, even darker and gloomier than the main hall) she saw that there were two men sitting with their backs against the far wall. It was Michael and Carl. They were drinking water from a plastic bottle which they passed between themselves.

'You okay?' Michael asked.

'I'm fine,' Emma replied. 'Mind if I come in?'

'Not at all,' said Carl. 'Everything calmed down out there?'

She stepped into the room, tripping over his outstretched legs and feeling for the nearest wall in the darkness. She sat down carefully.

'It's all quiet,' she said. 'I just had to get away, know what I mean?'

'Why do you think we're sitting in here?' Michael asked rhetorically.

After a short silence Emma spoke again.

'I'm sorry,' she said apologetically. 'Have I interrupted something? Did you two want me to go so you can...?'

'Stay here as long as you like,' Michael answered. Emma's eyes were slowly becoming accustomed to the darkness and she could now just about make out the details of the two men's faces.

'I think everyone's asleep out there. At least if they're not asleep then they're being very quiet. I guess they're all thinking about what happened today. I've just sat and listened to Jenny talking about...' Emma realised she was talking for the sake of talking and let her words trail away into silence. Both Michael and Carl were staring at her. 'What's the matter?' she asked, suddenly self-conscious. 'What's wrong?'

Michael shook his head.

'Bloody hell,' he sighed, 'have you been out there with Jenny all this time?'

She nodded.

'Yes, why?'

He shrugged his shoulders.

'Nothing, I just don't know why you bother, that's all.'

'Someone's got to do it, haven't they?' she replied nonchalantly as she accepted a drink from the bottle of water that Carl passed to her.

'So why does it have to be you? Christ, who's going to sit up with you for hours when you're...'

'Like I said,' she interrupted, 'someone's got to do it. If we all shut ourselves away in rooms like this when things aren't going well then we haven't got much of a future here, have we?'

Emma was immediately defensive of her own actions, despite the fact that she'd silently criticised herself for exactly the same thing just a few minutes earlier.

'So do you think we've got a future here then?' asked Carl. Now Emma really was beginning to feel uncomfortable. She hadn't come in here to be picked on.

'Of course we've got a future,' she snapped.

'We've got millions of people lying dead in the streets around us and we've got people threatening to kill each other because someone doesn't like soup. Doesn't bode well really, does it?' Michael mused.

Another silence.

'So what do you think?' Emma asked. 'You seem to have an opinion about everything. Do you reckon we've got any chance, or do you think we should just curl up in the corner and give up?'

'I think we've got a damn good chance, but not necessarily here.'

'Where then?' she wondered.

'Well what have we got here?' Michael began. 'We've got shelter of sorts, we've got limited supplies and we've got access to what's left of the city. We've also got an unlimited supply of dead bodies - some of them mobile - which are going to rot. Agree?'

The other two thought for a moment and then nodded.

'And I suppose,' he continued, 'there's also the flip-side of the coin. As good a shelter as this is, it's fast becoming a prison. We've got no idea what's around us. We don't even know what's in the buildings on the other side of the street.'

'But it's going to be the same wherever we go...' Emma remarked.

'Possibly. Carl and I were talking about heading out to the countryside earlier, and the more I think about it the more it seems to make sense.'

'Why?'

Carl explained, remembering the conversation he'd had with Michael a few hours ago.

'The population's concentrated in cities, isn't it? There will be less bodies out in the sticks. And less bodies equals less problems...'

'Hopefully,' Michael added cautiously.

'So what's stopping us?' Emma asked.

'Nothing,' Michael replied.

'Are you sure that you want to go?'

'Positive.'

'And what if no-one else does?'

'Tough. I'll go on my own.'

'And when are you going to go?'

'As soon as I can. I'd go tomorrow if I could.'

Emma had to admit that, arrogant and superior as he tended to sound, Michael's logic and reasoning made sense. The more she listened to and thought about his proposals, the more hopeful she became. Fired up with a new found enthusiasm and purpose, the three survivors talked through the first few long, dragging hours of the new day. By four o'clock that morning their plans were made.

12
Michael Collins

Bastards.

Spineless, fucking bastards.

Once I'd decided to leave that was it, I was going. It made so much sense. No-one could be sure what was going to happen next and no-one knew how safe we were going to be. Problem was the rest of them all seemed to agree that we should move on until the time came to actually do something about it. Until it was time to walk out the door they all agreed that getting out of the city made sense. When it came down to it though, none of them had the nerve to go. They were scared just sitting and waiting in the community centre for something to happen, but the thought of taking those first few tentative steps outside their new found comfort zone seemed to be even more terrifying. I stood there in the middle of the hall right in front of them all and told them why we should leave and like fucking sheep they nodded their heads and mumbled in agreement. Five minutes later though, when Paul Garner and Stuart stood up and had their say and told them why they thought it was better to sit still and wait for fucking eternity, the deal was done and the matter was closed. Suddenly it felt like it was me, Carl and Emma against the rest of them. I was beginning to identify more with the bodies outside on the streets than with the empty, lifeless bastards I found myself locked up with.

But that was it. Long and short of it, that was it. We could stay there and rot or we could go. It wasn't much of a choice.

That morning Emma stayed behind to pack our stuff together while Carl and I went out into the city to try and get everything we might need for our journey to God knows where. Once we were outside the stupidity and short-sightedness of the people hiding in the community centre became even more apparent. It was a bloody gold mine out there. Just about anything we wanted we could have, we just had to look for it. It was like shopping with a credit card that didn't have a limit, and the dead shop assistants were infinitely less irritating than they had been before they'd died. The strangest thing though was standing in the shops and looking out onto the silent streets. There were plenty of staggering bodies drifting about aimlessly. Truth be told, there wasn't much difference between the hordes of dead creatures today and the hordes of equally aimless consumers that had trampled the same streets less than a week earlier.

We found ourselves a decent sized car from a high-class garage. It was one of those people carriers with seven seats. We didn't have much stuff to take with us but it seemed to make sense to get the biggest car we could find. We decided that if push came to shove we could use it as a temporary shelter. We thought for a while about getting a Transit van or something similar but we decided against it. There didn't seem to be much point roughing it when we could have a little bit of comfort for no extra effort and at no extra risk.

We collected food and clothes because none of us had brought very much with us. From time to time while we were out in the open the option of actually going home to get our own things cropped up. At first I wasn't bothered about going back but Carl was certain that he didn't want to. He'd already told me a little about his wife and child and I understood why he didn't want to go anywhere near his place. I lived alone and the more I thought about it the more unnerving the thought of going back to my empty house seemed. The memories and emotions stored there were enough - I couldn't have coped if I'd left anyone behind. At the end of the day apart from my past all that was there were possessions which could easily be replaced. Just about anything I wanted I could take from the shelves of one of the desolate shops we looted.

I was losing all track of time. We had been up and out since nine o'clock but it felt like it was much, much later. During the week my days had lost all form, structure and familiarity. No-one slept much. People woke up whenever they woke up and kept themselves occupied as best they could until they couldn't keep their eyes open any longer. There were no set mealtimes, rest times or bedtimes, there was just time. Each hour dragged and seemed longer than the last.

Just before eleven Carl and I drove our silver van loaded with supplies back along the silent streets to the community centre.

13

Emma had managed to pack all her belongings into two carrier bags and a cardboard box. She did the same with Michael and Carl's things. Between the three of them everything they had was condensed into the sum total of five carrier bags and two boxes.

She breathed a sigh of relief at three minutes to eleven when Carl and Michael returned. The others had hardly spoken to her in all the time that the two men had been away from the community centre. It was almost as if she had suddenly ceased to exist. The rest of the survivors seemed to think that they were being abandoned, and Emma had real difficulty trying to understand why they felt that way. The invitation still stood for any of them - all of them if they wanted - to leave with Michael, Carl and herself. She guessed that the only thing stopping them was uncertainty and their personal and irrational fears of stepping outside the creaky wooden building. Countless times in those few hours she looked up and made eye contact with other people, only for them to look away again quickly. Countless times she heard people whispering behind her back. She knew that they were talking about her because nothing was private anymore. The eerie silence inside the hall amplified every spiteful word.

'Everything alright?' she asked as Michael parked the van in front of the building and clambered out and stretched.

'Fine,' he replied quietly, flashing her a quick and reassuring smile as he did so. 'You okay?'

She nodded.

Carl walked around from the other side of the van.

'We got everything we need,' he said. 'What do you think of the transport?'

She nodded again and slowly walked around the large family car. There were seven seats inside, two at the front, two at the back and three in the middle. The front two seats and the seat behind the driver's were empty. The others were piled high with supplies.

As she looked through the tinted glass windows it suddenly occurred to her that they were standing outside and, for the first time since it had all began, none of them seemed to be giving a damn about what had happened to the devastated world around them. They were surrounded by bodies - some still, some moving - and yet today she wasn't the least bit bothered. Perhaps it was because they were about to leave. Maybe deciding that she didn't need the protection of the hall anymore had subconsciously changed her way of thinking.

'Have any trouble while you were out there?' she asked, snapping herself out of her daydream.

'Trouble?' Carl replied, surprised. 'What kind of trouble?'

She shrugged her shoulders.

'I don't know. Christ, you spent the morning in the middle of a city full of walking corpses. I don't know what you saw. Did you...'

Michael interrupted.

'Nothing happened,' he said abruptly. 'There were plenty of bodies walking around, but nothing happened.'

'Not as many as I expected though,' Carl added.

'That's because they're starting to spread out,' Michael grunted as he shoved their carrier bags and boxes into the back of the van.

'Spread out?' said Emma.

'It's the blotting paper effect, isn't it?'

'Is it?'

Michael stopped and turned to face her.

'When all this started there was a high concentration of bodies in the middle of the city, wasn't there? People were at work and school, weren't they?'

'Yes...' she replied, unsure where the conversation was leading.

'So if those of them that are up and moving around are walking randomly, it stands to reason that they've spread out from the centre of the city like ink spreads across blotting paper.'

'I see...' she mumbled, far from convinced.

'It might take a while, but it's started and I bet that's what will happen.'

He returned his attention to loading the last two bags into the van. Emma continued to think, trying hard to follow through the route of his logic.

'So,' she eventually continued, 'if what you're saying is right, given time there could be equal numbers of bodies all over the country?'

Michael thought for a moment.

'Suppose so. Why?'

'Because if that's the case,' she said quietly, 'why the hell are we bothering to run?'

'We're not running,' he snapped, deliberately avoiding the very valid point of her comment. 'We're backed into a corner here. What we're doing is giving ourselves a chance.'

Sensing that the conversation had opened up a particularly unpleasant can of worms, he slammed and locked the van door and headed back inside.

The silence which greeted Michael as he walked back into the main hall was the most ominous silence he'd heard since he'd first arrived there days earlier. The rest of the survivors - all twenty or so frightened individuals - stopped and stared at him, Carl and Emma in unspoken unison. Some of those people hadn't acknowledged him in all the time they'd been at the community centre. Some hadn't even spoken a word to anyone since they'd got there. And yet, suddenly and unexpectedly, Michael got the distinct impression that it was the three of them against the rest. There was real animosity and anger in the room. It felt like betrayal.

The wave of hostility stopped Michael in his tracks. He turned around to face Emma and Carl. The three of them found themselves exposed and stood together in the centre of the room.

'What's all this about?' he asked, keeping his voice low.

'It's been like this since you went,' Emma replied. 'The rest of them seem to have a real problem with what we're doing.'

'Fucking idiots,' Carl snapped. 'It's because they know we're right. We should tell them that...'

'We'll tell them nothing,' Michael ordered. The surprising authority in his voice silenced and stunned Carl. 'Let's just go.'

'What, now?' Emma said, surprised. 'Are we ready? Do we need to...'

Michael glanced at her. The expression on his face left her in no doubt as to his intentions.

'What are we going to gain from waiting around?' he hissed. 'We're better off travelling in daylight so let's make the most of it. Let's get out of here.'

'Are you sure...?' Carl began.

'You sound like you're having doubts?' Michael snapped, the tone of his voice seeming almost to carry a sneer. 'You can stop here if you want to...'

Carl shook his head and looked away, feeling intimidated and pressured.

'Oh bollocks to it,' Emma said, her voice now a fraction louder. 'You're right. Let's just get out of here.'

Michael turned back to face the rest of the survivors who still stared at him and his companions. He cleared his throat. He didn't know what to say or why he was even bothering to try and say anything. It just didn't seem right to walk out without trying one last time to persuade the rest of them to try and see the sense in what they were doing.

'We're leaving,' he began, his words echoing around the cold wooden room. 'If any of you want to...'

'Fuck off,' Stuart Jeffries spat, getting up from his chair and walking up to Michael. The two men stood face to face. 'Just get in your damn car and fuck off now,' he hissed. 'You're putting us at risk. Every second you spend here is a second too long.'

Michael looked into his tired face for what seemed like an eternity. There were countless things he could have said to Jeffries and the others - countless reasons why they should follow and not stay locked in the community centre - but the anger bordering on hate in the other man's eyes left him in no doubt that to say anything would be pointless.

'Come on,' Emma said, grabbing his arm and pulling him away.

Michael looked around the room one last time and stared back at each one of the desperate faces which stared at him. Then he turned his back and walked.

Carl led the way out, closely followed by the other two. Just seconds after taking their first steps out into the cold afternoon air the door of the community centre was slammed and locked shut behind them. Sensing that there was no turning back (and feeling suddenly nervous and unsure) the three survivors exchanged anxious glances and climbed into the van. Michael started the engine and drove out towards the main road, pausing only to let a single willowy-framed, greasy-skinned body stagger oblivious past the front of the van.

14

Less than an hour into the journey and Carl, Michael and Emma found themselves wracked with fear and scepticism. Leaving the shelter had seemed like the only option but now, now that they had actually left the building and the other survivors behind them, uncertainty and unknowing had begun to set in and take over. Doubt which bordered on paranoia plagued Michael as he fought to keep his concentration and to keep the van moving forward. Problem was, he decided, they didn't actually know where it was they were going. Finding somewhere safe and secure to shelter had seemed easy at first but now that they were outside and could see the shattered remains of the world for themselves it was beginning to seem like an impossible task. The whole world seemed to be theirs for the taking but they couldn't actually find any of it that they wanted.

Emma sat bolt upright in the seat next to Michael, staring out of the windows around her in disbelief, looking from side to side, too afraid to sit back and relax. Before she'd seen it for herself it had seemed logical to assume that only the helpless population would have been affected by the inexplicable tragedy. The reality was that the land too had been battered, savaged and ravaged beyond all recognition. Countless buildings - sometimes entire streets - had been razed to the ground by unchecked fires which even now still smouldered. Almost every car which had been moving when the disaster had struck had veered out of control and had crashed. She counted herself lucky that she had been indoors and relatively safe when the nightmare had begun. She silently wondered how many other people that had died in a car crash or some other sudden accident might actually have gone on to survive had fate not dealt them such a bitter hand?

How many people who shared her apparent immunity to the disease, virus or whatever it was that had caused all of this had been wiped out through nothing more than misfortune and bad luck? Something caught her eye in a field at the side of the road. The wreckage of a light aircraft was strewn over the boggy and uneven ground at one end of a long, deep furrow. All around the wreck lay twisted chunks of metal which freely mixed with the bloody remains of the passengers the plane had been carrying. She wondered what might have happened to those people had they survived their flight? It was pointless to think about such things, but in a strange way it was almost therapeutic. It seemed to help just to keep her mind occupied.

With unnerving speed the three survivors found that they were becoming impervious to the carnage, death and destruction all around them. But, even though the sight of thousands of battered and bloodied bodies and the aftermath of hundreds of horrific accidents were now almost commonplace, from time to time each one of them still saw scenes that were so terrible and grotesque that it was almost impossible for them to comprehend what they saw. As much as he wanted to look away, Carl found himself transfixed with a morbid and sickening curiosity as they passed a long red and white coach. The huge and heavy vehicle had collided with the side of a red brick house. Carl stared in disbelief at the bodies of some thirty or so children trapped in their seats. Even though they were held tight by their seat belts, he could see at least seven of the poor youngsters trying to move. Their withered arms flailed around their empty, pallid faces, and the sight of the children made him remember Gemma, the perfect little girl that he had left behind. The realisation that he would never see or hold her again was a pain that was almost too much to bear. It had been hard enough to try and come to terms with his loss while he had been in the community centre but now, strange as it seemed, every single mile they drove further away made the pain even harder to stand. Sarah and Gemma had been dead for almost a week but he still felt responsible for them.

He'd just left them lying in bed together. He felt like he'd failed them.

Conversation had been sparse and forced since the journey had begun and the silence was beginning to deafen Emma. She could see that Michael was having to concentrate hard on his driving (the roads were littered with debris) and Carl seemed preoccupied but she needed to talk. The ominous quiet in the van was allowing her far too much time to think.

'Have either of you two actually thought about where we might be going?' she asked.

Neither of the men replied at first. Silently all three of them had been thinking about that question intermittently but there had been so many bizarre distractions that it had proved impossible for anyone to be able to decide anything.

'I've tried to think about it,' Carl admitted, 'but I can't think straight. I get so far and then I see something and...'

His words trailed away into silence. He sounded lost and helpless. Michael glanced into the rear view mirror and watched the other man's tired eyes as they darted anxiously around. He looked like a frightened little boy.

'Well we've got to decide something soon,' Emma said. 'We need some kind of plan, don't we?'

Michael shrugged his shoulders.

'I thought we'd got one,' he replied. 'Keep driving until we find somewhere safe and then stop.'

'But what does safe mean?' she asked. 'Is anywhere safe?'

'I don't know,' he sighed. 'You could argue we'd be safe anywhere. There's only the bodies that are moving to watch out for and they don't react to us.'

'But what about disease?' she continued. 'They're starting to rot.'

'I know they are.'

'So what are we going to do?'

He shrugged his shoulders again.

'There's not a lot we can do. We can't see the germs so we'll just have to take our chances.'

'So what you're saying is we could stop anywhere?'
He thought for a second.
'Yes.'
'So why haven't we? Why do we just keep driving and...'
'Because...' he snapped.
'Because we're too bloody frightened,' she interrupted. 'Because nowhere is safe, is it? Everywhere might well be empty and we might well be able to pick and choose but that doesn't matter. Truth is I'm too fucking frightened to get out of this fucking van and so are you two.'

With her sudden and unexpected admission (which both Michael and Carl silently agreed with) the conversation ended.

15

Three minutes past four.

The slow and laborious afternoon was drawing to a close and Carl knew that it would only be a couple of hours before the light began to fade. When he'd handed the driving duties over to Carl, Michael (who was now curled up on the empty seat in the back of the van, sleeping intermittently) had estimated that they should have reached the west coast in an hour or so. It had now been two and a half hours since they'd swapped places and still there seemed to be nothing ahead of them but endless road and aimless travelling.

It was a cool but bright afternoon. The brilliance of the sun belied the low temperature. It shone down from a slowly sinking position in a sky which was mostly blue but which was dotted with numerous bulbous grey and white clouds. The road glistened with the moisture which remained from a shower of rain they'd passed through a few minutes earlier.

Emma still sat in the front passenger seat, still sitting bolt upright, still scanning the world around them constantly, hoping that she would find them somewhere safe to shelter.

'Alright?' Carl asked suddenly, making her jump.

'What?' she muttered. She was miles away. She'd heard him speak but not heard what he'd said.

'I asked if you were alright,' he repeated.

'Oh,' she mumbled. 'I'm fine.'

'Is he asleep?' he asked, gesturing over his shoulder at Michael. Emma glanced back and shrugged.

'Don't know.'

At the mention of his name, Michael stirred.

'What's the matter?' he groaned, his speech slurred with exhaustion.

No-one bothered to answer him. He closed his eyes again and tried to sleep.

There was a hand-painted sign at the side of the road. It had been battered by the wind and was only partially visible. As they passed the sign Carl managed to make out the words 'cafe', 'turn' and '2 miles'. He hadn't had much of an appetite all day (all week if the truth be told) but at the thought of food he suddenly felt hungry. They did have some supplies with them in the van but in their rush to leave the city they had been left buried somewhere in amongst the various bags and boxes.

'Either of you two want anything to eat?' he asked.

Emma just grunted but Michael sat up immediately.

'I do,' he said, rubbing his eyes.

'I saw a sign for a cafe up ahead,' he mumbled. 'We'll stop there, shall we?'

There were empty grassy fields on either side of the uninterrupted road. There were no cars, buildings or wandering bodies anywhere to be seen. On balance Carl thought it was worth taking a chance out in the open. He needed a break. They all needed to stop for a while to try and get their heads together and decide what they were actually trying to achieve.

Suddenly interested in the day again, Michael stretched and looked around. He too noticed the lack of any obvious signs of human life. He could see a flock of sheep grazing up ahead. Up until that moment he hadn't stopped to think about the significance of seeing animals. In the city they'd seen the odd dog, and there had always been birds flying overhead, but the relevance of their survival had been lost on him because there had always been a million other confused thoughts running through his mind. Seeing the sheep in their ignorant isolation today forced him to think about it further. It must only have been humans that had been affected by the inexplicable tragedy. Whatever it was that had happened had left other species untouched. Their sudden arrival at the cafe interrupted his train of thought.

The tall white building appeared from out of nowhere. A large converted house that looked completely out of place in its lush green surroundings, it had been hidden from view by a row of bushy pine trees. Carl slowed the van down and turned left into a wide gravel car park, stopping close to an inconspicuous side door. He turned off the engine and closed his tired eyes. After hours of driving the effect of the sudden silence was stunning. It was like sitting in a vacuum.

Despite having been almost asleep only minutes earlier, Michael was by now wide awake and alert. Before Carl had even taken the keys out of the ignition he was out of the van and jogging over to the cafe door.

'Careful,' warned Emma instinctively.

Michael looked back over his shoulder and flashed her a brief but reassuring smile. The air was cold and fresh and he suddenly felt more relaxed and sure than he had done at any other time since they'd left the community centre.

He reached out and tried the door. It wasn't locked (it opened slightly inward) but it wouldn't open fully. He pushed against it with his shoulder.

'What's up?' asked Carl.

'Something's blocking it,' Michael replied, still pushing and shoving at the door. 'There's something in the way.'

'Be careful,' Emma said again. It was clear from the trepidation in her voice that she was nowhere near as comfortable with the situation as her two companions seemed to be.

Michael shoved at the door again, and this time it opened inward another couple of inches. He took a few steps back out into the car park and then ran at the door once more, this time charging it with his shoulder. This time the door opened just wide enough for him to be able to force and squeeze his bulky frame through into the shadowy building. He looked back at the others momentarily before disappearing inside.

'I really don't like this,' Emma muttered to herself, looking around anxiously. The cold wind blew her hair across her face and made her eyes water. She held her hand to her eyes to shield them from the sun and stared intently at the cafe door, waiting for Michael to reappear.

Inside the building he had found that the blockage preventing him from opening the door fully was the stiff and lifeless body of a teenage girl. She had fallen on her back when she'd died and his brutal shoving to get inside had forced her up and over onto her side, giving him those vital extra few inches space to squeeze through. He gingerly took hold of her left arm and pulled her out of the way. As he dragged the body clear he peered through a small square window and could see Carl and Emma standing in the car park waiting for him. He carefully laid the girl down out of the way and headed back outside.

'It's okay,' he shouted as he reappeared in the doorway. He had to shout to make his voice heard over the wind. 'It was just a body. I just...'

He stopped speaking suddenly. He could hear sounds of movement behind him. He could hear movement coming from inside the building.

'What's the matter?' Emma asked frantically as Michael half-ran and half-tripped back towards her.

Breathlessly he answered.

'In there,' he gasped. 'There's something in there...'

The three survivors stood in silence as a lone figure appeared in the dark shadows of the doorway. Its progress blocked by the lifeless body on the ground that Michael had moved, it turned awkwardly and stumbled out into the car park.

'Do you think it's...' Carl began.

'Dead?' Michael interrupted, finishing his sentence for him.

'It could be a survivor,' Emma mumbled hopefully although in reality she held out very little hope of that being the case.

From its stilted, uncoordinated movements Michael instantly knew that the figure which slowly emerged into the light was another one of the stumbling victims of the disaster. As it lurched closer Michael saw that it had been a woman, perhaps in her late fifties or early sixties, dressed in a gaudy and loose-fitting green and yellow waitress uniform. The remains of Tuesday morning's make-up was smudged across her wrinkled face.

'Can you hear me?' Emma asked. She knew in her heart it was pointless, but she felt that she had to try and force a response from the desperate figure. 'Is there anything we can do to...'

She let her words trail away into silence as the body approached. The world was silent save for the gusting wind and the relentless clump, clump of the creature's uncoordinated feet on the gravel as she took step after painful step towards the three survivors. The corpse tripped on an edging stone and fell towards Carl who instinctively jumped back out of the way. Emma leant down and helped her back onto her unsteady feet. The body walked slowly between them, completely oblivious to their presence, and then continued out towards the road. The road curved gently to the right but the woman's course remained relatively straight until she'd crossed the tarmac and become entangled in a patch of wiry undergrowth on the other side.

Michael and Emma watched the pathetic creature for a little longer. Michael couldn't help but think about what might happen to her. In his mind he pictured her staggering on through the dark night, through wind and rain, and he felt a sudden and surprising sadness. A poor defenceless old woman - a mother and grandmother perhaps - who had left for work last Tuesday just as she had done on any other day, she was now destined to spend what could be an eternity wandering without direction or shelter. He had managed to quickly build up a resistance to such thoughts and feelings in the city but now, now that they were out in wild, comparatively inhospitable surroundings, he found himself being deeply affected by the plight of the innocent victims of the disaster.

Carl had disappeared. Emma could see him moving around inside the cafe and she gestured to Michael to follow her into the building.

A short passageway led them to a large, dark and musty room which they cautiously entered. There were various bodies scattered around numerous tables and slumped awkwardly in comfortable chairs. Michael smiled morbidly to himself as he walked past the corpses of an elderly couple. They had been sitting opposite each other when they'd died. Alice Jones (that was the name on the credit card on the table) lay back in her seat with her head lolled heavily on her shoulders, her dry eyes fixed on the ceiling unblinking. Gravity had caught her husband somewhat differently. He was slouched forward with his face buried in the remains of a dry, mouldy serving of what was almost week-old scrambled eggs, sausage and bacon.

There was a noise from the kitchen area and Carl appeared carrying a large plastic tray.

'Found some food,' he said as he threaded his way over to the others through the confusion of corpses. 'Most of the stuff in there has gone bad. I managed to find some crisps and biscuits and something to drink though.'

Without responding Emma walked past the two men and made her way towards a large glass door at the end of the room. She pushed the door open and went back outside.

'Where the hell's she going?' Carl muttered.

Emma wasn't out of earshot.

'I'm not eating in there,' she shouted back into the building. 'You two can if you want.'

Michael looked around at his gruesome surroundings and obediently followed her back out into a grassy area beyond the car park. Carl also followed, a little slower than Michael because he was carrying the food and was having difficulty seeing his feet over the edge of the tray. Two bodies sitting in a bay seat by the window caught his eye. A woman and a man, both of whom looked like they'd been about his age, had been sitting next to each other when the virus had struck. Spread out over the table in front of them was a tourist map that was marked with spots and dribbles of dark dried blood. On the ground, twisted around his parents' feet and around the legs of their table, was a young

82

boy. His exposed face was frozen with pain and fear. At once all that Carl could see were the desperate faces of his own wife and child, and the sudden recollection of all that he had lost was almost too much to bear. With tears streaming down his cheeks he carried on out to the others, hoping that the gusting wind would hide his weeping from them.

Michael and Emma had sat down next to each other at a large wooden picnic table. Carl sat opposite them.

'You okay?' asked Michael.

'Does anyone want a can of coke?' Carl said, deliberately ignoring his question. 'There are some other cans inside if you'd prefer. I think I saw some bottled water...'

'Are you okay?' Michael asked again.

This time Carl didn't answer. He just nodded, bit his lip and wiped his eyes with the back of his sleeve. He began to busy himself by opening the food he'd brought outside.

'You look tired,' Emma said gently, reaching out and giving Carl's hand a quick and reassuring squeeze. 'Maybe we should stay here tonight. I know it's not ideal but...'

Her unexpected touch triggered a change in Carl. Suddenly, and without any warning, his defences seemed to crumble.

'Either of you two got kids?' he asked, his voice wavering and unsteady. Both Emma and Michael looked at each other momentarily and then shook their heads. 'I did. I had a daughter. The most beautiful little girl you've ever seen. She's got... I mean she had...'

'Hurts, doesn't it?' Emma said, sensing Carl's pain and sympathising (but not fully understanding) his obvious agony. 'My sister had two boys. Great lads, I saw them a couple of weeks ago and now...'

'Christ,' he continued, not listening to a word she'd said, 'they do something to you, kids. When we found out we we're expecting Gemma we were gutted - I mean absolutely fucking devastated. Sarah didn't talk to me for days and... and...'

'And what?' Michael pressed gently.

'And then she was born and everything changed. I tell you, mate, you can't understand what it's like until you've been there yourself. I watched that little girl being born and that was it. You never really know what life's all about until you've been there. And now she's gone... I can't fucking believe it. I feel so fucking empty and I just want to go back home and see her. I know she's gone but I want to see her again and just...'

'Shh...' Emma whispered. She tried desperately to think of something to say but instead settled on silence. She didn't fully appreciate the extent of Carl's pain, but she knew that nothing she could do or say would make him feel better.

'I'm fucking starving I am,' he sobbed, forcing the conversation to change direction. He grabbed a packet of biscuits and tore them open. A gust of wind picked up the empty cellophane wrapper and whisked it away.

As they ate Michael watched Carl sadly. He had always done his best to keep himself to himself and had often taken criticism from others for being so antisocial and insular in the past. Today though, watching his friend being torn apart with grief, he was strangely thankful that he had spent so much time alone and that he was not having to mourn a similar loss. True, he sometimes craved companionship (increasingly frequently as he'd got older), but Carl was obviously suffering with such excruciating pain that he found himself questioning the benefits of ever having been a family man. A like-minded friend had once said to him that they would never marry for that same reason. His friend had argued that after spending and sharing their adult life with one partner, the pain of any loss would have been too much to take and would have destroyed the memory of the years spent together. Watching Carl today, however, Michael thought how wrong his friend had been. Having a partner and a child seemed to have made Carl complete. True the pain was destroying him now, but would it have been any easier to have never experienced the love, memories and fond attachment that his family had obviously brought to him? Which was better, to be unfulfilled and never feel such attachments or to be complete for a while and then be torn apart with the agony of loss?

The further away from home and familiarity that Michael got, the more emotional and less self-assured he became.

The survivors sat and ate in virtual silence for half an hour. From where they were sitting they could see down along the side of the cafe. They could also see their well loaded van, and the thought of getting back behind the wheel and driving aimlessly again depressed each one of them. They knew that they had little option but to continue on their way but for a while the fresh air and open space was a refreshing change from the uncomfortable and musty confinement they had endured throughout the last week.

As was often the case, Emma was the first to disturb the silence.

'How are you two feeling?' she asked.

Neither man responded. Michael was deep in thought, playing with a broken can ring, and Carl was neatly folding an empty crisp packet. Both men waited for the other to answer.

'Do you still think we've done the right thing?'

Michael looked up at her with a puzzled expression on his face.

'Of course we have. Why, are you having doubts?'

'Not at all,' she answered quickly. 'It's just that we're sat out here and we don't seem to be making much progress. It'll be getting dark soon and...'

'Look, if push comes to shove we can sleep in the van,' Michael sighed. 'It won't be a problem. I know it won't be comfortable but...'

'I'm not worried,' she snapped, interrupting to justify her comments. 'I just think we should be on our way soon. The sooner we find somewhere to stop, the sooner we can get ourselves settled and sorted out.'

'I know, I know,' Michael mumbled, getting up from his seat and stretching. 'We'll get moving in a little while.'

With that he began to wander back down the side of the cafe towards the van. Emma stared after him. She found him a very strange man - equally inspiring and irritating. Most of the time he seemed cool, collected and level-headed, but there were occasions (like now) when he didn't seem to give a damn and his apathy was infuriating. Not for the first time in the last week their safety was on the line but Michael didn't seem the slightest bit bothered. She assumed it was because they hadn't yet found anywhere obvious to stop. If things weren't going Michael's way, she had noticed, he didn't want to know.

'You okay?' she asked Carl. He nodded and smiled. 'Arrogant sod, isn't he?'

Michael stopped walking when he reached the edge of the road in front of the cafe. He looked out across a lush green valley landscape and drew in several long, slow breaths of cool, refreshing air. He slowly scanned the horizon from left to right and then stopped and turned around with a broad grin plastered across his tired face. He beckoned the others to come over to where he stood. Intrigued and concerned in equal measures, Carl and Emma quickly jumped up.

'What's the matter?' Carl asked, his heart beating anxiously in his chest.

'Over there,' he replied, pointing out into the distance. 'Just look at that. It's bloody perfect!'

'What is?' mumbled Emma as she struggled to see what it was that he had found.

'Can't you see it?' he babbled excitedly.

'See what?' Carl snapped.

Michael moved around so that he was standing between the other two. He lifted his arm and pointed right across the valley.

'See that clearing over there?'

After a couple of seconds Emma spotted it.

'I see it,' she said.

'Now look slightly to the right.'

She did as instructed.

'All I can see is a house,' she said, dejectedly.

'Exactly. It's perfect.'

'So you found a house in the woods,' sighed Carl. 'Is that all? Bloody hell, we've passed a thousand houses already today. What's so special about this one?'

'Well you two had trouble seeing it, didn't you?'

'So?'

'So what does that tell you? What does the location of a house like that tell you?'

Emma and Carl looked at each other and shrugged their shoulders, sure that they were missing the point (if there was a point to be missed).

'No idea,' Emma muttered.

'It's isolated, isn't it? It's not easy to find. It's going to be right off the beaten track.'

'So, we're not trying to hide are we? There doesn't seem to be anyone left to hide from...'

Emma still couldn't understand what the big deal was. Carl on the other hand was beginning to get the idea.

'It's not about hiding, is it Mike?' he said, grinning suddenly. 'It's the isolation. People who lived in house like that must have been pretty self-sufficient.'

'That's exactly it,' Michael interrupted. 'Imagine this place in the winter. Christ, a couple of inches of snow and you're stuck where you are. And these people were farmers. They couldn't afford to be without heat and light, could they? My guess is that whoever lived in that house would have been used to being out on a limb and would have been ready for just about anything. I'll bet they've got their own power and everything.'

Emma watched the two men who had become much more animated than they had been at any other time in the last week.

'It's going to be hard enough for us to get there,' Carl continued. 'And you've seen the state of the poor sods left wandering the streets, haven't you? They'll never find us.'

'It's perfect,' Michael beamed.

16

After fighting for survival virtually every second of the way since the disaster had begun, a slice of good luck finally came the way of Michael, Carl and Emma. It really was nothing more than an unexpected chance. A welcome fluke.

They had been on the road again for just over an hour since leaving the cafe. Michael had certainly been right about the isolation of the house in the woods as it had proved impossible to find. It had taken them the best part of the last sixty minutes just to find the road which crossed the valley and their brief euphoria at finally seeming to have made some progress had once again quickly given way to desperation and melancholy.

The sides of the seemingly endless, twisting roads along which they travelled were lined with tall trees which made it virtually impossible to see very far into the distance in any direction. Irritation inside the van was rapidly mounting.

'This is bloody ridiculous,' Michael sighed. 'There must be something around here somewhere.'

Michael was driving again with Emma sitting directly behind. She leant forward and put a reassuring hand on his shoulder. He instinctively pulled away, annoyed and frustrated.

'Calm down,' she sighed, trying hard to soothe her companion's nerves despite the fact that her own were tattered and torn. 'Don't worry, we'll get there.'

'Get where? Fucking hell, all I can see are trees. I haven't got a clue where we are. We're probably driving in the wrong direction...'

'Got it!' Carl shouted.

'Got what?' Michael snapped.

Carl had been poring over the pages of a road atlas.

'I think I've found where we are on the map.'

'Well done,' he said sarcastically. 'Now can you find that bloody house?'

'I'm trying,' he replied. 'It's not easy. I can't see any landmarks or anything to check against.'

'So can you see any buildings round here?'

'Hold on...'

Carl struggled to focus his eyes on the map. He was being thrown from side to side as Michael followed the winding route of the narrow road.

'Anything?' Michael pressed impatiently.

'I don't think so,' Carl eventually replied. 'Look, can you slow down a bit? I'm having trouble...'

'Look, if you can't find any buildings on this road,' the other man interrupted angrily, 'do you think you could tell us how to get to another road that might actually lead somewhere?'

Another pause as Carl again studied the map.

'There's not very much round here at all...'

'Shit,' Michael cursed. 'There must be something...'

'Will you take it easy,' Emma said from the back. 'We'll get there.'

Michael thumped the steering wheel in frustration and then swung the van around a sharp bend in the road. He had to fight to keep control of the vehicle and then was forced to steer hard in the other direction to avoid driving into the back end of a car which had crashed into the hedge.

'If I've got this right then we should reach another bend in the road soon,' Carl said, sensing that they needed some definite direction. 'Just after the bend there's a junction. Take a right there and we'll be on a main road in a couple of miles.'

'What good's a main road? I just want a road with buildings on.'

'And I'm trying to find you one,' Carl shouted. 'Fucking hell, do you want to swap places 'cause all you've done is criticise everything I've tried to...'

'Bend coming,' Emma sighed, cutting right through their argument.

Without slowing down at all Michael steered round the sharp turn.

'Okay, here's the junction,' he said. 'Was it right or left here?'

'Right...' Carl replied. He wasn't completely sure but he didn't dare admit it. He turned the map round in his hands and then turned it back again.

'You're positive?'

'Of course I'm positive,' he yelled. 'Just bloody well turn right.'

Seething with anger and not thinking straight, in the heat of the moment Michael screwed up and turned left.

'Shit,' he hissed under his breath.

'You idiot, what the hell did you do that for?' Carl screamed. 'You ask me which way to go, I tell you, and then you go in the opposite bloody direction. Why bother asking? Why don't I throw this fucking book out of the window?'

'I'll throw you out of the fucking window,' Michael threatened. He became quiet as the road narrowed dramatically.

'Keep going,' suggested Emma. 'There's no way you're going to be able to turn the van around here.'

The width of the road narrowed alarmingly, and the tarmac beneath their wheels became potted and uneven.

'What the hell is this?' Carl demanded, still livid. 'You're driving us down a fucking dirt track!'

Rather than stop and admit defeat, Michael instead slammed his foot down harder on the accelerator, forcing the van up a sudden steep rise. The front right wheel clattered through a deep pothole filled with dark rain water which splashed up, showering the front of the van. He switched on the wipers to clear the muddy windscreen but, rather than clear the glass, they instead did little more than smear the greasy mud right across his field of vision, reducing his already limited visibility further still.

'There,' he said, squinting into the distance and looking a little further down the track. 'There's a clearing up ahead. I'll try and turn round there.'

It wasn't so much a clearing, rather a length of track where there was no hedgerow on one side and where there had once been a gate into an adjacent field. Michael slowed the van down to almost a dead stop and put it into first gear.

'Wait!' Carl shouted. 'Down there!'

He pointed through a gap in the trees on the other side of the road. Michael again used the wipers to clear the windscreen.

'What?' he asked, a little calmer now that they had stopped.

'I can see it,' Emma said. 'There's a house.'

Michael's tired and wandering eyes finally settled on the isolated building. He turned and looked at both Carl and Emma.

'What do you think?' Carl asked.

Rather than bother to answer he instead slammed his foot down on the accelerator again and sent the van flying down the track. Like a runner suddenly in sight of the finishing line there was a new found energy and steely determination about his actions.

A staggering body appeared from the darkness of the trees at the side of the track (only the fifth they'd seen since leaving the cafe) and wandered into the path of the van. His reflexes slowed by fatigue, Michael yanked the steering wheel to the left and swerved around the miserable creature, scraping the van against the hedge on the other side. For a fraction of a second he watched in the rear view mirror. The corpse stumbled on across the track and through the undergrowth on the other side, completely oblivious to the van which had just thundered past, missing it by inches.

Michael forced the van over another slight rise. Once over the top the survivors had a clear view of the building in the near distance. The track which they were following led directly to the front door of the large house.

'Looks perfect,' Emma said softly.

The uneven road became less defined with each passing metre. It swooped down through a dense forest in a gentle arc and then crossed over a little humped-back stone bridge. The bridge itself spanned the width of a gentle stream which meandered down the hillside.

'It's a farm,' Carl mumbled with remarkable perceptiveness as they passed an abandoned tractor and plough.

'Can't see any animals though,' Emma muttered, thinking out loud.

Michael wound down the window and sniffed the cool air. She was right - he couldn't see or smell a single cow, pig, sheep, chicken, duck or horse.

'Must have been an arable farm,' he said as he stopped the van in the centre of a large gravel yard, right in front of the house. Without saying anything else he climbed out and stretched, glad to finally be out of the driving seat.

The apparent tranquility of their isolated location belied the turmoil and devastation that they had left behind them. The three survivors stood together in silence and took stock of their surroundings. They were standing in a farmyard, about twenty metres square, boxed in by the stream, the farm buildings and the forest and littered with rusting farm machinery and unused supplies. On the furthest side of the yard (opposite to where the track crossed the bridge) were two dilapidated wooden barns. The farmhouse itself was a large and traditional brick-built building with a sloping grey roof which was dotted with green and yellow lichen. From the front the house appeared to be roughly rectangular. Three stone steps led up to a wooden porch which was the only protruding feature. Tacked to the side of the building was an out-of-place looking concrete garage with a grey metal door. Twisting ivy covered between a half and a third of the front of the building and the unchecked leaves had begun to crawl from the house across the roof of the garage.

'This looks perfect,' Emma continued to enthuse. 'What do you two think?'

As he was standing closest to her she first looked towards Michael for a response. Not for the first time today he seemed to be miles away, wrapped up in his own private thoughts.

'What?' he mumbled, annoyed that he had been disturbed.

'I said it looks perfect,' she repeated. 'What do you think, Carl?'

'Not bad,' he said nonchalantly, leaning against the side of the van. He was deliberately trying to hide the fact that being out in the open scared him. He didn't know who (or what) was watching them. 'It'll do for tonight.'

Michael slowly climbed the steps to the front door. He opened the porch and stepped inside. The other two watched from a distance, keen to know if anyone was home but too unsure to get any closer. Michael, on the other hand, was too tired to waste any more time. He banged on the door with his fist.

'Hello,' he yelled. 'Hello, is anyone there?'

Carl found the volume of his voice unsettling. He looked around anxiously.

When, after a few seconds, there had been no reply to his shouting and thumping, Michael tried the door. It was open and he stepped inside. Emma and Carl looked at each other for a moment before following him. By the time they were both standing in the hallway he had already been into every room downstairs and was working his way through the second storey. He eventually reappeared at the top of the stairs.

'Well?' asked Emma.

'It looks okay,' he replied breathlessly as he walked back down.

'Anyone in?'

He nodded and pointed towards a room on their right. Emma peered through the door into a large and comfortable sitting room. A single body - an overweight, white-haired man wearing a dressing gown, trousers and slippers - lay twisted painfully on the ground in front of an ornate open fireplace. Feeling a little safer now he knew that this was the only body, Carl went into the sitting room and walked over to the corpse. There was an unopened letter on the ground next to the man's lifeless hand.

'This must be Mr Jones,' he mumbled, reading from the address on the front of the envelope. 'Mr Arthur Jones, Penn Farm. Nice place you had here, Mr Jones.'

'No sign of Mrs Jones?' wondered Emma.

'Couldn't find anyone else,' Michael replied, shaking his head. 'And he looks too old for there to be any little Joneses here.'

Emma noticed that Carl had sat down next to the body. He was staring into its face.

'What's the matter?' she asked. No response. 'Carl, what's the matter?'

He shook his head, looked up at her and smiled.

'Sorry, I was miles away.'

Carl quickly looked away, hoping that the other two hadn't picked up on the sudden anxiety and unease he was feeling. Christ, he thought, he had seen literally thousands of dead bodies over the last few days, so why did this one in particular bother him? Was it because this had been one of the first bodies he'd actually sat down and looked at, or was it because this was the first body he'd seen with an identity? He knew the man's name and what he'd done for a living and they had broken into his home. It didn't feel right. He didn't believe in ghosts or anything like that but, at that moment, he was convinced that somehow Mr Jones would get his revenge on the three intruders.

Michael sat down in a comfortable armchair and shielded his eyes from the early evening sunlight which poured into the room.

'So will this do?' he asked. 'Think we should stop here?'

'There's plenty of room,' Emma replied, 'and there's the stream outside for water.'

'And it's not easy to get to,' Carl added, forcing himself to get involved in the conversation and ignore Mr Jones. 'Bloody hell, we had enough trouble finding it.'

'And it's a farm,' Michael said. 'There's bound to be much more to this place than just this house.'

'Like what?' Emma wondered. Michael shrugged his shoulders.

'Don't know,' he grinned. 'Let's find out, shall we?'

With that he jumped up from his seat and left the room. Carl and Emma followed him as he walked down the hallway with the entrance to the kitchen and the wooden staircase on his left and a succession of rooms on the right. He looked into (but didn't go into) a living room and a small office as he walked towards the back of the house. He stopped by the back door and looked back at the other two over his shoulder.

'There you go,' he said, grinning again. 'Told you. That should help.'

Intrigued, Carl and Emma peered past him. On the small lawn at the back of the house was a large gas cylinder mounted on a firm concrete base.

'Wonder what's in the shed,' Carl mumbled, looking into the trees at the bottom left hand corner of the garden.

'Probably just tools,' Emma guessed. 'You know, lawnmowers, that kind of thing.'

'Then what are those?' he said, nodding into a small store room to his left. Emma peered into the gloom and saw that everything she had thought would have been kept in the shed had been housed in this little room.

'Only one way to find out,' she said and she stretched past Michael and opened the door. She led the three of them across the lawn.

It was obvious that this was far more than just an ordinary garden shed. It was too big and strong to be a potting shed and too small to be anything to do with the farm stores. Carl pushed the door open and leant inside.

'What's in there?' Michael shouting, watching the other man with interest.

Carl reappeared.

'You won't believe this,' he gasped. 'It's only a bloody generator!'

'What? For making electricity,' Emma said stupidly.

'I bloody hope so,' Michael sighed under his breath. 'That's what they usually do.'

'Will it work?' she then asked, equally stupidly.

'Don't know,' Carl replied, 'I'll have a go at getting it going later.'

'We've got plenty of time to try,' Michael added as he turned and walked back towards the house. 'Think we should stop here then?' he asked sarcastically.

Neither Carl or Emma bothered to answer but it didn't matter. Individually they had all decided to stop the first moment they'd arrived. Penn Farm seemed the ideal place for them to sit and wait. What they would be waiting for, however, was anyone's guess.

17

Michael was asleep by eight o'clock. Curled up on a sofa in the sitting room of the rustic farmhouse, it was the best and most unexpected sleep he'd had since the disaster had begun. Fate had dealt everyone some bitterly cruel hands recently but, for this one man at least, a welcome respite in the nightmare had arrived.

The house was silent save for his gentle snoring and the muffled sounds of Emma and Carl's tired conversation. Although they were easily as tired as Michael, neither felt able to close their eyes for even a second. No matter how comfortable and peaceful their surroundings had unexpectedly become, they knew that the world beyond the walls of the building was as inhospitable and fucked up as it had been since the first minutes of the tragedy last week.

'I could have tried to get it going tonight,' Carl yawned, still talking about the generator in the shed behind the house. 'I just couldn't be bothered though. We've got plenty of time. I'll try it in the morning.'

Thinking about repairing the machinery had made him feel strangely relaxed. It reminded him of the job he used to do. He was looking forward to getting on with the job tomorrow and hoped that, for a short time at least, the grease and graft would allow him to imagine that he was back at work and that the last few days had never happened.

Emma and Carl sat on either side of the fireplace, wrapped up in their coats because the room was surprisingly cold. Michael had prepared a fire earlier but they had decided against lighting it for fear of the smoke drawing attention to their location. Their fear was irrational but undeniable. Chances were they were the only living people for miles around but they didn't want to take any risks, no matter how slight. Anonymity seemed to add to their security.

The large room was comfortably dark. A low, dancing orange light came from three candles which cast strange, flickering shadows on the walls. After an awkward silence that had lasted for a good ten minutes, Emma spoke.

'Do you think we're going to be alright here?' she asked cautiously.

'We should be okay for a while,' Carl replied, his voice quiet and hushed.

'I like it.'

'It's okay.'

The staccato conversation died quickly. Next time it was Carl who disturbed the quiet.

'Emma, you don't think...'

He stopped before he'd finished his question, obviously unsure of himself.

'Think what?' she pushed.

He cleared his throat and shuffled awkwardly in his seat. With some reluctance he began again.

'You don't think the farmer will come back, do you?'

As soon as he'd spoken he regretted what he'd said. It sounded so bloody ridiculous when he said it out loud but, nonetheless, the body of the farmer had been playing on his mind all evening. These days death didn't seem to have the same finality as it always had done before and he wondered if the old man might somehow find his way back to his home and try to reclaim what was rightfully his. He knew that they could get rid of him again if they needed to and that in a reanimated state he would pose little threat, but it was just the thought of the body returning which unnerved him. His thoughts were irrational but even so the hairs on the back of his neck had again begun to tingle and prickle with cool fear.

Emma shook her head.

'I'm sorry,' he blathered. 'Stupid thing to say. Bloody stupid thing to say.'

'Don't worry about it,' she insisted. 'It's okay.'

Emma turned away from Carl and watched a ghostly whisper of grey smoke snake away from the top of the candle nearest to her and dissolve into the air. She sensed that Carl was watching her and, for a moment, that made her feel suddenly and unexpectedly uneasy. She wondered if he could sense what she was thinking. She wondered if he knew that she shared his own deep, dark and unfounded fears about the body of the farmer. Logic told her that they would be alright and that he would stay down - after all, the bodies seemed to have risen *en mass* last week - they'd either dragged themselves up on that one cold morning or they'd stayed where they'd fallen and died. And even if Mr Jones did somehow rise up and start to walk again, his movements would be as random, stilted and uncoordinated as the rest of the wandering corpses. Pure chance was the only thing that would ever bring him back home. She knew that nothing was going to happen and that they were wasting their time thinking about the dead man but she still couldn't help herself.

'Alright?' Carl asked quietly.

She turned and smiled and nodded and then turned back and looked at the burning candle again. She stared into the flickering yellow flame and thought back to a couple of hours earlier when the three of them had shifted the body of the farmer and that of a farm hand that they'd found fallen at the side of the garage. Mr Jones had been the most difficult corpse to get rid of. He had once been a burly, well-built man who, she imagined, had worked every available hour of every day to ensure that his farm ran smoothly and profitably. By the time that Carl and Michael had got around to shifting his awkward bulk, however, his limbs had been stiffened and contorted by rigor mortis. She had watched with horror and disgust as one of the men had taken hold of his shoulders and the other his legs. With a lack of respect they had dragged him unceremoniously through what used to be his home. She recalled the look of irritation so clear on Michael's face when they hadn't been able to manoeuvre the farmer's clumsy bulk through the front door.

They had taken the two bodies into the pine forest which bordered the farm. Michael and Carl had shared the weight of the corpses (making two trips) and she had carried three shovels from the house. She remembered what happened next with an icy clarity.

After laying the bodies out on the ground Michael had turned to walk back towards the house. Emma and Carl had instinctively picked up a shovel each and begun to dig.

'What the hell are you doing?' Michael had asked.

'Digging,' Carl had replied. His answer had been factually correct, but he had completely missed the other man's point.

'Digging what?'

Thinking for a moment that he had been asked a trick question, Carl had paused before answering.

'Graves of course,' he replied before adding a cautious; 'Why?'

'That was what I was going to ask you.'

'What do you mean?'

Emma had been standing directly between the two men, watching the conversation develop.

'Why bother? What's the point?' Michael had protested.

'Pardon?' she'd interrupted.

'Why bother digging graves?'

'To put the bloody bodies in,' Carl snapped, annoyed that he was being questioned. 'Is there a problem?'

Instead of answering Michael had just asked another question.

'So when are you going to do the rest?'

'What?' Emma had sighed.

'If you're going to bury these two,' he had explained, 'then you might as well finish the job off and bury the fucking thousands of other corpses lying round the country.'

'Don't be stupid,' Carl had protested angrily. 'We can't...'

'For Christ's sake just look around you. There must be millions of bodies and not one of them has been buried. More to the point, none of them needs to be either...'

'Listen, we've taken this man's home from him. Don't you think that at the very least we owe him...'

'No,' Michael interrupted, his voice infuriatingly calm and level. 'We don't owe him anything.'

At that point he had turned and walked back towards the farmhouse. The light had started to fade with a frightening speed and he had almost been out of view when he'd shouted back to the others over his shoulder.

'I'm going back inside,' he'd yelled. 'I'm cold and I'm tired and I can't be bothered wasting any more time out here. There are all kind of things wandering round out here and I...'

'All we're doing is...' Carl had replied.

Michael had stopped and turned back around.

'All you're doing is wasting time. The two of you are standing out here risking your necks trying to do something that doesn't even need to be done. I'm going back inside.'

With that he had gone, and Carl and Emma had been left alone with the two lifeless bodies at their feet. They had stood together in silence, both unsure as to what they should do next. For a second Emma had been distracted. She thought she'd seen movement deeper in the forest. She wasn't sure, but she thought that she had caught a glimpse of another body staggering through the trees a short distance away. The thought of more bodies being close by made the cold night feel colder still and had returned her attention to the corpses on the ground.

Emma had been annoyed by Michael's attitude and manner, but what upset her most of all was the fact that he was right. He was cold, heartless and unfeeling but he was right. Whether they had wanted to bury the body out of duty to the farmer or out of instinct it didn't matter. The burial would have served no real purpose other than to make the two of them feel a little better and less guilty about what they were doing. But they were simply trying to survive. The farmhouse and everything in it was no use to Mr Jones any longer.

In the fading light they had reached a silent compromise. Rather than bury the bodies they had instead just placed a light covering of loose soil and fallen autumn leaves over the two dead men.

'What are you thinking about?' Carl asked, suddenly distracting Emma and bringing her crashing back into the cold reality of the living room.

'Nothing,' she lied.

Carl stretched out in the chair and yawned.

'What do we do next then?' he asked.

Emma shrugged.

'Don't know. If you're talking about tonight I think we should try and get some sleep. If you mean in the morning, I'm not sure. We need to decide if we're going to stay here first of all.'

'What do you think? Do you think we should stay here or...'

'I think we'd be stupid to leave right now,' said Michael, surprising the other two who turned to look at him. He had been sound asleep just a few moments earlier and his sudden interruption had startled Carl and Emma.

'How long have you been awake?' Carl asked.

'Not long,' he yawned. 'Anyway, in answer to your question, I think we should stay here for a while and see what happens.'

'Nothing's going to happen,' Emma mumbled.

'I bloody well hope you're right,' he said, yawning again. 'I think we should spend tomorrow trying to find out exactly what we've got here. If we're safe, sheltered and secure then I think we should stop.'

'I agree,' said Carl. He kept his motives hidden well. It wasn't that Carl particularly wanted to stay in the farmhouse, it was just that, for a few days at least, he didn't want to go anywhere else. In the journey from the city he had seen more death, carnage and destruction than he'd ever thought possible.

The old, strong walls of the house protected him from the rest of the shattered world.

'I'm going to bed,' Michael said as he stood up and stretched. 'I could sleep for a week.'

18

Emma was the first to wake up next morning. It was Saturday - not that it seemed to matter anymore - and she guessed by the amount of low light which was seeping in through the crack between the curtains that it was early morning, probably around four or five o'clock.

After a few seconds of disorientation she remembered where she was and how she'd got there. She gazed up at the ceiling above the bed she'd been sleeping on and stared at the numerous bumps, cracks and bubbles. Her eyes drifted towards the walls where, in the semi-darkness, she began to count patterns on the wallpaper. The design was made up of five different pastel-pink flowers (which looked grey in the half-light) printed on a creamy white background. The flowers were printed in a strict and repetitive rotational sequence.

Emma had counted twenty-three rotations of flowers on the wallpaper before she stopped to question what it was she was doing. She realised that, subconsciously, she had been filling her mind with rubbish. She realised that it was much easier to think about patterns on walls and other such crap than it was to have to think about what had happened to the world outside Penn Farm.

There was a sudden groaning noise from the side of the bed and she instantly froze rigid with fear. Lying perfectly still she listened intently. There was something in the bedroom with her. She was sure that she could hear something moving around on the floor next to the bed and for a moment she was too frightened to move. Her heart pounded in her chest with an anxious ferocity and she held her breath, petrified that whatever it was that was in there with her might sense her presence.

Ten long and terrifying seconds passed before she managed to pluck up enough courage to lean across to the side of the bed and look down. A wave of cool relief washed over her when she saw that it was Michael, asleep on the floor, curled up tightly in a thin sleeping bag. She lay back on the bed and sighed.

She was certain that Michael had begun the night sleeping somewhere else. They had talked together on the landing outside her room for a few minutes after Carl had gone to find a bed. There were four bedrooms in the house - three on the second floor and one in the attic - and she could clearly remember Michael going into one of the rooms adjacent to hers. So why was he sleeping on the floor next to her bed now? Was it because he thought that she might need him there for protection, or was it because he himself had found himself in need of company and reassurance in the dark hours of the night just passed. Whatever the reason she decided that it didn't matter. She was glad he was there.

By that point she was wide awake and there didn't seem to be any prospect of her getting back to sleep. Annoyed and still tired, she shuffled back over to the other side of the bed and swung her feet out over the edge. She lowered her feet down until they reached the bare varnished floorboards and then recoiled at the sudden chill which ran through her as her toes touched the ground. The temperature in the room was low and she was cold, despite the fact that she had slept virtually fully dressed. There were blankets and sheets on the bed, but she hadn't felt able to use them. She didn't know whether the bed had belonged to one of the bodies they'd left in the forest, and that thought had made her feel uneasy to the point that she hadn't felt comfortable enough to take off her clothes and sleep inside the bed. Still, even though she'd slept fully dressed on top of a dead man's bed, she'd been more comfortable there than at any other point in the last week.

Tiptoeing carefully so as not to wake up Michael, she crept around the cold room to the window and opened the curtains. Michael stirred and mumbled something unintelligible before rolling over and starting to snore gently, blissfully ignorant to the fact that Emma was watching him.

Leaning up against the cool glass she looked down onto a dull world. An early morning mist clung to the ground, settling heavily in every dip and trough. Birds sang out and flew between the tops of trees, silhouetted in black against the dull grey-purple sky. For a few short and blissful moments it was easy for Emma to believe that there was nothing much wrong with the rest of the world today. She hadn't often been up and about at four twenty-five (that was the precise time according to an alarm clock next to the bed) but she imagined that this was pretty much how every day must have started.

She spied a lone figure staggering aimlessly across a recently ploughed field just north of the farmhouse. She had seen thousands of the pitiful creatures over the last few days but she instantly decided that this one particular stumbling bastard was the one she hated the most. Her heart had sunk like a stone when she'd first spotted it tripping clumsily through the mist. If she hadn't seen it then perhaps she'd have been able to prolong the illusion of normality for a few minutes longer. But that was all it was - an illusion of a normality that was long gone and which would never be restored. And there she was, trapped in the same desperate and incomprehensible nightmare that she'd been stuck in last night and the night before that and the night before that... She began to cry and wiped her eyes, upset and annoyed. For a blissful few seconds everything had felt normal but now she felt like hell. She felt as cold, empty and lifeless as the body in the field.

'Everything okay?' a voice suddenly asked from the darkness behind her. Startled, Emma caught her breath and quickly span around. Michael stood in front of her, his normally bright eyes still dulled with sleep and his short hair matted and unruly.

'I'm alright,' she mumbled in reply, her heart still thumping.

'Did I scare you?' he wondered apologetically. 'I'm sorry, I tried to make as much noise getting up as I could but you...'

Emma shook her head, making it clear that it didn't matter. Her thoughts had been elsewhere. He could have screamed in her face and she wouldn't have noticed.

Michael took another step closer to her and she noticed that he too had slept in his clothes. She turned back to look out of the window and continued to scan the misty horizon, desperately hoping that she might catch sight of more movement. God, she hoped that they would see something else this morning. Not another one of the loathsome bodies though, she wanted to see something that moved with reason, purpose and direction like she did. She wanted to find someone else that was truly alive.

'What are you looking for?' Michael asked.

She shrugged her shoulders. She didn't want to answer him honestly.

'Nothing,' she grunted. 'There's no fucking point, is there? There's nothing left.'

Michael turned and walked silently out of the room, leaving her alone to look out over the dead world.

19

It was twenty past nine before Michael, Carl and Emma actually sat down together in the same room. They were in the kitchen. Carl and Emma sat in stony silence opposite each other around a circular pine table while Michael struggled to scrape together some breakfast from the meagre scraps remaining of the limited supplies they'd brought with them from the city.

The atmosphere at Penn Farm was heavy and subdued. Michael felt low - perhaps lower than he had done at any time during the last few days - and he was struggling to understand why. He'd expected to feel a little better today. The three of them had, after all, stumbled upon a place where they could shelter safely for a while. A place which offered isolation and protection and yet which was still comfortable and spacious. He looked out through the wide kitchen window and down onto the farmyard below and decided that it must have been the slight elation they'd felt last night that was making the cold reality of this morning so hard to accept.

The baked beans he had been cooking had started to stick to the bottom of the pan and spoil.

'Something burning?' Carl mumbled perceptively.

Michael grunted and stirred and scraped the beans with a wooden spoon. He hated cooking. The reason he was preparing the meal this morning was the same reason he'd been the first to cook food at the community centre back in Northwich. He had no community spirit and no real desire to please the others. Cooking was nothing more than a brief distraction. Rescuing the burning beans somehow stopped him from thinking about the world outside and all that he had lost for a few precious seconds.

Dejected and distant, he served up the food and carried the first two plates over to the table. Emma and Carl looked at the breakfasts which clattered down in front of them with disdain and disinterest as neither was feeling at all hungry. Each plate had on it a large serving of baked beans, a dollop of stodgy scrambled egg (prepared from a dehydrated mix usually used by mountaineers) and three hot dog sausages which had been boiled in brine. Emma managed half a smile in acknowledgement but Carl did not. He sniffed and stared at his food feeling exhausted and nauseous.

Emma picked up a fork and began to poke and prod gingerly at the food. She looked across at the other two and noticed that they were both doing the same. Each one of the survivors seemed to be trying their damnedest not to say or do anything that might result in them having to talk to or even look at the others. All three of them were being gripped tight and suffocated by a now familiar paradox - they each craved the security and normality of conversation, but they knew that such a conversation would inevitably lead to them talking about things that they were each doing their best to try and forget.

As the long minutes dragged on, Emma's patience wore thin. Eventually she cracked.

'Look,' she sighed, 'are we just going to sit here or should we actually think about doing something constructive today?'

Michael looked up and rubbed his tired eyes. Carl started to eat his food. Filling his mouth with burnt beans, undercooked sausage and powdered egg gave him an excuse not to have to talk.

'Well?' Emma pressed angrily.

'We've got to do something,' Michael quietly agreed. 'I don't know what yet, but we've got to do something...'

'We need some decent food,' she said, pushing her untouched breakfast away.

Michael thought for a moment.

'There's bound to be other things we need too.'

'Such as?'

'I don't know...clothes, tools, petrol...'

'We need to know what we've got here first.'

Carl watched Emma and Michael intently as they spoke, following the conversation, looking from face to face.

'You're right. First thing we should do is go through this house from top to bottom and see exactly what we've got. Space is going to be limited in the van so we don't want to be doubling up on anything.' Michael paused to take a breath. 'Carl, do you know what you'll need for the generator?'

Startled by the sudden mention of his name, Carl dropped his fork.

'What?'

Michael frowned.

'Do you know what you need to get the generator sorted?' he repeated, annoyed that the other man hadn't been listening.

He shook his head.

'No, not yet. I'll have a look later and try and work it out.'

'We should get it done straight after breakfast,' Emma suggested. 'I think we should check the house out from top to bottom then get out, get what we need and get back as quickly as we can.'

'The sooner we get started,' Michael added, 'the sooner we get back.'

He didn't need to say anything else. Emma was already up and out of her seat. She scraped her untouched food into a black plastic rubbish sack and swilled the plate in a bowl of cold water in the sink. Without saying another word she quickly smiled at the two men still sitting at the table and ran upstairs to start working, cleaning and searching her way through the farmhouse.

Prompted to move by Emma's sudden actions, Michael too jumped up and started to busy himself. Carl on the other hand was in no rush. He stayed sat at the table toying with - and occasionally eating - the cold food on his plate.

Last night the three survivors had made an unspoken agreement to stay at Penn Farm for the time being. It seemed relatively safe, secure and comfortable and had the potential to be much, much more. It was only as they scoured the house for supplies that the true potential of their location finally became apparent to Emma and Michael. Carl acknowledged it too, but he was still unsure. He wasn't yet completely convinced that they were safe anywhere.

Emma began at the top of the house and worked her way down. She started in an odd-shaped attic bedroom which Carl had quickly claimed as his own yesterday. The dull room was lit only by the light which trickled in through a small window at the front of the house. Other than a bed, a wardrobe and a couple of other items of furniture there was little of note to be found there.

Michael worked his way through the rooms on the second floor. Three more reasonably sized bedrooms and an old-fashioned but practical bathroom. He uncovered little that he didn't expect to find. Clothes (far too old, large and worn for any of them to consider wearing), personal possessions and trinkets and little else. As he sat on the edge of the large double bed that Emma had slept on last night and looked through an obviously antique jewellery box he found himself suddenly fascinated by the value of the items it held. Less than a month ago the rings, earrings, necklaces, bracelets and brooches (which, he presumed, had belonged to Mrs Jones - what had happened to her?) would have been worth a small fortune. Today they were worth nothing. Conversely the comfort of the wooden-framed bed he was sitting on made it worth millions in his eyes.

By the time Carl forced himself to get up and go outside the other two had almost finished. They met in the hallway and walked to the back door where they stood together and planned their next move. Buoyed by the unexpected novelty of finally having had something constructive and purposeful to do for a short while, Emma and Michael talked with what could almost have been classed as enthusiasm about the rest of the day which lay ahead of them. Michael had a grand plan to fill the van with supplies, make themselves safe in the grounds of the house and get the generator working. Much as it still reminded him of everything he'd lost, his aim was to get a television or stereo working by the time darkness fell. He wanted to bring beer back to the house so that he could drink and forget. He knew that it would only be an illusion of normality, and he also knew that when it finished the pain of reality would be almost unbearable, but that didn't seem to matter. He knew that the three of them were mentally and physically exhausted. If they didn't force themselves to stop soon then it would only be a matter of time before someone cracked. He was damn sure that, having survived so far, he wasn't about to go under.

20

Less than an hour later and Michael, Carl and Emma were ready to leave Penn Farm. Wrapped in as many layers of clothing as they could find, the three of them stood together at the side of the van and winced as a cold and blustery autumn wind gusted into their exposed and unprotected faces.

Doubt and uncertainty.

Their emotions had begun to take on an almost cyclical pattern. In turn they each felt utter desperation and fear and then sudden, short-lived elation and hope. They had spent the last week lurching from crisis to crisis. Since leaving the city those nightmare situations had been punctuated by brief moments of success and real achievement such as finding the house yesterday and realising its full potential this morning. As Michael had already discovered to his emotional cost, the temporary respite that those successes presented to them made the dark reality of their shattered lives all the more difficult to accept. No-one dared to think about what might happen next. No-one dared to think about what might happen tonight, tomorrow or the next day. As uncertain as anyone's future had always been, the survivors now seemed unable to look forward to their next breath of air with any certainty.

They had been standing in silence for almost five minutes when Michael managed to snap himself out of his trance and get into the van. Each one of them had a thousand and one unanswerable questions flying round their tired heads, and that constant barrage of questions seemed to prevent them from saying anything. Someone would think of something to say or something to ask, only to be distracted and thrown off track by another bleak and painful random thought.

Following Michael's lead Carl and Emma climbed into the van and sat down. Michael turned the key and started the engine. The noise made by the powerful machine echoed through the desolate countryside.

'Any idea where we're going?' Emma asked from the back of the van. She shuffled in her seat as she slid the precious key to the farmhouse into the pocket of her tight jeans.

'No,' Michael replied with admirable honesty. 'Have you?'

'No,' she admitted.

'Fucking brilliant,' Carl cursed under his breath as he leant against the window to his side.

Michael decided that whatever they did they weren't going to achieve anything by waiting. He slammed the van into gear and moved away down the long rough track which led to the road.

'I'm sure I used to come round here on holiday with my mum and dad when I was younger,' he sighed five minutes and three quarters of a mile further on.

'So do you know your way around?' Emma asked hopefully.

He shook his head and pulled out onto the smooth tarmac.

'No. What I do remember though is that there were loads of little towns and villages round here, all linked up by roads like this. If we keep driving in any one direction we're sure to find something somewhere.'

He began to push his foot down on the accelerator pedal, forcing the van along the twisting track.

'Hope we can remember the way back after this,' Emma mumbled.

'Course we will,' he replied confidently. 'I'll just keep going in one direction. We won't turn left or right unless we have to, we'll just go straight. We'll get to a village, get what we need, and then just turn around and come back home.'

Home. Strange word to use thought Carl because this definitely didn't feel like home to him. Home was a hundred or so miles away. Home was his modest three bedroom semi-detached house on a council estate in Northwich. Home was where he'd left Sarah and Gemma. Home was definitely not some empty fucking farmhouse in the middle of the fucking countryside.

Carl closed his eyes and rested his head against the cold glass. He tried to concentrate on the sound of the van's engine. For a few seconds the noise stopped him thinking about anything else.

Michael was right.

Within fifteen minutes of reaching the road they'd stumbled upon the small village of Pennmyre. As they approached they saw that it was not so much a village, more a short row of modest shops with a few car parking spaces and a pelican crossing. The silent hamlet was so small that the sign which said 'Welcome to Pennmyre - Please Drive Carefully' was just over a hundred meters from the one which read 'Thank You for Visiting Pennmyre - Have a Safe Journey'. But the compact size of the village was comforting. They could see it all from the main road. There weren't any dark corners or hidden alleys to explore.

Michael stopped the van halfway down the main street and climbed out, leaving the engine running in case they needed to get away at speed. On first impressions the sight that greeted them was disappointingly familiar. It was just what they had expected to find - a few bodies scattered on the pavement, a couple of cars crashed into buildings, pedestrians and each other, and the odd walking body, tripping and stumbling around aimlessly.

'Look at their faces,' Carl said as he stepped out into the cold morning air. It was the first time he'd said more than two words since they'd left the farmhouse. He stood on the broken white line in the middle of the road with his hands on his hips, just staring at the pitiful creatures that staggered by. 'Christ,' he hissed, 'they look fucking awful...'

'Which ones?' Emma wondered as she walked around the front of the van to stand close to him. 'The ones on the ground or the ones that are moving?'

He thought for a second and shrugged his shoulders.

'Both,' he eventually replied. 'Doesn't seem to be much difference between them anymore, does there?'

Emma shook her head slowly and looked down at a body in the gutter by her feet. The poor thing's lifeless face bore an expression of frozen, suffocated pain and fear. Its skin was tight and drawn and she noticed a peculiarly greenish tinge to its cold flesh. The first signs, she decided, of decomposition. Strange that the other bodies - those still moving around - had the same unnatural tinge to their skin too.

There was a sudden dull thump behind Carl and he span around anxiously to see that one of the awkward stumbling figures had walked into the side of the van. Painfully slowly it lurched around and then, quite by chance, began to walk towards the startled survivor. For a few long seconds Carl didn't react. He just stood there and stared into its cold emotionless eyes, feeling an icy chill run the entire length of his body.

'Bloody hell,' he hissed. 'Look at its eyes. Just look at its fucking eyes...'

Emma recoiled at the sight of the pathetic figure. It was a man who, she guessed, must have been about fifty years old when he'd died (although the unnatural tightness and hue of his skin made it difficult to be certain). The body staggered forward with stilted, uncoordinated and listless movements.

Carl was transfixed - his attention captured by a deadly combination of morbid curiosity and uneasy fear. As the cadaver approached he could see that both of the man's pupils had dilated to such an extent that the dull iris of each eye seemed almost to have disappeared. The eyes moved continually, never settling on any one object, and yet it seemed that whatever information was being sent from the dead eyes to the dead brain was not registering at all. The body moved ever closer to Carl, looking straight past him. It didn't even know he was there.

'Fucking hell,' Michael cursed. 'Watch out will you?'

'It's alright,' Carl sighed. 'Bloody thing can't even see me.'

With that he lifted up his arms and put a hand on each one of the man's shoulders. The body stopped moving instantly. Rather than resist or react in any way it simply slumped forward. Carl could feel the weight of the body (which was unexpectedly light and emaciated) being entirely supported by his hands.

'They're empty, aren't they?' Emma said under her breath. She took a few tentative steps closer to the corpse and stared into its face. Now that she was closer she could see a fine, milky-white film covering both eyes. There were open sores on its skin (particularly around the mouth and nose) and its greasy hair was lank and knotted. She looked down at the rest of the body - down towards the willowy torso wrapped in loose, dirty clothing - and stared hard. She was looking at the rib cage for signs of respiration. She couldn't see any movement.

Michael had been watching her as intently and with as much fascination as she'd watched the body.

'What do you mean, empty?' he asked.

'Just what I said,' she mumbled, still staring at the dead man. 'There's nothing to them. They move but they don't know why. It's almost as if they've died but no-one's told them to stop moving and lie still.'

He nodded thoughtfully and watched another one of the creatures as it wandered aimlessly across the road a little way ahead of the van. Carl again looked into the face of the body he was holding and then dropped his arms, allowing it to move freely again. The second he had released his grip the corpse began to stumble away.

'So if they're not thinking, why do they change direction?' he asked.

'Simple,' Emma answered. 'They don't do it consciously. If you watch them, they only change direction when they can't go any further forward.'

'But why? If they can't make decisions then they shouldn't be able to realise that they're stuck. When they hit a wall shouldn't they just stop and wait?'

She shrugged her shoulders.

'It's just a basic response, isn't it?' Michael said.

She nodded.

'Suppose so. It's just about *the* most basic response. Christ, even amoebas and earthworms can react like that. If they come across an obstruction then they change direction.'

'So what are you saying?' he pressed. 'Are they thinking or not thinking?'

'I'm not sure really...' she admitted.

'You sound like you're saying that they might still have some decision making capabilities...'

'Suppose I am.'

'But on the other hand they seem to be on autopilot, just moving because they can.'

Emma shrugged her shoulders again, becoming annoyed.

'Christ, I don't know. I'm just telling you what I think.'

'So what do you think? What do you really think has happened to them?'

'They're almost dead.'

'Almost dead?'

'I think that about ninety-nine percent of their bodies are dead. The muscles and senses have shut down. They're not breathing, thinking or eating but I think that there's something still working inside them. Something at their very base level. The most basic of controls.'

'Such as?' Michael asked.

'Don't know.'

'Want to take a guess?'

Emma seemed reluctant. She wasn't at all certain about what she was saying. She was improvising and having to think on her feet.

'I'm really not sure,' she sighed. 'Christ, it's instinct I suppose. They have no comprehension of identity or purpose anymore, they just exist. They move because they can. No other reason.'

Conscious that she had become the centre of attention, Emma walked away from the van towards the row of shops to her right. She felt awkward. In the eyes of her two companions her limited medical experience and knowledge made her an expert in a field where no-one really knew anything.

On the cold ground in front of a bakery the body of a frail and elderly old man struggled to pull itself up. Its weak arms flailed uselessly at its sides.

'What's the matter with it?' Carl asked, peering cautiously over Emma's shoulder.

'Don't know,' she mumbled.

Michael, who had followed the other two, nudged Emma's shoulder and pointed at an upturned wheelchair which lay a few metres away from the body. She looked from the chair to the body and back again and then crouched down. Fighting to keep control of her stomach (the rotting skin of the old man gave out a noxious odour) she pulled back one of his trouser legs and saw that the right leg was artificial. In its weakened state the body couldn't lift it off the ground.

'See,' she said, standing up again. 'Bloody think doesn't even know it's only got one leg. Poor bugger's probably been using a wheelchair for years.'

Disinterested in the crippled body and feeling nauseous and uneasy, Carl wandered away. He walked alone along the front of the row of silent shops and gazed sadly into the window of each building he passed. There was a bank - its doors wide open - and next to it an opticians. Two corpses sat motionless on dusty chairs waiting for appointments with their long since dead optometrist. Next to the opticians was a grocery store. Carl went inside.

Inside the shop was dank and musty. The pungent smell of rotting food tainted the damp air. The smell acted like smelling salts in suddenly reminding Carl of all that had happened. In a fraction of a second he was reminded of the nightmare of

Northwich, the loss of his family and everything else that had happened in the last week. He suddenly felt exposed, vulnerable and unsafe. Looking over his shoulder constantly he began to fill cardboard boxes with all the non-perishable food he could find in the tiny little store.

Emma and Michael arrived at the shop seconds later. In little more than a quarter of an hour the three of them had transferred much of the stock to the back of their van. In less than an hour they were back at Penn Farm.

21

Michael and Emma sat opposite each other at the kitchen table. It was almost four o'clock. Carl had been working on the generator outside for the best part of the afternoon. The back door was open. The house was freezing.

'There's got to be something driving them on,' Emma mumbled. 'I can't understand why they keep moving and yet...'

'Fucking hell,' Michael cursed, 'give it a rest, would you? What does it matter? Why should we give a damn what they do as long as they're not a danger to us. Christ, I don't care if I wake up to find a hundred and one of the fucking things stood around the house doing a bloody song and dance routine. As long as they don't come near me and...'

'Okay,' she snapped, 'you've made your point. Sorry if I don't share your short-sightedness.'

'I'm not short-sighted,' Michael protested.

'Yes you are. You don't give a damn about anyone but yourself...'

'That's not true.'

'Yes it is.'

'No it isn't. I'm looking out for you and Carl too. I just think we have to face facts, that's all.'

'We don't know any facts. We don't know fucking anything.'

'Yes we do,' he sighed. 'For a start it's a fact that it doesn't matter what's happened to the rest of the population as long as nothing happens to us. It's a fact that it doesn't matter why millions of people died. What difference would it make if we knew? What could we do? What if we found some fucking miracle cure? What are we going to do? Spend the rest of our lives sorting out fifty-odd million corpses at the expense of ourselves?'

'No, but...'

'But nothing,' he snapped.

'I can't help it,' she said quietly, resting her head in her hands. 'It's the medic in me. I've been trained to...'

'Forget all that,' he pleaded. Michael stared at Emma. She sensed his eyes burning into her and looked up. 'Listen to me,' he continued. 'Forget everything. Stop trying to work out what's happened and why. I'm not short-sighted and I'm not selfish, I'm a realist, that's all. What's gone is gone and we've got to make the most of what's left. We've got to say fuck everything else and try and build some kind of future for the three of us.'

'I know that,' she sighed, 'but it's not that simple, is it? I can't just turn away and...'

'You've got to turn away,' he said, slamming his hand down on the table and raising his voice. 'Christ, how many times do I have to say it, you've got to shut yourself off from the past.'

'I'm trying. I know I can't help anyone else, but I don't think you've thought about this like I have.'

'What do you mean?' Michael asked, sitting up in his seat. There was an equal mix of concern and annoyance in his voice.

'I want to make sure we're safe, same as you do,' she explained. 'But have you stopped to wonder whether it's really over?'

'What?'

'Who says that's the end of it? Who says that the bodies getting up and moving around last week was the final act?'

Michael realised what she was saying and a sudden cold chill ran the length of his spine.

'So what are you thinking?'

'I don't know,' she admitted, slouching forward again. 'Look, Mike, I think you're right, we have to look after ourselves now. But I need to know that whatever it was that happened to the rest of them isn't going to happen to me. Just because we've escaped so far doesn't necessarily mean we're immune, does it?'

'And do you think that we should...?'

Michael's words were cut short by a sudden loud crash from outside which echoed through the otherwise quiet house. He jumped up from his seat and ran out to where Carl was working. He found the other man sitting on the grass with his head in his hands. Through the half open shed door he could see a tool box on the ground which had clearly been kicked or thrown in anger.

'Okay?' he asked.

Carl grunted something under his breath before getting up and disappearing into the shed again.

'Is he okay?' Emma shouted from the safety of the back door.

Michael turned round and walked back towards her.

'Think so,' he sighed. 'Think he's having a few problems, that's all.'

She nodded thoughtfully and went back inside. Michael followed her into the sitting room. She sat down next to a large patio window and stared out onto the garden. It was a bright, sunny afternoon and she could see the shed from where she was sitting. Carl's tired shadow was clearly visible inside.

Cautiously (as he wasn't sure if he was disturbing Emma) Michael sat down on the arm of the sofa behind her. He picked up an old newspaper from a nearby coffee table, flicked through a few pages and then threw it back down again.

'Assuming we are immune and we do survive all of this...' he began quietly.

'Yes...' Emma mumbled.

'Do you think we'll be able to make something out of what's left?'

She thought for a moment.

'Don't know. Do you?'

He got up and walked to the other side of the room and leant against the wall.

'We can be comfortable here, I'm sure of that much. Christ, we could turn this place into a bloody fortress if we wanted to. Everything we need is out there somewhere. It's just a question of getting off our backsides and finding it...'

123

'Daunting prospect, isn't it?' she interrupted.

'I know. It's not going to be easy but...'

'I think the most important thing is deciding whether we want to survive, not whether we can.' She turned around to face Michael. 'Look, I know we could have anything - bloody hell, we could live in Buckingham bloody Palace if we wanted to...'

'...once we'd cleared out the corpses...'

'Okay, but you get my point. We *can* have anything, but we've got to ask ourselves if there's anything that will make any of this easier to deal with? I don't want to bust a gut building something up if we're just going to end up prisoners here counting the days until we die of old age.'

Michael sighed. Her honesty was painful.

'I agree. So what do you want? Accepting that we've all lost everything that ever mattered to us, what do you think would be worth surviving for now?'

She shrugged her shoulders and turned to look out of the window again.

'Don't know yet,' she admitted. 'I'm not sure.'

Michael's mind began to race. He hadn't dared to think about the future because, until yesterday, there hadn't seemed to be much chance of any of them actually having one. Ever the loner, however, he realised that there was in fact very little he needed. Shelter, food and protection, that was just about it. There were many aspects of his pre-disaster life that he was glad to finally have lost. Question was would time heal his, Carl's and Emma's mental wounds and allow them to make a life with what was left?

Their silent and personal thoughts were interrupted by another unexpected noise from outside. A roar of machinery followed by a low, steady mechanical chugging, followed by a scream of delight from Carl.

'Bloody hell,' Emma smiled. 'Will you listen to that!'

Michael left the room and was halfway to the back door when Carl appeared running the other way.

'Done it!' he gasped breathlessly. 'I've fucking done it!'

He slowed down, walked proudly into the kitchen and flicked the light switch on the wall. The fluorescent lighting flickered and jumped into life, filling the room with harsh, relentless and completely beautiful electric light.

22

The three survivors continued to work around the house until
just after nine o'clock that evening, the presence of electric light
having substantially extended the length of their useful day.
Once their supplies had been stored and the van and house made
secure for the night they stopped, exhausted. Emma made a meal
which they ate as they watched a video they'd found.

Michael, who had been sitting on the floor resting with his
back against the sofa, looked over his shoulder just after eleven
and noticed that both Carl and Emma had fallen asleep. For a
few moments he stared deep into their frozen faces and watched
as the flickering light from the television screen cast unnerving,
constantly moving shadows across them.

It had been a strange evening. The apparent normality of
sitting and watching television had troubled Michael. Everything
had seemed so very ordinary when they had started watching the
film an hour and a half earlier - within minutes each one of them
had privately been transported back to a time not so long ago
when the population of the country had numbered millions, not
hundreds, and when death had been final and inevitable, nothing
else. Perhaps the night felt so strange and wrong for that very
reason. The three of them had been reminded of everything that
they - through no fault of their own - had lost.

Michael found it disappointingly typical and increasingly
annoying that he had ended up thinking like that. Gone was the
time when he'd been able to enjoy the cheap and cheerful
comedy film such as the one he'd just sat through for what it was
- a temporary feel-good distraction, almost an anaesthetic for the
brain. Now just about everything that he saw, heard and did

seemed to spark off deep questions and fierce emotional debates inside him which he didn't want to have to deal with. Not yet, anyway.

His lack of concentration on the film had been such that he hadn't noticed it had finished until the end titles had been rolling up the screen for a good couple of minutes. Preoccupied by dark thoughts again he stayed sat on his backside, waiting for the tape to run out. As the music faded away and was replaced by a gentle silence he opened a can of beer and stretched out on the floor.

For a while he lay still and listened carefully to the world around him. Carl was snoring lightly and Emma fidgeted in her sleep but, other than that, the two of them were quiet. Outside there was the constant thumping and banging of the generator in the shed and he could hear a gusting wind, ripping through the tops of the tall pine trees which surrounded the farm. Beyond all of that Michael could just about hear the ominous low grumble of a distant but fast approaching storm. Through half-open curtains he watched as the first few drops of cold rain clattered against the window. The noise startled him at first and he lifted himself up onto his elbows. For a second he saw a definite movement outside.

Suddenly scared and nervous and pumped full of adrenaline, Michael jumped up, ran over to the window and pressed his face against the glass. He peered out into the dark night, hoping for a few anxious seconds that the mechanical noises being made by the generator had acted like the classical music had back in the city, attracting the attention of survivors who would otherwise have remained oblivious to their arrival at Penn Farm. He couldn't see anything. As quickly as he cleared the glass the rain outside and the condensation inside obscured his view again.

The others were still asleep. Thinking quickly Michael ran to the kitchen and picked up a torch that they had deliberately left on a dresser in case of emergencies. The light from the torch was bright and he followed the unsteady circle of illumination through to the back door of the house which he cautiously opened. He stepped out into the cold evening air and looked around, ignoring the heavy rain which soaked him.

There it was again. Closer this time. Definite movement around the generator.

With his heart thumping in his chest he made his way further into the garden towards the shed and then stopped when he was just a couple of metres away. Gathered around the walls of the small wooden building were four dishevelled figures. Even in the dim light and with the distraction of the wind, rain and approaching storm it was obvious that in front of him were four more victims of the disease, virus or whatever that had ripped through the population last week. Michael watched with curiosity and unease as one of the bodies collided with the door. Rather than turn and stagger away again as he'd expected it to have done, the bedraggled creature instead began to work its way around the shed, tripping and sliding through the mud.

Something wasn't right.

It took Michael the best part of a minute to decide what it was that was wrong, and then it hit him - they weren't going anywhere. The bloody things were moving constantly, but they weren't going anywhere. The movements of these corpses were as uncoordinated and listless as the hundreds of others they'd seen moving, but they were definitely gravitating around the shed.

When three out of the four bodies were around the back of the shed, temporarily out of the way, Michael pushed past the other one and opened the door. He slipped inside and, struggling to think over the deafening noise of the generator, he found the control panel that regulated the machine and switched it off.

After wiping his face and hands dry on a dirty towel and pausing to catch his breath, Michael went back outside.

By the time he'd shut the door to the shed he was alone. The four shadowy figures had drifted away into the darkness of the night.

23

Despite having gone to bed exhausted, Michael was awake, up and dressed by six o'clock the following morning. He had spent another uncomfortable and mostly sleepless night tossing and turning on the hard wooden floor at the side of Emma's bed. He was glad he'd woken up before she had. She hadn't said anything to make him think that she minded him being there, but he was quietly concerned as to what she thought his reasons were. Regardless of what she might or might not have been thinking, it made him feel much better not to be sleeping alone.

Even though his twenty-ninth birthday was now just a couple of weeks away, Michael had spent the last few dark hours curled up in fear like a frightened child. His mind had been full of the kind of irrational fantasies the like of which hadn't troubled him since he'd been eight or nine years old. In the early morning gloom he had hidden under his covers from monsters lurking under the bed and behind the wardrobe door and had found himself sitting bolt upright in the darkness, certain that something terrible and unidentifiable was coming up the stairs towards him. In his heart he knew that these were nothing but foolish thoughts and that the sounds he could hear were just the unfamiliar creaks and groans of the old house but that didn't make the slightest bit of difference. The fear was impossible to ignore. As a child there had always been the safety of his parents' room to rescue him from his nightmares but not today. Today there was nothing and no-one to help and the bitter reality beyond the door of the farmhouse was worse than any dark dream he'd ever had.

As soon as the morning light had begun to creep into the house he had felt more confident. The uncomfortable fear he'd experienced was quickly replaced by a uncomfortable foolishness leaving him feeling almost embarrassed that he'd been so frightened in the night. At one point in the long hours just passed, when the howling wind outside had been screaming and whipping through the trees with an incredible and relentless ferocity, he had covered his ears and screwed his eyes tightly shut, hoping with all his heart that he would fall asleep and wake up somewhere else. Although no-one else had seen or heard him, in the cold light of day he felt ashamed that he had allowed a chink to appear in his brash and arrogant exterior.

It was a strong, safe and sound house and Michael need not have worried. In spite of all that he had imagined in the darkness, nothing and no-one had managed to enter Penn Farm. Still drugged by sleep he stumbled into the kitchen and lit the gas stove. The constant low roar of the burner was strangely soothing and comforting and he was glad that the heavy silence of the early morning had finally been disturbed. Slightly more relaxed, he boiled a kettle of water and made himself a mug of strong black coffee which he quickly drank. He made himself some breakfast but couldn't eat much more than a couple of mouthfuls.

Bored, tired and restless, he desperately needed to find something to do. As he had already discovered to his cost recently, these days an unoccupied minute tended to feel like an hour and an empty hour seemed to drag on for more than a day.

A open door from the kitchen led to a large utility room which Michael wandered into aimlessly. He had spent some time in there yesterday, but no longer than half an hour. In the furthest corner of the room was a pile of empty cardboard boxes and other rubbish that the survivors hadn't yet been able to dispose of or find a home for. This had been the least important room in the house as far as the three of them had been concerned and, as such, they had paid it little attention other than to use it as a temporary store. Michael thought for a second or two about trying to sort the room into some kind of order but, if the truth be told, he couldn't be bothered. He wanted something to do, but it needed to be something interesting. He needed more than something that would just distract him. He wanted something that would grab his imagination and fully capture and hold his attention.

High on the wall opposite to the door he'd just walked through was a wooden shelf. Little more than a warped plank of wood held up by three rusty brackets, the shelf was piled high with junk. Curious, Michael dragged a chair across the room and climbed up to have a closer look. On first sight there seemed to be very little of any interest - some old garden tools and chemicals, faded and yellowed books and newspapers, glass jars full of nails, bolts and screws and the like - but then he came across an unexpected and unmistakable shape. It was the butt of a rifle. Cautiously he pulled the gun free and stood there, balancing precariously on the chair, admiring the cobweb and dirt covered weapon. Instinctively he reached up again and felt his way along the shelf, first to the left and then to the right of where he'd found the rifle. With his fingers at full stretch he grabbed hold of a dusty cardboard box which he dragged closer. Now standing on tiptoes with the rifle wedged under his arm he teased up the lid of the box and saw that it was full of ammunition. Like a child with a new toy he picked up the box, jumped down and carried everything back to the kitchen.

Emma got up at half-past eight and Carl rose three-quarters of an hour later. They found Michael sat at the kitchen table, carefully cleaning the rifle. He'd been working on it for over two hours and the job was almost complete.

Michael glanced up at Emma and noticed that she looked tired. He wondered whether she'd had as little sleep as he had. Although they'd only slept (or not slept) a few feet apart he hadn't dared disturb her in the darkness of the night.

'What are you doing?' she eventually asked him once she'd made and drunk a very necessary mug of coffee.

'I found this earlier,' he replied, stifling a yawn. 'Thought I'd have a go at cleaning it up.'

'What's it for?' Carl asked. Those were the first words he'd uttered since coming downstairs.

Michael shrugged his shoulders. Deadpan, and with a complete absence of any sarcasm or humour in his voice he replied.

'Shooting things,' he said. 'What else you going to use it for?'

'I know that,' he snapped, annoyed, 'but what are we going to use it for?'

He put the rifle down and looked up at Carl.

'Don't know,' he replied. 'Bloody hell, I hope we never need it.'

The rifle was clearly of interest to Carl. He sat down next to the other man and picked it up. Having spent all morning working on it, Michael seemed annoyed that someone else had dared to interfere.

'Put it down,' he said. 'I haven't finished with it yet.'

'You ever used one of these?' Carl asked, suddenly much more animated.

'No, but...'

'I have,' he continued to enthuse. 'Used to do some work for a bloke that used to shoot.'

'I don't like it,' Emma said from across the room. She was standing next to the sink. She couldn't have been any further away from the table. 'We don't need it. We should get rid of it.'

'I don't know. We don't even know if it's going to work yet...'

'Can't see any reason why it shouldn't,' Carl interrupted. 'Mind if I try it out?'

'Yes I do,' Michael protested. 'Bloody hell, I've spent bloody hours trying to get it...'

Carl wasn't listening. He jumped up from his seat, grabbed a handful of ammunition and headed for the front door. Michael looked over towards Emma. Surprised by his sudden disappearance they both stood still for a second before following him out.

By the time they reached the front door Michael could already hear the rifle being repeatedly cocked and fired. Fortunately Carl had been sensible enough to try and fire it before loading.

'Is he safe with that thing?' Emma asked quietly as they stepped out into a cold grey morning.

'Don't know,' Michael replied under his breath, still fuming that the other man had dared to take the rifle from him. He stared with piercing eyes as Carl loaded it.

'This is okay you know,' he babbled excitedly. 'This is just what we needed. You never know what's round the corner these days...'

'Don't know what frightens me more,' Emma mumbled, 'the fact that there are dead bodies walking round the countryside or him with that fucking gun.'

Michael managed half a smile which quickly disappeared when Carl lifted the rifle up and held it ready to fire. He pressed the butt hard into his shoulder, closed one eye and aimed into the distance.

'What the hell are you doing?' Michael demanded. 'Are you fucking stupid? All we need is for that bloody thing to blow back in your face and you're history...'

'It's okay,' he answered without moving or lowering the rifle. 'I know about these things. It won't blow back.'

'Just put it down will you?' begged Emma.

'Watch this. I'm going to get him...'

Puzzled, Michael stood behind him and looked along the barrel of the rifle. Carl was aiming through a gap in the trees, out towards a ploughed field a few hundred metres away. He squinted towards the horizon and saw that a lone figure was tripping clumsily through the uneven mud.

'Leave it, will you?'

'I'm going to get him,' he said again, shuffling his feet and getting the figure square in his sights. 'What's he going to do about it? Christ, he probably won't even know he's been shot.'

'You've got to hit him first,' Emma hissed cynically.

'Oh, I'll hit the bastard,' he said and, with that, he squeezed the trigger and fired.

For a long second the deafening sound of the shot rang out and echoed through the otherwise silent countryside.

'Missed him,' Carl spat, annoyed.

The figure in the field stopped moving.

'He's stopped,' Michael gasped. 'Fucking hell, he heard the shot. It's got to be a survivor.'

Stunned, Carl let go of the butt of the rifle and it swung down heavily to the ground. Still holding the barrel he took a few cautious steps forward.

'I didn't get him did I?' he asked anxiously. 'Shit, I was only trying to...'

'Shut up,' Michael snapped. 'You didn't get him.'

As they stared into the near distance the figure in the field began to move again. Instead of struggling on through the muddy fields, however, it had now changed direction. The bedraggled man was walking towards the house.

'He's coming this way, isn't he?' asked Emma, doubting what her eyes were telling her.

'Looks like it,' Carl mumbled in surprise.

Michael didn't say anything. He watched for a second longer until he was completely sure that the man was heading towards them before sprinting out to meet him. Apart from the survivors back in Northwich this was the first person they'd seen in a week who seemed actually able to react and respond to the outside world. He couldn't afford to let him out of his sight. And to think, moments earlier Carl had aimed a rifle at him.

Emma chased after Michael and Carl followed close behind.

The view from the farmhouse had been misleading. There was a hidden dip between Michael and the man which added an extra couple of hundred metres distance between them. Ignorant

to the uneven, clammy mud beneath his feet and to the pain of
the sprint and now to the climb back out of the dip, he continued
at speed, taking care to keep the lone stranger locked in his
sights every step of the way. He pushed himself to keep moving
faster and faster. He wanted to call out to him but he couldn't.
His mouth was dry and his heart was pounding was nervous
excitement.

'Hold on,' Carl moaned. He was a short distance behind
Emma. Not as fit as he would have liked to have been, he was
finding the running too much. Emma stopped and waited for him
to catch up, constantly keeping a close eye on Michael as she
did. She watched as he clambered over a metal five bar gate. He
was now in the same field as the man who continued to walk
closer and closer to him.

'You alright?' she breathlessly asked Carl.

He slowed down, shook his head and stopped next to her.
Doubled-over with exhaustion, he rested his hands on his knees
and sucked in as much cool, refreshing air as he could. He
looked up and watched as Michael stopped running and
approached the unknown man.

Michael wiped dribbles of sweat from his face and spat to
clear phlegm from his throat.

'Fucking hell,' he said between deep, forced breaths. 'Are
you okay? Christ the chances of us finding you like that must
have been...'

He suddenly lost his footing in the slimy mud and fell to
down his knees, landing at the feet of the other man. He looked
up into his face and, in a fraction of a second, all the hope and
elation he had felt suddenly disappeared. It was just another
corpse. The man's face was blank and cold and drained of all
emotion. His pockmarked skin was tight across his skull and had
a familiar grey-green hue and translucence. His dirty, ragged
clothes were loose and ill-fitting. He was as sick and diseased as
every other one of the lamentable bastards they had seen.

Dejected, Michael climbed to his feet and turned back to
shout the news to the others.

'It's no good,' he yelled, fighting to make his voice heard over a vicious, blustery wind. 'It's no fucking good. This bastard's just like the rest of them.'

Neither Emma or Carl could hear what he was saying. Confused, they watched as the scrawny man continued to move closer. He lifted his rotting head, seeming almost to be looking at Michael who was still facing the other way. The man's next movement was so unexpected that no-one, especially not Michael, had time to react.

The sound of a single sliding footstep squelching through the thick mud alerted him. He span around and found himself face to face with the foul creature. Before he could do anything it launched itself at him, grabbing hold of him with its emaciated arms. More from the surprise of the attack than its force Michael was sent slipping and sprawling to the ground. Suddenly forced into action, Carl sprinted to his friend's defence and grabbed the shoulders of the corpse that had now gripped hold of Michael tight with its skeletal fingers. Although weak and with little strength, the body held on with a savage and unexpected determination which proved difficult to break. Carl managed to pull its weakened frame up a little way, just far enough for Michael to be able to slide his hands under its bony abdomen and push it up and away. With one brutal and controlled show of force he thrust the body up into the air and rolled away to safety through the greasy mud.

'Okay?' Emma screamed, rushing to the Michael's side.

He wiped splashes of foul-smelling mud from his face and nodded, still fighting to catch his breath. Already tired from the run, the brutal speed and shock of the unexpected attack had winded him.

'I'm alright,' he gasped.

The body on the ground lay on its back, squirming and struggling to right itself again. It had just managed to haul itself up onto its elbows when Carl kicked it back down.

'Fucking thing,' he hissed. 'You stupid fucking thing.'

The body continued to twist and writhe. Oblivious to Carl's hate and comparative strength it again lifted itself up. Carl again kicked it back down.

'Fucking thing,' he spat for a third time before kicking the corpse in the side of the head. His boot collided with its left temple with a sickening thump and it stopped moving. A couple of seconds later it started again.

'Leave it,' Michael said. He had managed to stand and was being pulled back towards the house by Emma. 'Come on, Carl, just leave it.'

Carl wasn't listening. He began to lash out violently at the figure on the ground. He kicked it in the area of the left kidney, sending it rolling over and over away from him.

'Carl!' Emma pleaded. 'Carl, come on!'

She could clearly see hate and frustration in his face. He looked up at her for a fraction of a second before returning his attention to the rotting corpse in the mud. He spat into its vacant face before letting go with another brutal torrent of kicks. Oblivious to the battering it was taking, every time it was beaten down the creature continually tried to climb back up again. Dumbfounded, Carl took a breathless step backwards.

'Just look at this!' he shouted, pointing at the pathetic creature squirming in the mud. 'Will you just look at this fucking thing! It doesn't know when it's had enough.'

Emma could hear desperate, raw emotion clear in his voice. He sounded close to tears but she couldn't tell whether they were tears of pain, anger, fear or grief.

'Come on!' Michael yelled again. 'Don't waste your time. Let's get back to...'

He stopped speaking when he noticed that there was another figure in the field with them. Emma grabbed hold of his arm.

'Look,' she whispered, her voice barely audible.

'I see it. What the fuck is going on?'

The second figure was walking towards the survivors with the same slow, slothful intent as the first had just minutes earlier.

'There's another one coming, Carl,' Michael said, trying hard to control the rising panic in his voice.

'And another,' Emma gasped. A third creature was dragging itself up the field towards them.

Michael took her hand and half-helped and half-pushed her back over the gate.

'Get going,' he said quietly. 'Put your fucking foot down and get back to the house.'

'Okay,' she mumbled, her eyes filling with frightened tears. She clambered over the gate and took a couple of hesitant steps forward before pausing to look back. One last glance at the approaching bodies was enough. She turned and began running back towards the farmhouse for all she was worth.

'Carl!' Michael shouted. 'We're going. Pull yourself together...'

Carl looked up and finally saw the two corpses approaching. In a defiant last outburst of anger and frustration he kicked the still moving corpse in the head one more time. He caught it square in the face and felt bones shatter and break under the force of his boot. Thick crimson-black, almost congealed blood dribbled from a gaping hole where its nose and mouth had been. The creature finally lay still. Silently satisfied, Carl turned and ran after the others.

'I'm coming,' he yelled.

He sprinted back through the mud and hauled himself over the gate, almost losing his balance when a forth bedraggled body came at him from out of nowhere. He ran harder than he'd ever forced himself to run before, knowing full well that his life might depend on reaching the safety of the farmhouse.

By the time the three survivors had made it back to the house the first battered body in the field had dragged itself up onto its unsteady feet again. It turned awkwardly and followed eleven other bodies as they converged on the isolated building.

24

'What the fucking hell is going on?' Michael cursed as he pushed open the farmhouse door and ushered Emma inside. Carl followed seconds later and, as the second man entered the building, Michael slammed the door shut behind him and locked it. Emma slid down the wall at the bottom of the stairs and held her head in her hands.

'Christ knows,' she sighed, exhausted and out of breath.

Carl barged back past Michael to peer through one of the small glass windows in the front door.

'Shit,' he hissed under his breath. 'There are loads of them out there, bloody loads of them. I can see at least ten from here.'

He seemed strangely fascinated by everything that was happening outside. While Emma and Michael were content to shut the door and lock themselves away from the rest of the nightmare world, Carl was pumped full of adrenaline. Almost ready, it seemed, for a fight.

Michael sat down on the stairs next to Emma and gently rested his hand on her shoulder.

'They've changed,' she said, her head still held low. 'I don't know what's happened or why but they've changed.'

'I know. I saw it last night,' he whispered, 'when you and Carl were asleep.'

Emma looked up.

'What happened?'

'I went out to shut off the generator and there were four of them hanging around outside the shed.'

'You didn't say anything...'

'I didn't think anything of it until now. Anyway, as soon as I switched off the generator they disappeared.'

'Don't think they're coming any closer,' Carl said, his face still pressed hard against the glass, still ignorant to their conversation. 'Looks like they're starting to move away again.'

'Which way are they going?' Michael asked.

'Not sure. Might be heading towards the back of the house.'

'Back to the generator?' Emma wondered.

'Could be, why?'

She shrugged her shoulders and held her head again.

'Don't know,' she mumbled, rubbing her tired and tearstained eyes. 'Last night, did those bodies leave as soon as the generator was switched off?'

'I think so,' Michael replied.

'Well that's it then, isn't it?'

'What?' he pressed, suddenly feeling a little foolish and confused because although she seemed to understand some of what was happening, he didn't have a clue. He respected Emma's opinion but wished that he could understand for himself what was happening to the once human shells wandering around the desolate countryside. She may only have been a part-qualified doctor (if that) but that part-qualification seemed to make her the last surviving authority on what remained of the human condition.

'They're starting to regain their senses.'

'But why? Why now?'

'I don't know. Remember how they suddenly got up and started moving around?'

'Yes...'

'So this must be the same thing.'

'What the hell are you talking about?' Carl interrupted, turning from events outside to face the others and join their conversation.

'Don't know really,' she admitted. 'Perhaps they weren't as badly damaged as we first thought.'

'Jesus,' he laughed, unable to believe what he was hearing. 'They couldn't have been much more badly damaged, could they? They we're dead for Christ's sake!'

'I know that,' she sighed. 'So maybe it's just a small part of them that's survived. The only reactions we've seen have been basic and instinctive. I was taught that there's a lump of jelly right in the middle of the brain that might be responsible for instinct. Maybe that's the part of them that's still alive?'

'But they didn't attack me last night, did they?' Michael reminded her. 'I walked right past those bastards and...'

'Perhaps they were only just starting to respond last night? This is a gradual thing. From what you've told me it seems possible that they've only been like this for a few hours.'

'This sounds like bullshit,' Carl snapped angrily.

'I know it does,' Emma admitted, 'but you come up with a better explanation and I'll listen. One morning everyone drops down dead. A few days later, half of them get up and start walking around again. A few days after that and they start responding to the outside world and their eyes and ears start working again. You're completely right, Carl, it stinks. It does sounds like bullshit...'

'But it's happening,' Michael reminded him. 'Doesn't matter how ridiculous or far-fetched any of it sounds, it's happening out there.'

'I know, but...' Carl began.

'But nothing,' he interrupted. 'These are the facts and we've got to deal with them. Simple as that.'

The conversation ended abruptly and the house became deathly silent. The lack of noise unnerved Carl.

'So why did that thing attack you?' he asked, looking directly towards Michael for answer he knew the other man could not give.

'Don't know,' he admitted.

'I'm sure it's sound they respond to first,' Emma said. 'They hear something and turn towards it. Once they see what it is they try and get closer.'

'That makes sense...' Michael began.

'Nothing makes sense,' Carl muttered. Ignoring him, Michael continued.

'The noise from the generator last night, the gunshot this morning...'

'So we've just got to stay quiet and stay out of sight,' she sighed.

'And how the hell are we going to do that?' Carl demanded, suddenly and unexpectedly furious. 'Where are you going to get a fucking silent car from? What are we going to do, go out to get our food on fucking push-bikes? Wearing fucking camouflage jackets?'

'Shut up,' Michael said, calmly but firmly. 'You've got to try and deal with this, Carl.'

'Don't patronise me you bastard,' Carl hissed.

'Look,' Emma snapped, standing up and positioning herself directly between the two men, 'will both of you please shut up? It's like Michael says, Carl, we've got no option but to try and deal with this as best we can...'

'So what are we going to do then?' he asked, a little calmer but with his voice still shaking with an equal mixture of frustrated anger and fear.

'We need to get more supplies,' Michael said quietly. 'If they are becoming more aware and more dangerous all the time then I think we should go out right now and get as much stuff as we can carry. Then we should get ourselves back here as quickly as we can and lie low for a while.'

'And how long is that likely to be?' Carl asked, clearly beginning to wind himself up again. 'A week, two weeks? A month? Ten fucking years?'

'I don't know,' the other man replied, equally agitated. 'How the hell should I know that?'

'Shut up!' Emma yelled, immediately silencing the other two. 'For Christ's sake, if neither of you can say anything without arguing then don't bother saying anything at all.'

'Sorry,' Michael mumbled, running his fingers through his matted hair.

'So what *are* we going to do?' she asked.

Rather than answer or take any further part in the increasingly difficult conversation, Carl walked away.

'Where are you going? Carl, come back here. We need to talk about this.'

Halfway up the stairs he stopped and turned back around to face her.

'What's left to talk about? What's the point.'

'The point is we've got to do something and I think we should do it now,' Michael said. 'We don't know what's going to happen next, do we? Things could be a hundred times worse tomorrow.'

'He's right,' agreed Emma. 'We've got enough stuff here to last us for a few days but we need enough to last us weeks. I think we should get out now and barricade ourselves in when we get back.'

'What do you mean?' asked Carl, now much quieter and calmer. He sat down on the stair he'd been standing on. 'I don't want to shut myself away in here...'

'Maybe we shouldn't,' Michael said. 'Maybe we should try it a different way, try and seal off the farm from the outside.'

'And how are we supposed to do that?' Emma wondered.

'Build a fence,' he replied, simply.

'It'd have to be a fucking strong fence,' Carl added.

'Then we'll build a fucking strong fence,' Michael explained. 'We'll get whatever materials we need today and make a start. Face it we're not going to find anywhere better to stay than this place. We need to protect it.'

'We need to protect ourselves,' said Emma, correcting him.

'Let's go,' he said, picking up the keys to the van from a hook on the wall by the front door.

'Now?' said Carl.

'Now,' he replied.

Michael opened the door and made his way to the van, stopping only to pick up the rifle from where Carl had left it in the yard in front of the house.

25

Carl drove the van while Michael and Emma sat in the back together drawing up a list of everything they could think they might need. It had been a conscious move by Michael to hand the keys over to the other man. He hadn't liked the way Carl had been acting this morning. Sure all three of them were right on the edge at the moment, but his position seemed more precarious than that of the other two. There was an undeniable air of uncertainty and fear in his voice every time he spoke. Michael's logic was that by distracting him and giving him a definite role to concentrate on, his mind would be occupied and any problems could be temporarily avoided. He could sympathise with the poor bastard entirely. He knew that he personally could just about handle what was going on around him at the moment, but if anything else happened he wasn't so sure that he'd be able to cope.

Less than two minutes trying to draw up the list and the two survivors stopped, both of them quickly realising that it was a waste of their precious time and that they couldn't afford to even try and be specific anymore. Truth was they couldn't risk wasting time trying to find the things they thought they might need, instead they had no option but to fill the van with whatever they could lay their hands on and only stop when there wasn't space for anything else.

Carl drove towards the village of Byster at a phenomenal speed. Michael silently wished that he would slow down but he knew that he wouldn't. He'd found himself accelerating at a similar rate whenever he'd driven recently. Driving was deceptively difficult because although silent, every road was strewn with hundreds upon hundreds of random obstacles - crashed and abandoned cars, burnt out wrecks and the remains of collapsed buildings. There were scattered, motionless corpses and scores of other wandering bodies everywhere. When Michael had driven he'd found that a nervous pressure had forced him to keep accelerating. He felt sure that Carl was feeling that same clammy, noxious fear too.

Before they reached the village they passed a vast, warehouse-like supermarket, brightly painted and completely at odds with the lush green countryside which surrounded it. Carl slammed his foot on the brake, quickly turned the van around and drove back towards the large building. It was a crucial find. They guessed that pretty much everything they needed would be inside. More importantly, filling the van with supplies there meant that they didn't need to get any closer to the centre of the village. More to the point, it meant that they could keep their distance from the sick and diseased remains of the local population.

'Brilliant,' Carl said under his breath as he pulled into the car park and slowed the van down. 'This is fucking brilliant.'

He gently turned the steering wheel and guided their vehicle round in a wide and careful arc. Other than four stationary cars (two empty, one containing three motionless bodies and the other a charred wreck) and a single body which tripped and stumbled towards them they seemed to be alone.

'You want to get as close as you can to the main doors,' Michael advised from his position behind Carl. 'We want to be out in the open as little as possible.'

Carl's immediate response was to do and say nothing. After thinking for a couple of seconds he put the van into first gear and pulled away again. He turned away from the building and then stopped when the glass entrance doors were directly behind him.

'What's he doing?' Emma asked quietly.

'I think he's going to reverse back,' Michael replied, his voice equally low. 'It's what I'd do. If I was driving I'd try and get us almost touching the doors so that...'

He stopped speaking suddenly when Carl jammed the van into reverse gear and slammed his foot down on the accelerator pedal. The force of the sudden and unexpected movement threw Emma and Michael forward in their seats.

'Jesus Christ!' Michael screamed over the screeching of tyres tearing across the car park. 'What the hell are you doing?'

The other man didn't answer. He was looking back over his shoulder, looking past Emma and Michael and towards the supermarket doors. The engine whined as the van hurtled back towards the silent building.

'Carl!' Emma protested uselessly. She turned to look behind her and then crouched down with her hands over her head as she braced herself for impact. The van smashed into the plate glass doors and then stopped suddenly - the ear splitting noise of the engine immediately replaced by the deafening crash of shattering glass and the ominous groan of metal on metal. Carl pressed hard on the brake and Michael looked out of the window to his side. The van had stopped a third inside the building and two thirds out in the car park. They were virtually wedged in the doorway.

'You stupid fucking idiot!' Emma screamed.

Ignoring her, Carl turned off the engine, opened the tailgate using a control lever by his right foot, took the keys from the ignition and then clambered out over the back seats. He stepped out into the supermarket, his boots crunching and grinding jagged shards of glass into the marble floor.

'Good move,' Michael mumbled under his breath as he watched Carl. He quietly acknowledged that the other man's unorthodox parking, whilst battering the exterior of their van, had made their situation infinitely easier. Not only had he got them safely inside the building, he'd also managed to block the entrance at the same time, and the entrance would stay blocked until they decided to leave. He was impressed, but he didn't want Carl to know that he approved. Michael felt sure that he was having real difficulty in coming to terms with recent events and he thought it was important to keep his feet firmly planted on the ground. If he boosted his confidence by applauding his risky and very direct actions what would he do next?

Michael followed Carl out into the supermarket and Emma followed a few seconds later.

'Bloody hell,' she scowled, screwing up her face in disgust.

'Stinks, doesn't it?' Carl said, turning back to look at the others.

Michael covered his nose and took a few cautious steps further forward. The air was heavy with the sickening stench of rotting food and rotting flesh. More than just unpleasant, the obnoxious smell was stifling and suffocating. It hung heavy in the air and he could feel it coating his throat and dirtying his clothes and hair. It was making Emma retch and heave. She had to fight to control the rising bile in her stomach.

'We should get a move on,' Michael suggested. 'We don't want to be here any longer than we need to be.'

'I agree,' Emma said. 'I can't stand much of this...'

Her words were viciously truncated as she was knocked off balance by a lurching, staggering figure which appeared from out of nowhere. The stumbling creature had silently dragged itself along an aisle of rapidly decomposing food. Emma screamed and instinctively pushed the corpse away and down to the ground. Michael stood and watched as the remains of a gaunt, mousy-haired shop-assistant lay still for a second before its withered arms and legs began to flail around again as it desperately tried to haul itself back up onto its unsteady feet. Before it could get up he kicked it in the face and it dropped back down again.

'We should have a look around,' he said, anxiously looking from side to side. 'There's bound to be more of them in here.'

He was right. The deafening crash of the van as it ploughed through the glass doors had attracted the unwelcome attentions of a further five ragged cadavers which had been trapped inside the building. The clumsy remains of four shop staff and one delivery driver slowly advanced towards the three survivors. The battered body on the floor reached out a bony hand and grabbed hold of Michael's leg. He shook it free and kicked the creature in the head again.

'Fuck this,' he spat. 'We've got to shift them.'

He looked around again and spied a set of double doors behind a bakery display piled high with stale, mouldy bread. Without saying anything else he took hold of the body at his feet by its shoulders and dragged it across the floor. He kicked open the doors and threw the remains of the man into a room filled with cold, lifeless ovens. Making his way back towards Emma and Carl, he caught hold of the next closest corpse (a check-out operator) and disposed of it in exactly the same way.

'Carl,' he yelled as he made his way towards the third creature. 'Grab hold of another one, will you? If you're quick they don't have time to react.'

Carl took a deep breath and grabbed hold of the nearest corpse in a tight headlock. With its thrashing limbs carving desperate, uncoordinated arcs through the stagnant air he hauled it over to the bakery and pushed it through the double doors. It collided with the body of the dead check-out operator which, a fraction of a second earlier, had managed to lift itself back up onto its feet.

Sensing that quick action was needed, Emma ran over towards the others and shoved through the doors the remains of an elderly cleaner who, unbeknownst to Carl, had been staggering dangerously near. She dropped her shoulder and charged at the pitiful figure. The unexpected force of the impact sent the shuffling carcass (which had all the weight and resistance of a limp rag-doll) flying into the bakery.

In less than three minutes the survivors had cleared the main area of corpses. Once the last one had been safely pushed through the double-doors Michael wheeled a line of twenty or so shopping trolleys in front to prevent them from pushing their way out.

'Let's get a move on,' he said breathlessly as he wiped his dirty hands on the back of his jeans. He stood up straight and rested his hands on his hips. 'Just get whatever you can. Load it into boxes and pile it up by the van.'

In silence they began to work.

As Michael packed tins of beans, soup and spaghetti into cardboard boxes he nervously looked around. The cold, emotionless faces of the bodies in the bakery stared back at him through small square safety-glass windows in the doors. They were still moving continually. They were clamouring to get out but didn't have the strength to force themselves free. Were they watching him? Had they not acted quickly in locking the bastard things away, would they have attacked them in the same way that
the lone body in the field had attacked him earlier?

'Jesus Christ,' Carl said suddenly.

He was standing at the opposite end of the building to Michael and Emma, close to where the van had smashed through the entrance doors. His voice echoed eerily around the vast and cavernous room.

'What is it?' Emma asked, immediately concerned.

'You don't want to know what's going on outside,' he replied ominously.

Emma and Michael looked at each other for a fraction of a second before dropping what they were doing and running over to where Carl was standing.

'Shit,' Michael hissed as he approached. Even from a distance he could see what had happened.

Carl had been about to start loading the boxes into the back of the van when he'd noticed a vast crowd of diseased and rotting bodies outside. Their cold, dead faces were pressed hard against the windscreen and every other exposed area of glass. More of the creatures tried unsuccessfully to force their way through the slight gap between the sides of the van and the buckled remains of the supermarket doors.

Emma stared through the van at the mass of grotesque faces which stared back at her with dark, vacant eyes.

'How did they...?' she began. 'Why are there so many of them...?'

'Heard us breaking in, didn't they,' Michael whispered. 'It's silent out there. They'd have heard the van and the crash for miles around.'

Gingerly Carl leant inside the van and looked around.

'There are loads of the fucking things here,' he hissed, his voice just loud enough for the others to hear. 'There's got to be thirty or forty of them at least.'

'Shit,' Michael cursed.

'What?' Emma asked.

'This is just the start of it,' he replied. 'Fucking hell, that was a hell of a noise we made getting in here. The whole building's probably been surrounded by now.'

For a few dangerously long seconds the three survivors stood together in silence. They exchanged awkward, uncertain glances as each one waited for one of the others to make a move.

'We've got to get out of here,' Carl eventually said, stating the obvious.

'Have we got everything we need?' Michael asked.

'Don't care,' the other man snapped. 'We've just got to go.'

Michael immediately began to load boxes and bags of food and supplies into the van.

'You two get inside,' he said as he worked.

Carl loaded another two boxes and then clambered back through to the driver's seat.

'I'll get the engine going,' he shouted.

'Leave it,' Emma shouted back. 'For God's sake, leave it to the last possible second will you. The more noise we make the more of those bloody things we'll have to get through.'

He didn't say anything as he climbed through the gap between the front seats and slid down into position. On Michael's instruction Emma followed and lowered herself into the passenger seat, equally silent. The two of them stared in abject horror at the wall of dead faces gazing back at them. Trying hard to concentrate, Carl attempted to put the key into the ignition. He was shaking with fear. The more he tried to ignore the bodies and keep his hands steady, the more they shook.

'Last couple of boxes,' Michael yelled as he crammed more and more into the back of the van. He'd left just enough space for him to be able to climb inside and pull the tailgate shut.

'Forget the rest of it,' Emma shouted. 'Just get yourself inside.'

Carl managed to force the key into the ignition. He looked up and to his right. One of the closest bodies in the wretched throng lifted a clumsy hand into the air above its head. It slowly drew its weak and diseased fingers together to form an emaciated fist which, without warning, it brought crashing down on the driver's door window.

'Michael,' he shouted, his voice wavering with strained emotion. 'Are you in yet?'

'Almost,' the other man replied. 'Last box.'

Carl watched as a second body lifted its hand and smashed the side of the van. Then another and another. The reaction spread through the ragged bodies like fire through a tinder-dry forest. Within seconds the inside of the van was ringing with a deafening crescendo of dull thumps and relentless crashes. He turned the key and started the engine.

'I'm in,' Michael yelled as he hauled himself into the van. He reached out and grabbed hold of the tailgate which he pulled shut. 'Go!'

Carl pushed down on the accelerator and cautiously lifted his foot off the clutch. For a second there was no response then a slow, jerking movement as the van inched forward, shackled by the twisted metal remains of the supermarket entrance doors. Another lurch forward and they were free from the door but still progress was difficult, the sheer volume of bodies surrounding the front and sides of the vehicle preventing them from moving away at speed. Terrified, Carl pushed harder on the accelerator and lifted his foot completely off the clutch and this time the van moved away freely. The bulk of the bodies were brushed away to the sides but many others were dragged down under the wheels.

'Bloody hell,' Michael mumbled, watching events behind them through a small gap between boxes and bags of food.

'What's the matter?' Emma asked.

'They won't lie down,' he said. 'The bastards just won't lie down.'

He stared in horror and total disbelief as the crowd surged after them. Although their slow stagger was obviously no match for that of the van, the relentlessness and pointless persistence of the rotting gathering caused an icy chill to run the entire length of his spine. There was no point in them following the van, but still they came.

'Almost there,' Carl said under his breath as he steered towards the car park exit.

'Keep going,' Emma yelled, her voice hoarse with emotion. 'For Christ's sake don't stop.'

A single solitary figure stumbled out in front of the van and, rather than waste precious seconds trying to avoid the woman's body, Carl instead ploughed straight into it. The momentum of the van carried the corpse along for a few meters before it slipped down under the front bumper and was crushed beneath the wheels. As they left the car park and turned onto the road, Michael continued to watch the battered body on the ground. Its legs were smashed and shattered - that much was clear - and yet it still tried to move. The surging crowd tripped and stumbled over it ignorantly but still it continued to move oblivious. Reaching out with twisting, broken fingers, it dragged itself along the ground, inch by inch by inch.

26
Michael

I didn't know the true meaning of the word fear until we were on our way back to the farm. It was only then that the reality of our situation came crashing down around me. For the last few days life had begun to feel almost bearable - we had lived with our incredible situation for almost a week and the initial shock and desperation had, for a while, begun to subside and had been replaced by something resembling a sense of purpose. We had found ourselves somewhere safe where we could hide together and sit out the storm that had destroyed the rest of the world around us. But the bodies in the field and the visit to the supermarket had changed all that. Suddenly, having found some protection, we were exposed and vulnerable again. And the situation seemed to be deteriorating with each passing hour, practically each minute. As we drove back along roads strewn with rotting human remains and other wrecked remnants of society, I began to wonder what was next. How could things get any worse? The bodies were becoming more violent and unpredictable with each passing hour. If they were ready to tear us apart today, what would they be like tomorrow?

Once we'd made it back to the farm we quickly unpacked the van. We literally threw the boxes and bags into the house. I watched Emma and Carl as we worked and I could see that they were obviously as terrified as I was. The fear was impossible to hide. Every unexpected movement caused us to freeze and catch our breath and every sudden sound made our hearts miss a collective beat. Even the rustle of the wind through the bushes was no longer just an innocent background noise. Instead it had become a whispered warning and reminder to be constantly on our guard.

A few long hours later and the three of us found ourselves sitting around the kitchen table.

'So what are we going to do?' I asked. I couldn't just sit there and wait any longer.

Carl shrugged his shoulders and Emma did the same. To her credit she did at least answer me.

'Don't know,' she mumbled.

I had been thinking about our situation constantly, but I hadn't yet managed to come up with any constructive ideas other than to lock all the doors and sit and hide in the dark and wait. It wouldn't achieve anything, but at that moment it seemed to be the easiest option.

'We'll be alright if we can keep them away from the house,' Emma said a short while later.

'And how are we going to do that?' I instinctively asked.

'Build a wall or a fence?' she offered.

We had discussed building some kind of barrier before, and it still seemed sensible.

'I don't want to go out there again today,' Carl grumbled pathetically.

'Neither do I but if we don't do something,' I said, 'then we really are going to be trapped here. We won't be able to risk making a sound.'

'So how are we supposed to build a fence without making any noise?' Emma asked. A valid question to which I didn't have an answer.

'And what are we going to use to build this barrier?' Carl added.

Another question that I couldn't answer.

'I don't know,' I replied honestly. 'I suppose we'll just have to use whatever we can find lying around. This is a farm for Christ's sake. There's bound to be plenty of stuff if we look for it...'

Emma picked up a pen and a scrap of paper from the table. She began to sketch a very simple outline of the house.

'You know,' she mumbled as she drew, 'there wouldn't be as much work to do as you'd think. Look, we could build something from the wall of the house down the length of the yard, then take it straight across to the stream.'

It took a couple of seconds for me to understand what she was saying. From her rough sketch nothing was immediately apparent until she turned it around. As soon as I had my bearings and could associate the drawing with the house, the forest, the generator and the stream and bridge, it started to make sense. By using the barriers that we already had, we could cut down the amount of work we had to do virtually by half. At the moment the bodies still had trouble walking and moving with any co-ordination - there was no way that they'd be able to cross the stream. It wasn't particularly deep or wide but it was difficult enough for them to keep their balance on dry, solid ground.

'So what do we use to build this fence?' Carl asked again.

I thought for a few seconds.

'Doesn't have to be a fence, does it?'

'What do you mean?' he asked, confused.

'It just has to be a barricade,' I explained with a hundred and one ideas suddenly flooding into my mind. 'All we want to do is stop those things getting close to the house, isn't it? Doesn't matter how we do it. We could build a fence, dig a trench or just park cars and tractors around the place. That would be enough to keep them out.'

'You're right,' Emma agreed.

'Okay so they're strong in numbers,' I continued, 'but individually they're easy to stop. Emma, I watched you shoulder-charge the body of man twice your size today and you virtually threw it across the room.'

My mind was racing. It all seemed so simple and so obvious. Build a fence down from the side of the house to the bottom of the yard and then across until it meets the stream. Use the bridge as an entry point and block it off somehow. Do the same at the

156

back of the house and take the barrier out far enough to enclose the generator shed and the gas tank. Simple. Safe.

I took the paper and pen from Emma and began to draw over her basic markings. Perhaps feeling as if I was taking over, she stood up and walked away. Sensing that the conversation had ended (not that he had contributed much anyway) Carl also got up from his chair and left the room.

For a short time my planning and sketching brought a welcome distraction from the nightmare that was the outside world.

With my mind occupied the time passed relatively quickly. Before I knew it the morning had ended and we were well into the afternoon. Both Emma and Carl had found other ways and means to occupy themselves and I had been left alone in the kitchen to think and to plan.

By half-past two I had reached the stage where I knew exactly what I wanted to do and how I wanted to do it, but I wasn't sure what materials we had to use. Perhaps foolishly, I picked up the rusty rifle from where we'd left it lying on one of the kitchen units and went outside.

There were no bodies to be seen. The afternoon was dry and clear but cold. As summer had faded and died and autumn had arrived the temperature had dropped steadily. There was a light breeze rustling through the trees and bushes but otherwise the world was silent.

In the two large barns at the side of the yard I found some timber and a few fence posts. There was also some barbed wire. While I was there I looked at the barns themselves. They appeared strong but not indestructible. The wooden walls and the sheets of corrugated metal on the roof of each of the dull buildings also looked like they were going to be useful. On top of all of that I discovered numerous bits and pieces of farm equipment scattered around the place. I didn't know what half of it was for, but I knew that all of it could be used in someway to build a barrier between us and the rest of the diseased population.

I began to walk back towards the farmhouse feeling unusually calm and assured. The terror and stomach-wrenching fear of the morning had, for a time at least, subsided and been put to one side. The respite didn't last long. The light was beginning to fade and, as night rapidly approached, a single innocent and unexpected thought wormed its way into my tired brain and slowly and systematically destroyed the confidence and sense of purpose that I had spent the previous hours silently building up inside me.

I thought about a friend from work.

Just for a fraction of a second I pictured her face, and the memory of all that I had lost and left behind suddenly returned. With this torrent of unexpected memories came an equally unexpected torrent of pain and raw emotion.

For what felt like hours I sat alone on the steps outside the porch of the farmhouse and wept. I pictured the faces of my family and friends, of my colleagues from work, my customers, the people at the garage who had fixed my car a couple of weeks ago, the woman who'd sold me a paper on the morning it had all begun... as I saw each one of them the bitter realisation that they were gone forever felt like nails being driven into my flesh. And each dull pain was followed by a second hurt. While everyone I knew lay rotting in the streets - either lying motionless on the ground or dragging themselves around in endless agony - I had survived. Why me? Why should I have lived over all those others? I thought about my two brothers - Steven and Richard. I hadn't seen them for a couple of months. I hoped that they were like me and that they had survived. The thought of them being like those fucking monsters I'd seen this morning was too much to take...

But what could I do?

Why should I feel this way?

There was nothing I could have done to have changed any of it.

I picked myself up and went indoors. I was filled with a deep hurt that I knew would never completely disappear. But I owed it to myself to try and build something from what was left.

27

The barrier around the house took the three survivors all of the following day to complete. They worked almost constantly - beginning just after the sun first rose and only stopping when the job was finally done. As the light had faded the work had become harder to concentrate on and finish. Carl, Michael and Emma had each individually struggled to keep focussed on the task at hand and to ignore the mounting fear that the approach of darkness brought. The fear of drawing attention to themselves was constant and relentless. Throughout the day the generator had remained switched off. As far as was possible they worked in the safety of a shroud of silence.

Despite his earlier apparent apathy, Carl worked as hard as the other two to complete the vital barrier. For much of the time Emma stood guard with the rifle and, in some ways, that job proved to be the hardest of all. She had never held a loaded firearm before and, although Carl had shown her how to load, prime and fire the weapon, she doubted she would actually be able to use it should the need arise. Frustrating, often contradictory thoughts flooded her mind with an infuriating regularity. She had come to despise the wandering corpses which dragged themselves lethargically through the remains of her world. They were now so sick, diseased and dysfunctional that it had become almost impossible for her to comprehend the fact that a short time ago they had each been human beings with names, lives and identities. And yet, should one of them stumble into her sights, she wondered whether she would be able to pull the trigger and shoot it down. She wasn't even sure whether a bullet would have any effect. She had witnessed those creatures being battered and smashed almost beyond recognition, only to continue to move constantly, seemingly ignorant to the pain that their injuries and sickness must surely have caused. No matter what physical damage was inflicted, they carried on regardless.

It was fortunate that the house was so isolated. In the long hours spent outside only a handful of bodies had appeared. Whenever they became aware of movement the three survivors would drop their tools and disappear into the silent shadows of the farmhouse and wait until the withered creatures passed or became distracted by another sound and drifted away again.

Michael had impressed himself with his ingenuity and adaptability. As he had planned, they had used the stream as a natural barrier along one side of the farmhouse, building up the bank on their side with rocks and boulders from the water. Using the tall doors from one of the barns they had created a strong, padlocked gate across the stone bridge which spanned the width of the water. Two thick and removable crossbeams provided additional strength and security for the hours they would spend locked away inside the farmhouse. Much of the walls and roofs of the two barns had been stripped to provide extra materials to construct and reinforce the vital boundary. Now the remains of the buildings stood dejected and abandoned outside the fence, the bare bones of their empty frames reaching up into the air like the ribs of an animal carcass stripped of flesh.

In other places the barrier was little more than a collection of carefully placed obstructions. Piles of farm machinery and unneeded bags of chemicals were arranged to create a hopefully impenetrable blockade. Michael judged the success of each section of barrier by whether he could get through or over to the other side. If he had trouble then the tired and sickly bodies would surely have no chance.

As Monday evening drew to a close and the early dark hours of Tuesday morning approached, Michael stood outside checking and rechecking that the barrier was secure. Everything he could find that they wouldn't need was placed against the fence or used to build it higher. As he worked in his cold isolation it occurred to him that it was one week to the day since the nightmare had begun. The longest seven days of his life. In that time he had experienced more pain, fear, frustration and outright terror than he would ever have thought possible. He refused to allow himself to think about what might be waiting for him tomorrow.

28

Wednesday night. Nine o'clock.

Michael cooked a meal for himself, Carl and Emma. He seemed to have allowed himself to relax slightly now that there was a decent physical barrier between them and the rest of the world. Emma noticed that he had now started to occupy his time by doing odd jobs around the house. She had casually mentioned that a shelf in an upstairs room was coming loose from the wall. By the time she'd next walked past the room Michael had completed the repair. Each one of the survivors had an increasing, burning desire - almost a guttural, basic need in fact - to keep themselves occupied. Keeping busy helped them to forget (almost to the point of denial) that the world outside their door had crumbled and died.

The three of them had been sitting in the kitchen for the best part of two hours before the meal was ready and Michael was finally in a position to serve dinner. It was the longest length of time that they'd willingly spent in each other's company since the trip to Byster a few days earlier. The atmosphere was subdued and low as was to be expected. Conversation was sparse. Michael busied himself cooking (as usual), Emma read a book and for the most part, Carl did very little.

Emma found some wine. She had discovered a few bottles hidden in a dusty rack wedged between two kitchen units and she'd wasted no time in uncorking a bottle of white and pouring out three large glasses, passing one each to Carl and Michael. Carl normally didn't drink wine but tonight he was ready to make an exception. He wanted to get drunk. He wanted to be so fucking drunk that he couldn't remember his own name. He wanted to pass out on the kitchen floor and forget about everything for as long as was possible. He wasn't even that bothered about waking up the next morning.

The food was good - probably the best meal they'd eaten together - and that, combined with the wine, helped perpetuate an uneasy sense of normality. That sense of normality, however, had the unwanted side effect of helping them to remember everything about the past that they had been trying to forget. Michael decided that the best way of dealing with what they'd lost was to try and talk about it.

'So,' he began, chewing thoughtfully on a mouthful of food as he spoke, 'Wednesday night. What would you two usually have been doing on a Wednesday night?'

There was an awkward silence. The same awkward silence which always seemed to descend on any conversation that dared to broach the subject of the way the world had been before last Tuesday.

'I'd either have been studying or drinking,' Emma eventually replied, also sensing that it made sense to talk. 'Or probably both.'

'Drinking midweek?'

'I'd drink any night.'

'What about you, Carl?'

Carl toyed with his food and knocked back a large mouthful of wine.

'I was on call,' he said slowly. He was obviously unsure about talking about the past. He had only just begun to speak and it was already hurting him. 'I couldn't drink in the week but I'd make up for it at the weekend.'

'Were you a pub or a club man?' Emma asked.

'Pub,' he replied, very definitely.

'So what about your little girl?'

There was an awkward pause and Emma wondered whether she'd gone too far and said the wrong thing. Carl looked down at his food again and swallowed a second mouthful of wine, this one emptying the glass. He grabbed hold of the bottle and helped himself to a refill before continuing.

'Sarah and me used to walk down to the local in the afternoon,' he began, his eyes moistening with tears. 'We were part of a crowd. There was always someone in there we knew. We'd start drinking around three or four o'clock and then leave just before closing. There were always kids Gemma's age there. They had a play area and she had her friends and they used to...'

When the pain became too much to bear he stopped and drank more wine.

'Sorry,' Emma mumbled instinctively. 'I shouldn't have said anything. I wasn't thinking.'

Carl didn't respond.

'Why shouldn't you have said anything?' Michael asked.

'What?'

'Why are you apologising? And why don't you want to talk about it, Carl?'

Carl looked up and glared at the other man with tears of pain streaked down his face.

'I don't want to talk because it fucking well hurts too much,' he spat, almost having to force the words out. 'You don't know how it feels.'

'I've lost people too...'

'You didn't lose a child. You don't know how that feels. You couldn't.'

Michael knew he was right. He wasn't sure whether it was sensible or stupid, but he desperately felt that he should force this conversation to continue. He had decided that they wouldn't be able to move on and make something of the rest of their lives until they'd managed to sweep away the remains of the past.

Carl was staring into space again.

'I'd give anything to be back in lectures again,' Emma sighed. 'Stupid isn't it? Before I used to do anything I could to avoid them, now I just want to...'

'You just can't imagine what this feels like,' Carl said under his breath, interrupting her. 'This is killing me.'

165

'What is?' Michael pressed gently.

'Every morning I wake up and I wish that it was over and I was dead,' he explained. 'Every single day the pain is worse than the last. I still can't accept that they've gone and I just...'

'It hurts now but it will get easier,' the other man said, beginning to regret his earlier words. 'It must get easier over time, it must...'

'Will it? Know that for a fact do you?'

'No, but I...'

'Just shut your mouth then,' Carl said, his voice suddenly surprisingly calm and level. 'If you don't know what you're talking about, don't say anything. Don't waste your fucking time trying to make me feel better because you can't. There's nothing you can say or do that will make any of this any easier.'

With that he got up and walked away from the table without saying another word. For a few long seconds the only sounds to be heard in the house were heavy, lethargic footsteps as Carl dragged himself upstairs and shut himself away in isolation in his room.

A short while later Michael opened another bottle of wine. He didn't ask, he just poured Emma another glass. She didn't resist.

'Really fucked up there, didn't I?' he said quietly.

She nodded.

'We both did. It's obvious he's struggling. I should never have asked him about his little girl.'

Michael immediately became defensive again.

'Maybe not, but I still think he's got to talk,' he explained. 'Jesus, we can't move on until we've dealt with everything that's happened. We can't start to build anything up until we've sorted out everything that...'

'Have you dealt with everything then?' she asked, cutting across him.

He paused for a moment and then shook his head.

'No,' he admitted. 'Have you?'

'I haven't even started. To be honest I don't even know where to start.'

'I think we should all start with what hurts the most. With Carl it's his daughter. What about you?'

She drank more wine and considered his question.

'Don't know really. Everything hurts.'

'Okay, so when does it get to you the most?'

Again she couldn't answer.

'Don't know. I was thinking about my sister's kids yesterday and that really bothered me. I didn't see them that often, but the thought that I might not see them again...'

'Where did they live?'

'Overseas. Jackie's husband got moved to Kuwait with his job for a couple of years. They were due to come back next summer.'

'They still might.'

'How do you reckon that then?'

He shrugged his shoulders.

'We still don't know for certain that any other countries have been affected by this, do we?'

'Not for sure, but...'

'But what?'

'But I think we would have heard something by now, don't you?'

'Not necessarily.'

'Oh, come on, Michael. If there was anyone left we would have heard something. You said as much back in Northwich last week.'

At the mention of the name of the town they'd fled from Michael immediately began to think about the crowd of survivors left behind in the shabby surroundings of the Whitchurch Community Centre. He pictured the faces of Stuart, Ralph, Kate and the others and wondered what had become of them. Fortunately, before he had time to think too much, Emma asked another question.

'So what about your family then?'

'What about them?'

'Who do you miss the most? Did you have a partner.'

Michael took a deep breath, stretched and yawned and then ran his fingers through his hair.

'I had been seeing a girl called Marie for about six months,' he began, 'but I haven't thought about her at all.'

'Why not?'

'We split up three weeks ago.'

'Do you miss her?'

'Not any more. I don't miss my best friend who she was screwing either. There are plenty of other people I miss more.'

'Such as?'

'Such as my mum. Last night when I was trying to get to sleep I was thinking about her. You know that feeling you get when you're just about to go to sleep and you think you can hear a voice or see a face or something?'

'Yes.'

'Well I thought I heard my mum last night. I can't even tell you what it was I thought she'd said. I just heard her for a split second. It was like she was lying next to me.'

'That was me,' Emma smiled, trying desperately to make light of a conversation that was becoming increasingly morose.

Michael managed half a smile before returning his attention to his drink. Emma studied him intently. A very private and independent man from day one, she was beginning to see signs that there might be more to him than she first thought. He was blunt, opinionated and occasionally aggressive, but she was beginning to see that despite his seemingly self-centred emotions he was genuinely concerned about Carl's and her own welfare.

The conversation in the kitchen continued as long as the wine lasted. As time passed by their discussions became less in-depth and focussed and more trivial and trite to the point where, by the early hours of Thursday morning, almost everything they talked about was insignificant and inane.

During the hours they spent together, Emma and Michael learnt about each other's strengths, weaknesses, hobbies, interests, phobias and (now pointless) aspirations and ambitions.

They talked about their favourite books, films, records, televisions programmes, concerts, musicians, actors, foods, politicians, authors and comedians. They learnt about other redundant aspects of each other's lives - their religious beliefs, their political views and their moral standings.

They finally made their way up to the bedroom they innocently shared just before two in the morning.

29

Carl spent many hours during the days which followed shut away in isolation in his attic bedroom. There hadn't seemed to be much point in coming out. What was there to do? Sure he could talk to Michael and Emma, but why bother? Every conversation, no matter how it began, seemed to end with the three of them each drowning privately in complete and absolute negativity. They either ended up talking about how little they had left or how much they had lost. It hurt Carl too much to talk anymore. He decided that it was easiest for all concerned if he just didn't bother.

His bedroom was wide and spacious, spanning virtually the entire length of the house. Being high up it was relatively warm and comfortable and, most importantly to Carl, it was isolated. There was no need for anyone to come upstairs for any reason other than to see him. And as no-one had any need to see him, no-one came upstairs at all. That was the way he was beginning to like it.

Although twee and old-fashioned, the bedroom seemed to have been recently used. When they'd first arrived there Carl had decided that it had been used as a temporary base for a visiting grandchild, perhaps sent to the countryside to spend his or her final summer holiday on the farm. The furniture was sparse - a single bed, a double wardrobe, a chest of drawers, two brightly painted stools, a bookcase and a battered but comfortable sofa. On top of the wardrobe Carl had found a wooden box containing a collection of toys, some old books and a pair of binoculars which, once he'd cleaned the lenses, he had used to watch the world outside his window slowly rot and decay.

It was approaching half-past three in the afternoon and he could hear Emma and Michael working outside in the yard. He felt absolutely no guilt at not being out there with them because he couldn't see any point in anything that they were doing. He was happy to sit back and do nothing. Okay it was boring, but what else was there to do? Nothing seemed to be worth any risk or effort.

He didn't even know for sure what day it was.

He sat on a stool near to the window and, for a couple of seconds, tried to work out whether it was Friday, Saturday or Sunday. Back when life had been 'normal' and he'd been at work, each day had its own 'feel' and atmosphere - the week would begin with the dragging purgatory that was Monday morning and then slowly improve as Friday evening and the weekend approached. None of that seemed to matter anymore. Each new day was the same as the last. Yesterday was as frustrating, dull, grey and pointless as tomorrow would surely also be.

Today - whatever day it was - had been fairly warm and clear for the time of year. Perched on one of the wooden stools with the binoculars held up to his eyes he had been able to see for miles across rolling fields. The world was so still and free of distractions that, even from a distance, he could make out minute detail such as the dramatic tower and steeple of a far-off church. As the sun began to slowly fade below the horizon he watched as the colour faded from the steeple and it became an inky dark shape silhouetted against the light purples and blues of the early evening sky. Strange, he thought, how it all looked so calm and peaceful. Underneath the cover of apparent normality the world was filled with death, disease and destruction. Even the greenest and purest, seemingly untouched fields were breeding grounds filled with fermenting disease and devastation.

A short distance before the church Carl could see a straight length of road lined on either side with narrow cottages and shops. The stillness of the scene was suddenly disrupted when a scrawny dog ran into view. The nervous creature slowed down and crept breathlessly along the road, keeping its nose, tail and belly low and sniffing bodies and other piles of rubbish as it moved, obviously hunting for food. As Carl watched the dog stopped moving. It lifted its muzzle and sniffed the rancid air. It moved its head slowly (obviously following some out of view movement) and then cowered away from something in the shadows. The dog jumped up and began to bark furiously. Carl couldn't hear it, but he could tell from its defensive body position and the repeated angry jerks of its head that it was in danger. Within seconds of the first sound the dog had attracted the attention of some fourteen bodies. With a vicious, instinctive intent and a new found speed, they surrounded the helpless creature and set upon it. Between them the corpses tore the animal limb from limb.

Even after all that he had seen - the destruction, the carnage and the loss of thousands of lives - this sudden and unexpected attack shocked Carl. The bodies were becoming more alert and more deadly with each passing day. They now seemed to be grouping together and moving in packs, animal instinct driving them on.

He couldn't understand why Michael and Emma were bothering to make such an effort to survive. The odds were stacked against them. Where was the point in trying to carve out a future existence when it was so obviously a pointless task? Everything was ruined. It was over. So why couldn't they just accept it and see the truth like he could? Why continue to make such a fucking noise about nothing?

Carl knew that there would never be a salvation or escape from this vicious, tortured world and all he wanted to do was just stop and switch off. He wanted to let down his guard for a while and not have to look constantly over his shoulder. In the dark hours he spent alone he came to the conclusion that he'd never again find such peace until his life was over. But even death no longer brought with it any certainty.

***

Outside in the enclosed area in front of the house Michael was working on the van. He had checked the tyres, the oil, the water level and just about everything else he could think of checking. The importance of the van to them could not be overestimated - without it they would be stranded. Without it they would be trapped at Penn Farm, unable to fetch supplies (which they knew they would have to do at some point in the near future) and unable to get away should anything happen to compromise the safety of their home. And they had almost come to think of it as a home too. In a world full of dark disorientation, within the safe and sturdy walls of the farmhouse they had at last found a little stability.

'Next time we're out we should get another one of these,' Michael said as he ran his hands along the buckled driver's side wing of the van. He made it sound as if they could just run down to the shops when they next felt like it. His casual tone completely belied the reality of their situation.

'Makes sense,' Emma agreed. She was sitting on the stone steps leading up to the front door. She'd been sitting there for the last hour and a half, just watching as Michael had worked.

'Perhaps we should try and get something a little less refined,' he continued. 'This thing has been fine, but if you think about it, we need something that's going to get us out of any situation. If we're somewhere and the roads are blocked, chances are we'll need to find another way to get away. We could end up driving through fields or...'

'I can't see us leaving here much. Only to get food or...'

'But you never know, do you? Bloody hell, anything could happen. The only thing we can be certain about anymore is that fact that we can't be sure of anything.'

Emma stood up and stretched.

'Silly bugger,' she smiled.

'I know what you're saying though,' he continued as he gathered together his tools and began to pack them away. 'If we stay here we could do pretty much anything. We could build a brick wall round the house if we wanted to. Really keep those bastards out.'

Emma didn't respond. She stood at the top of the steps and looked down across the yard and out towards the rapidly darkening countryside.

'Light's fading,' she mumbled. 'Better get inside soon.'

'I don't think it makes much difference anymore,' Michael said quietly, climbing the steps to stand next to her. 'Doesn't matter how dark it is, those bloody things just don't stop. It might even be safer out here at night. At least they can't see us when its dark.'

'They can still hear us. Might even be able to smell us.'

'Doesn't matter,' he said again, looking into her face. 'They can't get to us.'

Emma nodded and turned to walk inside. Michael followed her through into the house.

'Carl's in, isn't he?' he asked as he pushed the door shut.

Emma looked puzzled.

'Of course he's in. He hasn't been out of his bloody bedroom for days. Where else do you think he's going to be?'

He shrugged his shoulders.

'Don't know. He might have gone out back. Just thought I'd check.'

She shook her head and leant against the hall wall. The house was dark. The generator hadn't yet been started.

'Take it from me,' she said, her voice tired and low, 'he's inside. I looked up at the window and saw him earlier. He was there again with those bloody binoculars, face pressed against the glass. Christ alone knows what he was looking at.'

'Do you think he's alright?'

Emma sighed at Michael's question. It was painfully obvious to her that Carl was far from alright. It was equally obvious that his temperament and stability appeared to be wavering more and more unsteadily each day.

Michael sensed her frustration.

'He'll come through this,' he said optimistically. 'Give him time and he'll get over everything that's happened.'

'Do you really think so?' Emma asked.

Michael thought for a moment.

'Yes... why, don't you?'

She shrugged her shoulders and disappeared into the kitchen.

'Don't know. He's really suffering, that much I'm sure about.'

'We've all suffered.'

'I know that. Bloody hell, we've had this conversation again and again. He lost more than we did. You and I lived on our own. He shared every second of every day with his partner and child.'

'I know, but...'

'But I'm not sure if you do. I'm not sure if I fully understand how much he's hurting. I don't think I ever will.'

Michael was beginning to get annoyed and he wasn't completely sure why. Okay so Carl was hurting, but no amount of hoping, praying and crying would bring back anything that any of them had lost. Hard as it sounded, he knew that the three of them could only survive by looking forward and forgetting everything and everyone that had gone.

He watched as Emma took off her coat, hung it up in the hallway and then lit a candle and walked upstairs.

Left alone in the darkness, Michael listened to the sounds of the creaking old house. A strong wind had begun to blow outside and he could hear the first few spots of a heavy shower of rain hitting the kitchen window. In cold isolation he thought more about Carl and, as he did, so his frustration and concern continued to increase. It wasn't just about Carl, he decided. The well-being of each of the survivors was of paramount importance to *all* of them. Life was becoming increasingly dangerous by the day and they couldn't afford to take any chances. They all needed to be pulling in the same direction in order to continue to survive. For the first time since this had all begun it had stopped happening. It was beginning to feel like he was with Emma and that Carl just happened to be there as well, distant and superfluous.

He knew that they were going to have to pull him into line.

Carl was their glass jaw. He was fast becoming their Achilles heel and every time they left the safety of the house he was dangerously exposed.

30

The earlier wind and rain had quickly developed into a howling storm. By half-past ten the isolated farm was being battered by a furious gale which tore through the tops of the surrounding trees and rattled and shook sections of the hastily constructed barrier around the building. Constant floods of driving, torrential rain lashed down from the ominous, swirling clouds overhead, turning the once gently trickling stream beside the house into a wild torrent of white water.

For the first time in several days the survivors had started up the generator. It had seemed sensible to presume that the noise of the squally weather would drown out the constant mechanical thump of the machinery. Sick of sitting in darkness, Michael had decided that it was worth taking the risk for a little comfort.

Relatively relaxed and oblivious to the appalling conditions outside, Michael, Emma and Carl sat in the living room together watching a video in the warmth of an open fire. Michael was quickly bored by the video - a badly dubbed martial arts film which he'd seen several times since they'd taken it from the supermarket in Byster - and yet he was pleased to be sitting where he was. Whilst what remained of the population suffered outside, he was warm, dry and well fed. Even Carl had been tempted down from the attic. Their evening together had provided a brief but much needed respite from the alternating pressure and boredom of what remained of their lives.

Emma found it hard to watch the film. Not just because it was one of the worst films she'd ever had the misfortune to see, but also because it aroused a number of unexpected and uncomfortable emotions within her. Whilst doing a good job of distracting her from everything that was happening around her for a time, the film also reminded her of the life she used to lead. She couldn't really identify with anything - the characters, their accents, the locations, the plot and the incidental music all seemed alien - and yet at the same time it was all instantly familiar and safe. In a scene depicting a car chase through busy Hong Kong streets she found herself watching the people in the background going about their everyday business instead of the violent physical action taking place in the foreground. She watched the people with a degree of envy. How novel and unexpected it was to see a clean city and to see individuals moving around with reason and purpose and acting and reacting with each other. Emma also felt a cold unease in the pit of her stomach. She couldn't help but look into the faces of each one of the actors and think about what might have happened to them in the years since the film had been made. She saw hundreds of different people - each one with their own unique identity, family and life - and she knew that virtually all of them would by now be dead.

The end of the film was rapidly approaching, and a huge set-piece battle between the hero and villain was imminent. The filmmakers were less than subtle in their attention grabbing techniques. The main character had driven into a vast warehouse and now found himself alone. The lighting was sparse and moody and the overly dramatic orchestral soundtrack was building to an obvious crescendo. Then the music stopped suddenly and, as the hero of the film waited for his opponent to appear, the house became silent.

Emma jumped out of her seat.

'What's the matter?' Michael asked, immediately concerned.

For a few long seconds she didn't answer. She stood still in the middle of the room, her face screwed up with concentration.

'Emma...' Michael pressed.

'Shh...' she hissed.

Oblivious and disinterested, Carl cocked his head to the right so that he could see past Emma who was standing in the way of the television.

She looked frightened. Michael was worried.

'What is it?' he asked again.

'I heard something...' she replied, her voice low.

'It was probably just the film,' he said, trying desperately to play things down. His mouth was dry. He felt nervous. Emma wasn't the type to make a fuss for no reason.

'No,' she snapped, scowling at him. 'I heard something outside, I'm sure I did.'

The film soundtrack burst into life again, startling her. With her heart in her mouth she reached down and switched off the television.

'I was watching that,' Carl protested.

'For fuck's sake, shut up,' she barked at him.

There it was again. A definite new and indistinct noise coming from outside. It wasn't the wind and it wasn't the rain and she hadn't imagined it.

Michael heard it too.

Without saying another word Emma ran from the living room into the dark kitchen. She quickly threaded her way around the table and chairs to the window and craned her neck to see outside.

'Anything there?' Michael asked, close behind her.

'Nothing,' she mumbled. She turned and headed out of the room towards the stairs. She stopped when she was halfway up and turned back to face Michael. 'Listen,' she whispered, lifting a single finger to her lips. 'There, can you hear it?'

He held his breath and listened carefully. For a few moments he couldn't hear anything other than the wind and rain and the constant rhythmic mechanical thumping of the generator. Then, just for a fraction of a second, he became aware of the new noise again. His ears seemed to lock onto the frequency of the sound and it somehow rose up and became distinct from the rest of the melee. As he concentrated the noise washed and faded and changed. In turn it was the sound of something being clattered against the wooden gate over the bridge, then another, less obvious noise, then more clattering and thumping. Without saying another word he ran towards Emma and pushed his way past her. She followed as he disappeared into their bedroom. By the time she entered the room he was already standing on the far side, looking out of the window in utter disbelief.

'Bloody hell,' he said as he stared down. 'Just look at this...'

With some trepidation Emma walked across the room and peered over his shoulder. Although it was pitch-black outside and the driving rain blurred her view through the glass, she could clearly see movement on the other side of the barrier. Running the entire length of the barricade were vast crowds of bodies. They had often seen one or two of them there before, but never this many. They had never seen them in such vast and unexpected numbers.

'There are hundreds of them,' Michael whispered, his voice hoarse with fear, 'fucking hundreds of them.'

'Why?' Emma asked.

'The generator,' he sighed. 'Even over the weather they must have heard the generator.'

'Christ.'

'And light,' he continued. 'We've had lights on tonight. They must have seen them. And there was the smoke from the fire...'

Emma shook her head and continued to stare down at the rotting crowd gathered round the house.

'But why so many?' she wondered.

'Think about it,' Michael replied. 'The world is dead. It's silent and at night it's dark. I suppose it just took one or two of them to see or hear us and that was enough. The first few moving towards the house would have attracted the next few and they would have attracted the next and so on and so on...'

As the two of them looked down at the hordes of corpses, one of the creatures standing on the stone bridge spanning the stream lifted its emaciated arms and began to shake and bang the wooden gate.

'What's going on?' Carl asked having finally dragged himself out of his seat and upstairs.

'Bodies,' Michael said quietly. 'Hundreds of bodies.'

Carl crept forwards, dragging his tired feet on the ground, and looked out over the yard.

'What do they want?' he muttered under his breath.

'Christ knows,' Michael cursed.

The other man stared down at the heaving crowd with a morbid curiosity. Emma turned towards Michael and took hold of his arm.

'They won't get through, will they?' she asked.

He felt that he should try and reassure her but he couldn't lie.

'Don't know,' he replied with a brutal honesty.

'But they haven't got any real strength, have they?' she said, trying hard to convince herself that they were still safe in the house.

'On their own they're nothing,' he muttered. 'But there are hundreds of them here tonight. I've got no idea what they're capable of in these kind of numbers.'

Emma visibly shuddered with fright. Her fright instantly became icy fear as the moon broke through a momentary gap in the heavy cloud layer and illuminated even more of the desperate figures staggering through the fields surrounding the farm and converging on the house.

'Shit,' snapped Michael anxiously.

'What are we going to do?' Emma asked. She looked down and watched as part of the crowd lining the stream-come-river surged forward. Several of the creatures, their footing already unsteady in the greasy mud, fell and were carried away by the foaming waters.

Michael looked up into the clouds and ran his fingers through his hair, trying desperately to clear his mind and shut out all distractions so that he could think straight. Then, without warning, he ran out of the bedroom and sprinted down the staircase and along the hallway to the back door. Taking a deep breath he unlocked the door and ran over to the shed which housed the generator. The conditions were atrocious and he was soaked through in seconds. Ignorant to the cold and the vicious, swirling wind, he flung open the wooden door and threw the switch which stopped the machine, suddenly silencing its constant thumping and plunging the farmhouse into complete darkness in one single movement.

Emma caught her breath at the moment the lights died. The darkness explained Michael's sudden disappearance and she ran out to the landing to make sure that he had made it safely back inside. She was relieved when she heard the back door slam shut and lock.

'You okay?' she asked as he dragged himself breathlessly back up the stairs.

He nodded and cleared his throat.

'I'm okay.'

The two survivors stood at the top of the stairs, holding each other tightly. Save for the muffled roar of the wind and rain outside the house was silent. The lack of any other sound was eerie and unnerving. Michael took old of Emma's hand and led her back to the bedroom.

'What the hell are we going to do?' she whispered. She sat down on the edge of the bed as Michael looked out of the window.

'Don't know,' he answered, instinctively and honestly. 'We should wait and see if they disappear before we do anything. There's no light or noise to attract them now. They should go.'

'But what are we going to do?' she asked again. 'We can't live without light. Christ, winter's coming. We'll need fire and light...'

Michael didn't reply. Instead he simply stared down at the crowd of decomposing corpses. He watched the bodies in the distance, still dragging themselves towards the house, and prayed that they would become disinterested and turn away.

Emma was right. What quality of life would they have hiding in a dark house with no light, warmth or other comfort? But what was the alternative? On this cold and desolate night there didn't seem to be any.

Rapidly becoming sick of it all, Michael turned away from the window, took Emma's hand and led her out of the room. The temperature was low and to hold her close was comforting and reassuring.

Carl remained alone in the bedroom, leaning against the window, watching the milling crowds beyond the barricade with fear, unease and mounting hate. He hadn't even noticed that the other two had left the room.

31

Emma finally managed to fall asleep a little after two o'clock the following morning but she was awake again by four.

Her bedroom was dull and cold. She woke up with a sudden start and sat bolt upright in bed. The air around her face was icy and her breath condensed in cool clouds around her mouth and nose.

Since arriving at the farm she and Michael had shared this room. There was nothing sinister or untoward about Michael's presence there - he continued to sleep on the floor in the gap between the bed and the outside wall and he discreetly looked away or left the room whenever she dressed or undressed. Neither had ever spoken about their unusual sleeping arrangements. Both of them silently continued to welcome the warm comfort and security of having another living, breathing person close nearby.

This was the first morning that Michael hadn't been there when she'd looked. He often rose first but, until this morning, she'd always been aware of him getting up and leaving the room.

She instinctively leant over to her right (as she often did first thing) and, finding it hard to focus her eyes in the early morning gloom, stretched out her arm, hoping that her outstretched fingers would reach the reassuring bulk of her sleeping friend. This morning, however, her tired eyes had not deceived her - where she had expected to find Michael she instead found only his crumpled sleeping bag. He had definitely been there when she'd gone to bed because she could clearly remember hearing him snuffling and snoring as he had drifted off to sleep beside her. She leant across a little further, picked up the empty sleeping bag and pulled it close to her face. It smelled of Michael, and it was still warm from the heat of his body.

No need to panic, she thought.

Had it been any later then she wouldn't have been unduly worried, but it was only four o'clock. Perhaps he hadn't been able to sleep. Maybe he'd just gone elsewhere because he'd been restless and he hadn't wanted to wake her up.

Regardless of the reason, Emma got up and pulled on a nearby pair of jeans and a thick towelling dressing-gown which she had left draped over the back of a chair on the other side of the bed. She tiptoed across the dark bedroom with arms stretched out in front of her to give guidance and balance. The varnished floorboards were cold beneath her bare feet and she shivered as she reached out to open the door.

There was considerably more light on the landing. The thick curtains drawn across her bedroom window had blocked out almost all of the early morning light. She glanced up the short flight of stairs which led to Carl's attic room and saw that his door was open. Unusual, she thought. With Carl becoming more of a recluse with each passing day, she had become used to not seeing or hearing him before midday. At the moment the last thing he seemed to want was any contact with Michael or herself, especially at this time of the morning.

She crept along the landing to the top of the staircase and peered down to the hallway.

'Michael,' she hissed. The deathly quiet of the building amplified her voice to an unexpectedly loud volume.

No response.

'Michael,' she called again, this time deliberately a little louder. 'Michael, Carl...where are you?'

She waited for a moment and concentrated on the silence of the house around her, hoping that the ominous quiet would soon be shattered by a reply from one of her two companions. When no such reply came, she took a couple of cautious steps forward and called out again.

'Michael,' she called for the forth time, her voice now at full volume. 'Christ, answer me, will you?'

Another step forward. She stopped again and waited and listened. She lifted her foot to take a further step but then, before she could put it down again, the oppressive quiet was shattered by a dull thump from outside. She froze, routed to the spot in fear. She had heard that sound last night.

Another thump.

Another.

Another.

Then suddenly the sound of a thousand bodies beating their rotting fists against the barrier round the house.

Desperate, Emma ran downstairs. The relentless noise coming from outside was increasing in volume. It was different this morning, harsher and already much, much louder than last night. Last night the bodies had hammered against the gate with tired, clumsy hands. This morning they sounded more definite. This morning they sounded purposeful.

'Michael,' she hissed again, still no closer to finding either of her companions. She looked up and down the empty hallway for any signs of life.

The noise outside reached an almighty crescendo and then stopped. Confused and terrified, Emma ran to the front door and stared out over the yard.

The gate across the bridge was down.

A vast torrent of stumbling bodies was surging towards the house.

Seconds later and there was another noise, this time from the kitchen. It was the cracking of glass. Emma ran into the room and then stopped dead in her tracks. Pressed hard against the wide kitchen window were countless diseased and decomposing figures. Pairs of cold, clouded and expressionless eyes followed her every move and the remains of numb, heavy hands began to beat against the fragile glass. In abject horror she watched as a series of jagged cracks quickly worked their way across the window from the bottom right to the diagonally opposite corner.

Emma turned and ran. She tripped on a rug in the hallway and half-sprinted, half-fell into the living room, landing in an uncoordinated heap on the carpet. She looked up and saw through the French windows that more rotting faces were staring back at her from outside this room. Forgetting about Michael and Carl, she knew that her only chance was to barricade herself in Carl's attic bedroom - the highest and, she hoped, safest part of the house.

As she sprinted back down the hallway towards the stairs the front door burst open under the force of a thousand desperate bodies outside. Like a dam that had broken its banks, in seconds an unstoppable flood of abhorrent creatures were inside. She struggled to push past the first few corpses and get to the staircase. She ran up the stairs and then paused for a fraction of a second to look back down. The whole of the lower floor of the house was carpeted with a seething mass of writhing, rotting bodies.

She ran into her room (as it was the closest) and slammed the door shut behind her. Struggling in the darkness, she threw a chair out of the way and kicked her way through a pile of Michael's discarded clothes. Once she'd reached the window she threw back the curtains and looked outside to see her worst nightmare made reality. The barrier around the house was down in at least three places that she could see. Countless figures continued to stagger towards the house and the yard was a heaving sea of bodies. The van - her only means of escape - was hopelessly surrounded. Beyond the remains of the fence, for as far as she could see in all directions, hundreds of thousands of shadowy figures traipsed relentlessly towards Penn Farm.

There was a sudden crashing noise behind her and Emma span round to find herself face to face with four corpses. She could see more of them on the landing, the sheer volume of bodies having forced them into the room. The nearest of the group of four - something that had once been a Policeman - stared at her for a moment before lurching forward. She screamed and tried desperately to open the window.

As the bodies approached she turned and kicked the first creature square in its withered and rotting testicles. It didn't flinch or show the slightest flicker of emotion. Instead it reached out for her with vicious, talon-like fingers and caught hold of her hair, yanking her down onto the bed.

As the first sharp claws tore into her skin the nightmare ended.

32

The dream terrified Emma.

She woke up drenched in an ice-cold sweat and, for a few uncertain moments, was almost too afraid to move. Once she had managed to convince herself that it had only been a dream and that she was safe (or as safe as she could expect to be), she leant over to her right to check that Michael was still lying on the floor beside her. A wave of cool relief washed over her as she reached out her hand and rested it on his shoulder. She held it there for a few seconds until she was completely sure that all was well. The gentle, rhythmic movements of his body as he breathed were remarkably calming and reassuring.

In the days, months and years before her world had been turned upside down Emma had often tried to analyse the hidden meaning of dreams. She had read numerous books that offered explanations for the metaphors and images which filled her mind while she slept. Her dreams had changed since they'd arrived at Penn Farm. There was nothing subtle or hidden in the visions she'd seen in her sleep this morning. They showed her, in no uncertain terms, a terrifying version of the future. A version of the future which could so quickly and easily come to be.

Climbing out of bed (and taking care not to disturb Michael as she did so) Emma made her way over to the window and threw back the curtains. She kept her eyes screwed tightly shut for a few seconds - partly because of the bright light flooding in through the glass but mostly because she was afraid of what she might see outside. She breathed a heavy sigh of relief when she finally dared to open her eyes and saw that only thirty or forty figures remained on the other side of the barrier. The majority of the crowd that had gathered last night had wandered away into the wilderness again, perhaps having been distracted by some other sound or movement. Since they had switched off the generator the farmhouse had, to all intents and purposes, appeared to be as dead and as empty as any one of the hundreds of thousands of other buildings dotted around the countryside.

Emma heard noises downstairs. It was almost eight o'clock and the fact that it was now a reasonable hour to be getting up coupled with the fact that she knew the barrier round the building was still intact, gave her a comforting feeling of security and protection. Feeling certain that all was well within the house, and still taking care not to disturb Michael, she pulled on some clothes and made her way downstairs. She found Carl in the kitchen.

'Morning,' she said as she walked into the room. She yawned and stretched. Other than mumbling something indistinct Carl didn't stop or look up from what he was doing.

Emma stood and watched him for a moment. He was fully dressed and had obviously washed and shaved. He was searching through the kitchen cupboards and had collected a pile of food and supplies on the table.

'What are you doing?' she asked cautiously.

'Nothing,' he muttered, still not looking up at her.

'Doesn't look like nothing to me.'

Carl didn't reply.

Sensing his very obvious reluctance to talk, Emma walked round him and made her way over to the cooker. She lifted the kettle and shook it. Happy that there was enough water inside she put it down again and lit the gas burner. The kettle and stove were cold and unused. Whatever it was Carl was doing was obviously important because he hadn't bothered to make himself a drink since getting up. One thing that the three survivors had quickly found they had in common was a need to get a hot drink inside them before they could function in the morning.

'Want a coffee?' she asked amiably, determined not to let his hostility deter her.

'No,' he replied abruptly, still avoiding eye-contact. 'No thanks.'

Emma shrugged her shoulders and spooned coffee granules into two mugs.

There was an oppressive atmosphere in the room. The only noise came from the kettle boiling on the stove. Carl continued to look through the cupboards and drawers. Emma felt uneasy. He was obviously up to something but he clearly didn't want to talk and she couldn't think of a subtle way of asking him what it was that he was doing. She quickly came to the conclusion that she should just ask outright again, and that she should keep asking until she got the answers she wanted.

'Carl,' she began, 'what exactly are you doing? And please don't insult my intelligence by telling me it's nothing when it's bloody obvious that it's not.'

He continued to ignore her.

Emma noticed that there was a well-packed rucksack resting against a wall in the store room adjacent to the kitchen.

'Where are you thinking of going?' she asked.

Still no response.

The kettle began to boil. Emma made a cup of coffee for herself and one for Michael. She sipped at her scalding hot drink and looked directly at Carl over the brim of her mug.

'Where are you going to go?' she asked again, her voice deliberately low and calm.

Carl turned his back to her and leant against the nearest kitchen unit.

'I don't know,' he eventually replied. Emma guessed that he was lying. It was obvious that although he feigned nonchalance, he knew exactly where he was going and what he was planning to do.

'Come on,' she sighed, growing tired. 'Do you really expect me to believe that?'

'Believe what you want,' he snapped. 'Doesn't matter to me.'

'You can't leave the house, it's too dangerous. Bloody hell, you saw how many of those things managed to get here last night. If you really think that you...'

'That's the whole fucking problem, isn't it?' he said, finally turning round to face her. 'I saw how many bodies were here last night - too bloody many. It's not safe to stay here anymore.'

'It's not safe anywhere these days. Face it, Carl, this place is as good as you're going to get.'

'No it isn't,' he argued. 'We're out on a limb here. There's nowhere to run. If that fence comes down we're completely fucked...'

'But can't you see that we can get over that? When they're here in large numbers we just shut up and sit tight. If we stay silent and out of sight for long enough they'll disappear.'

'And is that what you want? Are you happy to sit and hide for hours every time those bloody things get close? They're getting stronger everyday and it won't be long before...'

'Of course it's not ideal, but what's the alternative?'

'The alternative is to go back home. I know Northwich like the back of my hand and I know that there are other survivors there. I think I'll have more of a chance back in the city. It was a mistake coming out here.'

Emma struggled to comprehend what she was hearing.

'Are you fucking crazy?' she stammered. 'Do you know the risks you'd be taking by...'

'Emma, I'm going. If you haven't got anything constructive to say then do me a favour and don't say anything at all.'

'But have you thought this through? Do you really believe this is the right thing to do?'

'There's safety in numbers,' he said, turning his back on her again. 'Those bloody things proved it last night, didn't they? More survivors has got to equal more of a chance in my book...'

'You're wrong,' Michael interrupted. He was standing in the kitchen doorway. Neither Emma or Carl knew how long he'd been there or how much he'd heard. He leant against the door frame with his arms crossed in front of him.

Carl shook his head.

'Leaving here would be a fucking stupid thing to do,' Michael added.

'Staying here seems like a fucking stupid thing to do too,' he snapped back.

Michael took a deep breath and walked further into the kitchen. He sat on the edge of the kitchen table and watched the other man as he tried desperately to busy himself and avoid eye contact with the other two survivors.

'Convince me,' Michael said as he took his coffee from Emma. 'Just how much have you thought about this?'

For a second Carl was angry, feeling that Michael was patronising him. But then he decided that he sounded as if he was at least going to listen to what he had to say.

'I've thought long and hard about it,' he replied, 'this isn't something that I've just decided to do on a whim.'

'So what's your plan?'

'Get back to Northwich and try and get to the community centre. See who's still there...'

'And then?'

'And then find somewhere secure to base myself.'

'But you said you didn't want to lock yourself away and hide. Aren't you just going to be doing that somewhere else instead of here?' Emma asked.

'There's a council works depot between the community centre and where I used to live. There's a bloody ten foot wall right the way around it. Once we're in there we're safe. There's trucks and all kinds of things there.'

'How you going to get in?'

'I'll get in.'

'And what if there's no-one at the Community Centre?'

'I'll keep going to the depot on my own.'

Michael stopped asking questions and sat and thought for a few seconds.

'So when were you thinking of going?' he wondered.

'We've got to go out for supplies at some point in the next few days,' Carl answered. 'I figured I'd try and get some transport while we were away from the house and then I'll take it from there.'

'We could go and get supplies today,' Michael said, surprising Emma who looked at him with an expression of utter disbelief on her face.

'What the hell are you doing?' she hissed at him. 'Christ, are you thinking of going too?'

Michael shook his head.

'Seems to me that you're going to go whatever we try and say or do to stop you.'

Carl nodded.

'I'd go now if I could.'

'Then there doesn't seem to be any point in Emma or I wasting our time trying to persuade you that you're making a mistake.'

'I don't think I am. You are right though, you'd be wasting your time.'

'And if we try and stop you leaving we'll probably end up beating the crap out of each other and the net result will still be that you leave. Am I right?'

'You're right.'

He turned to face Emma.

'So we don't have a lot of choice, do we?'

'But, Mike, he'll end up dead. He won't last five minutes out there.'

Michael sighed and watched Carl disappear into the store room.

'That's not our problem,' he said. 'Our priority is to keep ourselves safe, and if that means that Carl leaves then Carl leaves. Think of him as a homing pigeon. We send him on his way today and, with a little luck, if things don't work out he'll bring the rest of the survivors from Northwich back here with him if he manages to find them.'

Emma nodded. She understood everything he said but still found it hard to accept.

'He's a stupid fucking idiot,' she hissed under her breath.

33

Once it had been accepted that Carl's leaving for the city was inevitable the survivors quickly forced themselves into action. He was keen to get away as quickly as he could and Michael and Emma were keen to make the most of having him around. A trip away from the house was essential to all of them whether they were staying or going. Having three pairs of hands instead of two meant that theoretically Michael and Emma could collect more supplies and so defer their next excursion for a few precious days and hours longer.

On a cold and wet Sunday morning they returned to Pennmyre, the first place they had visited after stumbling upon Penn Farm last week. The tension in the van rose quickly as they approached the main street of the village. It came as no surprise that as the sound of the engine shattered the fragile silence, the unwanted interest of scores of deplorable creatures nearby was aroused. Too afraid to move at first for fear of being swallowed up by the diseased crowds that had quickly gathered all around them, Emma, Michael and Carl were forced to wait for over an hour in the back of their battered vehicle, crouching silently on the floor, hidden under blankets and coats until the bodies had drifted away.

Michael had parked close to a small supermarket. Once the crowds around the van had dispersed Emma carefully opened the van door nearest to the building and quietly disappeared inside. While Michael and Carl began their search for alternative transport she collected as many tins of food and other non-perishable supplies as she could find and loaded them into the back of the van. Each movement she made was slow and considered. Every step was carefully co-ordinated so that she remained silent and out of sight of the rest of the world.

There were two large garages near to the supermarket. Michael quickly found a Landrover that suited his needs and set about finding the keys from the office and ensuring that the tank was filled with petrol. He siphoned extra fuel from other vehicles scattered around the forecourt and loaded them into the back of his new transport in metal cans. As he worked he watched the occasional body stagger by. He was sure that one or two of them saw him. He guessed that they were used to seeing bodies moving and that their rotting brains were not been able to distinguish between him and the millions of other sickly bodies still dragging themselves along the silent streets. Sound still seemed to be their main stimulus.

By chance Carl stumbled across the perfect machine to get him to the city. In a dark and narrow alley between two shops he found a motorbike. It looked well maintained and powerful and, although his experience of riding motorbikes was limited, he knew that it would be ideal. It would give him far more speed and manoeuvrability than any four-wheeled vehicle could. He found the keys to the bike in the pocket of a leather-clad corpse nearby. With trepidation (but understanding the need for protection and not having the time or inclination to look elsewhere) he then stripped the leathers from the decaying body and gingerly removed its helmet. The head of the cadaver was withered and light and the flesh unexpectedly dry and discoloured. Not daring to start the engine, he released the brake and pushed the bike back to the supermarket where Emma and Michael waited anxiously for him.

Emma climbed into the driver's seat of the van as he approached, keen to get away.

'Got this,' he whispered. 'Should do me.'

She nodded but did not say anything. The reasons for her silence were twofold. Primarily she didn't want to attract the attention of any body wandering nearby but, also, she didn't have anything she wanted to say to Carl. As the morning had progressed she had silently become more and more incensed by his selfish intentions. Not only did she think he was a fool for even thinking about going back to the city, but she also decided that he was a weak and uncaring bastard for leaving her and Michael. Three was a safe number - if one of them was injured then the other two could help. Left alone with Michael, she knew that they would be in serious trouble if anything happened to either of them. And the chances of Carl surviving on his own in an accident were next to nil. By leaving he was putting them all at risk.

'What do you think of this?' Carl whispered to Michael as he returned to the van. Michael couldn't even pretend to be interested in either the bike or Carl. He grunted in resentful acknowledgement.

'Ready to get going?' he then asked, clearly directing his question towards Emma. She nodded.

'I'm ready.'

'I've found a Landrover,' he continued. 'You start the van up and I'll try and get it going. If it works I'll lead, if not get ready to let me back inside.'

She nodded again. Her throat was dry and her heart had started to thump in her chest. She knew that as soon as they started the first engine they would be engulfed by bodies.

'I'll follow on behind,' Carl said.

'Whatever,' Michael muttered as he jogged back over to the Landrover.

Once he was inside the vehicle Carl climbed onto the bike and waited. Emma looked across to the garage and waited for Michael to settle himself. He shuffled in his seat, put the key in the ignition and then put his thumb up to Emma. She started the van and within a couple of seconds the first bodies had arrived, lurching towards the survivors from all directions. Michael started the Landrover and inched forward over the high kerb and down onto the road. Carl started the bike, taking three attempts before the spluttering engine burst into life after the best part of two weeks of idleness. The deafening roar from the engine seemed to attract the attention of every corpse for miles around. A vast crowd surged towards the scene as fast as their rotting legs would carry them.

As body after relentless body collided with the sides of the Landrover, Michael put his foot down and carved a bloody path through the pitiful creatures. Emma did the same, following in his wake, and then Carl attempted to move forwards. The bike was powerful - far more so than he had expected - and the unexpected force caught him off guard. For a second he almost lost control. He paused and steadied himself. The nearest corpse lurched towards him, catching hold of the back of his jacket more through luck than judgement. Terrified, Carl lifted his feet from the ground and accelerated away from the remains of the desolate, dead village, leaving the body behind reaching out after him.

A few miles had been driven before Carl had developed enough confidence to try and use the bike to its full potential. He raced with the van and the Landrover, overtaking and then dropping back, cutting between them and weaving his way through the wrecks, bodies and ruins which lay in his path. By the time they'd reached the track which led from the main road back up to Penn Farm he felt confident enough to surge ahead. He drove across the stone bridge, unlocked the gate and waited for Emma and Michael. The second they were both through and safely within the confines of the barricade he slammed the heavy gate shut and snap-locked the eight chunky padlocks which they used to keep it secure. Already there were bodies close by - perhaps the remains of last night's crowds. As he closed the gate he saw twenty or thirty shadowy shapes appear from the forest and start to stumble towards the house, hopelessly following the bike, van and Landrover. Although still clumsy and lethargic, they moved with an unnerving determination and reason. A week ago they had wandered aimlessly and without direction. This morning it was clear that the creatures had a purpose.

Carl wheeled the bike closer to the house and knelt down and began to check it over for signs of obvious damage. He didn't want to go inside just yet. Now that his decision to leave the house was certain he felt disconnected from the others. He no longer belonged at the farm. It felt almost as if he shouldn't be there any longer and he felt alone and strangely superfluous. Out of the corner of his eye he noticed that Emma was walking over to speak to him and, for a second, that made him feel slightly better.

'You okay?' she asked.

He stood up and brushed himself down.

'I'm alright,' he replied. 'You?'

She nodded. Her voice was tired and emotionless. Carl sensed that she was talking to him more out of duty than any real desire to.

'Look,' she began, 'I know you've said that you're sure about this, but have you stopped to think...'

'I don't want to hear this,' he snapped, interrupting and silencing her words.

'You don't know what I was going to say...'

'I can guess.'

She sighed and turned away. After thinking for a second or two she turned back, determined to make her point.

'Are you sure about what you're doing?'

'As sure as anyone can be about anything at the moment...'

'But you're taking such a chance. You don't have to leave. We could stay here for a while longer and maybe go back to the city later. We could bring the others back here. There might even be more of them by then...'

'I've got to leave. It's not just about surviving anymore, I've already done that.'

'So why are you going?'

'Take a look around you,' he sighed, gesturing towards the house and the barrier which surrounded it. 'Is this enough for you? Does this give you all the protection and security you need?'

'I think we're as safe as we can be...'

'I don't. Christ, last night we were surrounded.'

'Yes, but...'

'Just answer me this, Emma. What would you do if those things got through the barricade and got into the house?'

Emma struggled to answer.

'What would happen? As far as I can see you wouldn't have many choices. You could lock yourself into a room and sit tight or you could try and get to one of your vans and try and get away that way. Or you could just run for it.'

'You'd have no chance on foot.'

'That's exactly my point. This house is surrounded by miles and miles of absolutely fucking nothing. There's nowhere to run to.'

'But we don't need to run...' Emma protested, raising her voice.

'But you might. Back in the city there are a hundred places to hide on every street. I don't want to spend the rest of my time locked away in this bloody house.'

Emma sat down on the steps in front of the house, dejected and frustrated. Michael was busy working to unload the supplies from the back of the van. He already seemed to be doing his level best to ignore Carl.

'I'm worried about you, that's all,' Emma said quietly. 'I just hope you realise that if anything happens to you on your own, that's it.'

'I know that.'

'And you're still willing to take the chance?'

'Yes,' he said, simply and definitely.

Carl leant against the bike and looked deep into Emma's face. It was the first time for days that the two of them had made anything resembling real, purposeful contact with each other. Looking into his dull, tired eyes, Emma felt her earlier anger mellowing and mutating into something that resembled pity. The man standing in front of her was nothing more than a shell. He was less than half the man he had been when they'd first met. He had lost everything including, it seemed, all direction and reason. She knew that he wasn't bothered about surviving anymore. All his talk of finding shelter and of reaching the survivors was bullshit. She knew in her heart that all he wanted to do was go home.

34

'Planning on leaving tonight then?' Michael asked.

An hour after returning from Pennmyre and Carl was still outside, getting ready to go and refuelling the bike and loading his few belongings. He looked up and nodded at Michael.

'Might as well,' he quietly replied.

'Sure you want to take the risk?'

He shrugged his shoulders.

'We're all taking risks whatever we do,' he answered. 'I don't think it matters anymore.'

'Well I think you're asking for trouble. You should at least wait until the morning when it's...'

'I'll be alright,' he insisted.

'Fine.'

Michael sat down on the damp ground near to the bike. He looked around the yard, first quickly checking that the barrier round the house seemed secure and then looking up high, staring into the trees surrounding, listening to drops of water from the earlier heavy rainfall dripping down from leaf to leaf to leaf before falling to the ground.

'Look,' he said, sensing that he had a duty to again try and persuade the other man not to leave, 'are you sure you know what you're doing?'

Carl sighed.

'Christ, not you as well. I had enough bullshit from Emma earlier...'

'It's not bullshit. We're just worried that...'

'Worried that what?'

'I don't know,' he lied, feeling awkward and reluctant to reveal his true feelings. 'I guess we're just worried that you're doing the wrong thing. I've heard everything you've said about wanting to go back to the community centre and I understand why you think you need to go but...'

Carl stopped what he was doing and looked at Michael. 'But...?'

'I think you're confused. I think you've been through too much to cope with and you're having trouble dealing with it all. I don't think you're capable of making the right decisions at the moment and...'

'I'm not a fucking lunatic if that's what you think,' Carl snapped, his voice surprisingly calm, 'I know exactly what I'm doing. The fact is I just don't feel safe here. And before you say it, I know we're not safe anywhere anymore, but I obviously feel differently about this place than you two do. That excuse for a fence we built doesn't make me feel any better...'

'That excuse for a fence,' Michael interrupted, annoyed, 'kept a thousand of those bastards out last night.'

'I know, but there are millions of them out there. Eventually they're going to get through.'

'I don't agree.'

'We'll put a bet on it now and I'll come back next year and see how you're doing.'

Michael didn't find Carl's attempt at black humour amusing.

'Okay, so we're not as isolated as we thought we were here, but we've done alright so far, haven't we?'

'Better than I ever thought we would,' he accepted.

'So why leave now? You're going to get ripped to pieces out there.'

Carl thought for a moment. He had done a good job of keeping his true feelings and emotions hidden from the other two for most of the last week. The pair of them had been so wrapped up in building and protecting their precious ivory tower that they seemed to have forgotten everything else that was ever important.

'I just want to go back to somewhere I know,' he eventually admitted. 'I know I'm taking a massive chance but I think it's worth the risk. If I'm going to spend the rest of my days hiding from those bloody things out there, I might as well hide somewhere close to the place I know best, somewhere I actually want to be.'

'But think about the other risks,' Michael said, his voice tired and low. 'Think about the bodies that are just lying rotting on the ground. Every city will be filled with disease.'

Carl just shrugged his shoulders.

'I don't know anything about that and there's nothing I can do about it anyway. I used to mend fucking twenty-ton presses for a living, doesn't matter if you tell me there's germs and disease about because I can't do anything about it. I'll have to take my chances there just the same way you and Emma will do here.'

'But we're not taking chances...'

'How do you know that? How do you know that there isn't cholera, typhoid or a thousand other diseases that we've never even heard of already here in the air or in the stream or...'

Michael knew he was right. There was no point in arguing.

'You don't have to go,' he said, quickly deciding to change tack completely. 'Please stay here with us. Just do me a favour and think about it for a couple of days at least will you?'

Carl shook his head.

'All I've done this last week is think about this. Look, it's nothing personal. You were the one who kept telling us how important it was to look after ourselves, weren't you?'

'Yes, but...'

'So can't you see that's all I'm doing. You keep doing what's best for you and Emma, and I'll look after myself. We all might be gone tomorrow...'

'Don't talk like that,' Michael interrupted, suddenly angry. 'You can't talk like that if...'

Ignoring him, Carl continued.

'We might all be gone tomorrow but the three of us might still be around in ten years time. I just can't lock myself away in here and sit and wait for something to happen. If all we're going to do is cower and hide for the rest of our lives then we might as well just end it now.'

'I understand what you're saying,' Michael sighed, accepting that nothing he could say or do would persuade Carl to stop. 'I understand completely, but I still think you're a stupid fucking bastard.'

'That's your opinion.'

Michael stood up and took a step closer before stopping again.

'Just stay a little longer, will you? Things might be different again in the morning.'

Carl looked up and managed half a smile.

'That's what scares me,' he mumbled, sounding tired and resigned. 'I can't stay. I have to go.'

Sensing that to prolong the conversation any longer would be pointless, Michael turned and walked back to the house.

By six o'clock Carl was ready to leave. His bike, loaded up with his bags, stood next to the gate. Dressed in the leathers and boots taken from corpse in Pennmyre earlier in the day, and carrying the freshly disinfected crash helmet in his hand, he stood at the front door of the farmhouse with Emma and Michael. This was it. He knew that there was no turning back, and no point in delaying the inevitable.

He glanced at the other two.

'Ready?' Emma asked.

He nodded and swallowed. His mouth was dry.

It was a cold night with a relentless, biting wind. Emma zipped up her fleecy jacket and thrust her hands deep into her pockets.

'Last time I ask,' Michael said, fighting to make himself heard over the wind, 'are you sure about this?'

Carl nodded again.

'Better get on with it,' he said and with that he pulled on his crash helmet. The helmet helped to make him feel further detached from the other two, and that sudden perception of distance made it easier to take the first step and leave.

The three survivors walked together towards the bike.

'I'll open the gate,' Michael said. 'You wheel the bike through and start it. Once I hear the engine and see you move, I'm locking up. Okay?'

Carl raised a leather clad hand and lifted his thumb to show that he understood. He took one last look over his shoulder at the farmhouse he was leaving and climbed onto the bike. He flicked up the kick-stand with his foot and rolled forward a couple of tentative meters.

'Wait by the house,' Michael said, gesturing for Emma to get back and out of the way. They had no idea what would be waiting for them on the other side of the gate on the bridge. Keen to put maximum distance between her and the rest of the world beyond the barricade, Emma slowly walked backwards towards the house. She watched intently as Michael carefully unlocked each of the eight padlocks and lifted the wooden bar which secured the gate.

'Ready?' he asked.

Carl stood astride the bike, his hands tightly gripping the handlebars. He nodded.

Slowly and cautiously, Michael pushed open one side of the gate. Carl rolled the bike forward again until he sat on the other side of the bridge. Again he glanced over his shoulder and saw that the other man had also taken a few steps forward. He kept hold of the edge of the gate in his hand, ready to slam it shut as soon as Carl had gone. They had only been out there for a few seconds but already Michael could see movement in the bushes.

A few seconds later and it was done. Carl lifted his foot and slammed it down on the pedal, starting the bike. The mighty engine spluttered and roared into life sending a cloud of fumes and heat billowing towards Michael. As the first few inquisitive corpses emerged from the shadows of the forest Carl accelerated away. As he pulled the gate closed Michael saw the bike swerve as Carl avoided the first body to have staggered into his path. With shaking hands he lowered the wooden bar back into place and snap-locked each of the heavy padlocks.

Emma was standing just a few feet behind Michael. He turned around and her sudden unexpected appearance startled him. He caught his breath and then, instinctively, reached out and held her tight. The warmth of her body was reassuring. He rested his head on her shoulder and cried silent tears for the man who had just left Penn Farm. Michael put his tears down to the wind but he knew in his heart that there was more to them. He found himself suddenly wracked with guilt at having let the other survivor leave.

Such was the silence of the evening that almost ten minutes had passed before the sound of Carl's engine had finally faded away into the night. Emma shivered as she imagined the effect that the noise would have on the lamentable remains of the population of the shattered world through which Carl was now travelling. The roar of the engine and the light from the headlamp would attract the attention of hundreds, probably thousands of bodies, every last one of which would stagger after Carl until he was out of view or earshot. But he would have to stop the bike eventually. What would happen then? It didn't bear thinking about.

It was a bitterly cold night.

Once they were completely sure that they could no longer hear the distant sound of the motorbike, Emma and Michael went inside and locked the door of the farmhouse behind them.

35

Carl raced along countless twisting, turning narrow roads, hoping and praying that he was still travelling in the right direction, hoping and praying that he would soon see a road sign or some other signal to confirm that he was heading the right way. He needed to find the motorway which would take him south-east, almost directly into the heart of Northwich. It was bitterly ironic that he now found himself desperate to return to the city which he, Emma and Michael had earlier been so keen to escape from.

Driving at speed in the dark was harder and required more concentration than he had expected. He found it difficult to get used to the motorbike - it had been some ten years since he'd ridden one regularly and, even then, the bikes he had been used to were nowhere near as powerful as this one. The state of the roads made the journey even more hazardous. Although devoid of any other moving traffic, they were littered with haphazard piles of rubbish, twisted, rusting vehicle wreckage and rotting human remains. As well as the countless motionless obstructions, Carl was constantly aware of shadowy bodies all around him. Although they could do nothing to harm him while he travelled at speed, their ominous presence alone was enough to distract and unnerve him. He knew that one slip was all that it would take. One lapse of concentration and he could lose control of the bike. If that happened he knew that he would have just seconds to get himself back in command of the powerful machine before the bodies arrived.

The motorcycle's bright headlamp was powerful enough to illuminate a sizeable area of the devastated world through which he travelled. In spite of all that he had seen over the last few hours, days and weeks, some of the sights he witnessed through the inky blackness chilled him to the bone. As he drove towards a car facing towards him, the dead driver lifted its rapidly decomposing head and stared at him. In the fraction of a second he saw it, he knew that the body had not looked past him, it had looked directly at him. In those lifeless, dull eyes he saw both a complete lack of emotion and, at the same time, a paradoxical savage intent which chilled him to the bone. Such abhorrent visions, and the fact that he knew he was utterly alone for the first time since his nightmare had begun, made the cold, dark night seem colder and darker still.

Thousands upon thousands of pathetic, straggling bodies turned and stumbled towards the source of the sound that shattered the otherwise all-consuming silence. Most of the time they were too slow and, when they finally arrived at where the bike had just been, Carl was long gone. Occasionally, however, fate and circumstance contrived to allow some of the bodies to get dangerously close to him. He quickly learnt that the best way to deal with them was simply to plough straight through them with relentless ferocity. The empty corpses offered no resistance. The shadowy silhouette of a dead young woman stumbled out into the middle of the road and began to walk towards the rapidly approaching bike. Rather than waste time and effort by swerving to avoid her, Carl instead forced the bike to move faster and faster. He collided with the body full-on. It was rotten and decayed and completely disintegrated on impact.

Other than the light from the bike the world was swathed with a virtually impenetrable darkness. The only other light came from the full moon which occasionally dared to peer out from behind a cover of thick, swirling cloud. The sharp light which then spilled down on the world was cold and cruel. The shadows it cast made the grotesque sights which surrounded Carl seem even more unbearable.

He knew that he could not afford to stop - not even for the briefest of moments.

Carl knew that he had no option but to keep moving forwards. Even if he decided to turn around and head back to Penn Farm he would have little chance of alerting Emma and Michael to his return. Crowds of bodies would be upon him before he'd be able to get through the gate or cross the stream.

He had no choice but to keep going until he reached the safety and security of the survivors' base in Northwich.

He wished they'd never left the city.

36

The farmhouse felt as cold and empty inside as the rest of the world was outside. For hours Michael and Emma sat together in total darkness and almost complete silence, both of them thinking constantly about Carl. Whilst they could understand why he had decided to leave, neither could fully agree with what he'd done. Michael's home seemed a million miles away to him but he knew in his heart that there was nothing worth going back there for. All that he had left behind was familiarity, property and possessions and none of that counted for anything anymore. Sure there were things which had a sentimental value attached that he wished he had with him now, but even those few precious belongings weren't worth risking his life for. Nevertheless he accepted that Carl had been forced to leave far more behind than he or Emma had. Returning to Northwich would never bring his family back but, if it meant that he could be at peace with himself for the rest of his days, Michael guessed it would be worth taking the chance.

Without the generator working the house was dark, cold and uninviting. By late evening the gloom was such that Emma and Michael could hardly see each other despite the fact that they were sitting at opposite ends of the same room. Conversation was sparse. Although both thought of a thousand and one things they wanted to say to the other, neither dared say a word. Both survivors felt disconsolate and empty. Regardless of the fact that Carl had spent most of the last few days locked away in private in his room, it was painfully obvious that he was missing. Everything felt incomplete. Nothing felt the same anymore. And more than that, all that Emma and Michael could think about was what might be happening to their companion out on the road. The more they both thought about it the easier it became to accept what he had done and why he'd done it. The painful part was not knowing whether or not he was still alive. Was he still driving towards Northwich? Had he arrived? Was he with the survivors or had something happened to him along the way? Had the numbers of bodies in the city proved too much for him to deal with? No matter how hard they tried, neither Michael or Emma could clear these constant dark thoughts from their minds. The oppressive atmosphere eventually proved too much for Emma. She went up to the bedroom, preferring for a while to be alone.

At midnight Michael had also had enough. He'd spent the last fifty minutes dozing intermittently in his chair and yawning. Each yawn had been long and persistent and they had followed one after the other after the other, leaving his head spinning and his eyes watering. He desperately wanted to sleep but did nothing about it, despite Emma having gone upstairs over an hour earlier. For a while he wondered whether it would even be worth the effort of going up to bed. Once there would he be able to switch his mind off for long enough to be able to sleep? He could have slept in the chair he was sitting in but it was uncomfortable and he would have woken up stiff and aching and still tired. A few minutes after twelve he forced himself to get up and go upstairs.

For some reason Michael decided to try and sleep in another room. He and Emma had slept in the same room every night since they'd arrived at Penn Farm. Although he desperately wanted both her company and the reassurance of her presence, tonight he decided that it would be better if he slept elsewhere. Whether he was silently following some subconscious and misguided moral code he didn't know and he didn't care. Whatever the reason for using another bedroom it didn't work. On his own in the dark he couldn't even bring himself to shut his eyes for more than a couple of seconds, never mind sleep. Less than an hour after first climbing the stairs he lit a candle and quietly traipsed back down again. Trying hard not to make any more noise than was absolutely necessary he made himself a drink, lit a fire in the hearth and sat down to read a book.

Twenty minutes later Emma (who had also been unable to sleep and who had become understandably concerned when she'd heard noises downstairs) tiptoed into the living room. Finding Michael curled up in a ball on a rug in front of the fire she reached out and gently shook his shoulder.

'Fucking hell!' he screamed out, spinning round and sitting up in a single frightened movement. 'Jesus, you scared the shit out of me. I didn't know you were down here.'

Taken aback by the unexpected strength of his reaction, Emma sat down on the nearest chair. She brought her knees up under her backside and consciously tried to shrink her body down to the smallest possible size. In spite of the fire the house was still bitterly cold.

'Sorry,' she mumbled. 'You looked like you were asleep.'

'You're joking aren't you? I haven't slept a bloody wink all night.'

'Me neither.'

Michael finished his drink, stretched and looked around the living room. The house felt much bigger tonight - perhaps even too big - and Carl's sudden leaving was the obvious reason why that seemed to be the case. The room they sat in was filled with random flickering shadows from the fire, trapped indoors as the curtains at all of the windows had been drawn tightly shut. The survivors were afraid to let even the thinnest sliver of light escape out into the night for fear of attracting more of the wandering bodies to the house. When they needed to speak to each other Emma and Michael both instinctively talked in hushed whispers which echoed around the empty house, and when they needed to go into another room they crept through quietly, taking care not to make a single unnecessary sound. They didn't dare do anything that might alert the outside world to their presence at the farm and the constant oppression was making Michael feel claustrophobic. He wanted to scream or shout or play some music or laugh or do pretty much anything other than sit there and watch the hands on the clock on the wall slowly march round another hour. But they both knew that they couldn't afford to take any chances.

Michael glanced over at Emma sitting curled up on the chair. She looked tired and sad. Her eyes were heavy and she was deep in thought.

'Come here,' he said warmly, holding out his arms to her.

Not needing any further encouragement, she slid down from the chair and sat next to him. He gently put his arms round her shoulders and pulled her close. He lightly kissed the top of her head and held her tight.

'It's bloody cold tonight,' she whispered.

'You tired?' he asked.

'Knackered,' she admitted. 'You?'

'The same. Can't sleep though.'

'Nor me. Too much going round my mind. I can't switch off.'

'Don't need to ask what you're thinking about, do I?'

She shook her head.

'Not really. Difficult to think about anything else, isn't it?'

Michael held her a little tighter still.

'Just wish he'd stopped,' he said, his voice suddenly sounding unexpectedly strained and cracked with emotion. 'I still think I should have stopped him. I should have locked the stupid bastard in his room and not let him leave. I should have...'

'Shh...' Emma whispered. She pulled back slightly from Michael to allow herself to look deep into his eyes. The low orange flames of the fire highlighted glistening tears which ran freely down his face. 'There was nothing that either of us could have done and talking like this is just pointless, we've already had this conversation. We both know we would have done more harm than good if we'd tried to stop him...'

'I just wish he was here now...' Michael continued, having to force his words out between sobs and deep breaths of air.

'I know,' she whispered, her voice soothing and low.

The two friends held each other tightly again. After a brief moment of awkwardness and reluctance they finally both began to cry freely. For the first time since they had lost everything on that desperate autumn morning two weeks ago, they both dropped their guard, relaxed and cried. They cried for all they had lost and left behind, they cried for their absent friend and they cried for each other.

The unexpected and much needed outpouring of emotion which Emma and Michael shared acted as a relief valve - diffusing otherwise insurmountable pressure, soothing troubled minds and breaking down unnecessary (and imaginary) barriers. Once their tears had dried (it could have been minutes or hours later - neither was completely sure) they began to relax and then, gradually, to talk freely again. Michael made them both a drink of hot chocolate which they drank together as they watched the fire die.

'You know,' Michael yawned, lying on his back and watching the shadows flickering on the ceiling, 'I'd have bought a house like this if I could have afforded it.'

Emma, lying at right angles to him with her head resting on his stomach, smiled to herself.

'Me too.'

'Really?' he asked, lifting himself up onto his elbows and looking across at her.

'Yes, really,' she replied. 'It's a dream house, isn't it. A lick of paint and it could be beautiful.'

He sighed and yawned again.

'Apart from half a fucking million rotting bodies on the other side of the fence it's okay, isn't it,' he mumbled sarcastically.

Emma ignored him. She tried to stifle a yawn but couldn't.

'I'm tired,' she said.

'Want to go to bed?' he asked.

'No point. I won't sleep.'

'Me neither.'

His elbows aching, Michael lay back down again. He scratched the side of his face and then rubbed his chin. He hadn't shaved for three or four days. He couldn't remember exactly how long it had been but it didn't seem to matter. He put his hands behind his head and basked in front of the fire.

'If it wasn't for the bodies,' he said, his voice quiet, 'then I could put up with this.'

'What do you mean?'

'Don't get me wrong, I wish everything was back as it was,' he explained. 'All I'm saying is that I could deal with it all a lot better if the dead bodies had stayed dead. I can handle there being only a handful of us left, I'm just having trouble coping with the fact that it's a constant fucking battle.'

'It's not a battle.'

'Yes it is,' he insisted. 'Of course it is. If we want food then we have to fight for it. We have to sneak out, grab as much as we can and then sneak back like bloody mice. If we want heat and light then we have to be ready to be surrounded by those frigging things outside. It's a fucking battle and it's not fair.'

For a second Michael sounded like a spoilt child. But Emma knew that he was right and she agreed with everything he said. Had it not been punishment enough to have lost everything that ever mattered to them? Why now did they have to continue to suffer like this?

'And what really gets me,' he continued, 'is the fact that the bloody things are already dead. You can't kill them. I bet if you put a fucking bullet between their eyes they'd still keep coming at you.'

Emma didn't respond. She knew it was important for him to talk but this was a conversation that she didn't particularly want to prolong. She reminded herself that it was obviously doing Michael good. For too long they had each kept their fears and emotions bottled up for fear of upsetting the other two and disturbing the fragile peace and shelter that they'd found at Penn Farm. In the last twenty-four hours Carl had proved that holding onto private pain and frustration was not necessarily the best thing to do. His internal conflict and personal torture had driven him to take action which, from where she was standing, appeared tantamount to suicide.

'Want another drink?' Michael asked, disturbing her train of thought.

'What?' she mumbled, only half-listening.

'I asked if you wanted another drink.'

'No thanks. Do you want one?'

He shook his head.

'So why did you ask then?'

'Don't know. Just something to say I suppose.'

'What's wrong with saying nothing.'

Michael covered his eyes.

'Too quiet,' he replied.

'And what's wrong with silence?'

'It lets you think too much.'

'Don't you want to think?'

'No, not any more. I want a break from thinking.'

'But that's a stupid thing to say. You're always thinking, aren't you?'

He yawned, stretched his arms and then pulled them back and covered his face again.

'There's thinking and there's thinking, isn't there?'

'Is there?'

'Of course there is. Have you ever sat down with a group of friends and talked about nothing in particular?'

'Yes...'

'Have you ever had one of those pointless conversations where you spend hours discussing really bloody stupid things? You know, when you find yourself arguing about the colour of your favourite superhero's shorts or something like that?'

Emma smiled.

'I can't ever remember talking about superhero's shorts, but I know what you mean.'

'I remember when I was a kid, in the summer holidays, we'd get up early and disappear into the park for hours. We'd be there for most of the day and we wouldn't actually do anything. We'd walk around and play and fight and...'

'You need to switch off,' Emma said as Michael's voice trailed away into silence. 'We both do. We weren't designed for this kind of life. Your mind and body can't cope if you keep going at full speed all the time.'

'So when are you and me going to switch off then?' he asked. 'When are we going to be able to do something without worrying about the consequences?'

'Don't know.'

'Because I think you're right, we're both going to need to, Em. I think that somehow we're going to have to try and find a way to do it.'

'Meditation,' Emma suggested. 'We could meditate in shifts.'

'Are you taking the piss?'

'No, I'm serious. Like you say, we've got to learn to switch off and disconnect from everything. If we don't then one or even both of us will probably lose it big time.'

'So when was the last time you managed to switch off and disconnect?' he asked, semiseriously.

Emma thought carefully for a couple of seconds.

'About six months ago,' she laughed.

Once their frustrations had been aired and discussed, Michael and Emma talked for hours. Their long and rambling conversation covered everything and nothing.

'We're you born in Northwich, Mike?'

'Just outside. What about you?'

'No, I just studied there.'

'Did you like it?'

'It was okay.'

'Just okay?'

'Yes, it was okay.'

'I liked it. Alright so it had it's fair share of penthouses and it's fair share of shit-holes but everywhere does. It was home.'

'I much prefer being out in a place like this. Not at the moment, of course, but before all this happened I was always happier out in the country away from the noise and the concrete and the people.'

'And me. I used to try and get away as often as I could. I'd just get in the car and drive for a couple of hours and see where I ended up. I'd go and lie down in a field or walk along a river or something...'

'Didn't go fishing did you?'

'No, why?'

'Because I hate fishing. It's a bloody barbaric sport.'

'Bloody boring sport.'

'I used to camp. I'd pack a rucksack and a tent and catch a lift to somewhere remote.'

'And then what would you do.'

'Nothing.'

'Emma, do you miss the television?'

'I miss the noise and normality of it, but not much else.'

'I miss the weather.'

'The weather?'

'I never realised how much I relied on weather forecasts until now. I really miss knowing what the weather's going to do next.'

'Doesn't matter anymore though, does it?'

'Suppose not. It didn't really matter anyway but I still want to know.'

'Just looking at the telly switched off reminds me of everything that's gone now.'

'Did you used to watch a lot of films?'

'I used to watch more films than anything else.'

'And I bet you never really listened to the radio.'

'No, not very often. Why?'

'I've got this theory that people who watched a lot of films and who didn't listen to the radio always had strong personalities.'

'How do you work that out?'

'Because you're the kind of person who knows what you want if you don't listen to the radio. If you listen to the radio you have to sit through hours of crap music, crap adverts and pointless conversations just to get to hear to a couple of minutes of something you like.'

'I suppose. I'm not convinced though.'

'I never listened to the radio, not even in the car. I was always a CD or cassette man. You always knew where you were with a cassette.'

'So how's this all going to end, Em?'

'What do you mean?'

'I don't know. Are things ever going to sort themselves out?'

'I doubt it. Bloody stupid question really.'

'I know, sorry.'

'I think it'll get worse before it gets any better.'

'Think so? Shit, how could it get any worse?'

'Disease. There are millions of bodies lying rotting in the streets, aren't there?'

'What about insects then?'

'What about them?'

'Rotting bodies and more disease is going to mean more insects, isn't it?'

'It might do. Probably.'

'And rats. There are going to be fucking hundreds of rats about in the cities.'

'Emma, is there anybody you can think of that you're glad is dead?'

'Bloody hell, what kind of a question is that?'

'Come on, be honest. Is there anyone out of all the people you knew who you're actually glad is dead?'

'No. Christ, you're sick at times.'

'No I'm not, I just don't bother with bullshit. There were a few people in my life who I'm happy aren't about anymore.'

'Like who?'

'I worked with a bloke who was a complete bastard. He had a wife who just doted on him. She'd have done absolutely anything to make him happy. She had two part-time jobs as well as looking after three kids.'

'And what did he do?'

'Nothing. Absolutely bloody nothing. He was qualified and everything, just couldn't be bothered to get off his backside and do anything with his life.'

'So why did you want him dead? What did he ever do to you?'

'I didn't say I wanted him dead. He didn't do anything to me.'

'So why did you hate him?'

'I didn't say I hated him. He used to be quite a laugh actually.'

'So why are you happy he's dead?'

'Don't know really. He just always pissed me off. Suppose it was because I couldn't be that way. He was just a waste of space. He didn't add anything to his family, he just took from them. It never seemed right.'

'Do you think you would have got married?'

'Don't know. Probably. I would have liked to have settled down and had a family eventually.'

'So did you ever get close?'

'No. I always thought I'd know instantly when I met the woman I was going to marry, but it never happened.'

'I got engaged when I was eighteen.'

'How old are you now? Christ, I can't believe I've never asked your age before.'

'I'm twenty-three.'

'So why didn't it work out?'

'Because I was left doing all the work while he sat on his backside, same as your mate and his wife. Jesus, he broke my heart. I would have done just about anything for him but he wasn't prepared to do anything for me.'

'So you must be glad that he's not around?'

'Not really. Actually I still miss him.'

Another hour and the virtually constant stream of questions, revelations and personal admissions had all but dried up. By three o'clock the two of them were sprawled out together on the rug in front of what remained of the fire, relaxing in the fading warmth of the lightly glowing embers. Michael woke up when Emma shuffled in her sleep and snored. In turn his sudden startled movements woke her.

'You okay?' he asked as he untangled himself from her legs. Their bodies had become innocently twisted together in the night.

'I'm alright,' she mumbled, her words dulled with sleep.

Michael dragged himself up onto all fours and shuffled round until he was in a similar position to Emma. Exhausted, he collapsed back down next to her. He instinctively reached out and put his arms around her body, holding her tightly and subconsciously shielding and protecting her from anything that might happen in the remaining dark hours of the night.

37

By three-thirty Carl was fast approaching the outskirts of the city of Northwich. He had driven at an increasingly cautious speed - as his journey had progressed, so his fatigue had mounted. As his tiredness had climbed towards dangerous levels he had been forced to concentrate even harder, and that extra concentration quickly drained his already severely depleted reserves of energy and determination.

As the dark shadows of the once familiar city engulfed him, his heart began to pound in his chest with more and more force and confusing, conflicting emotions constantly raged through his tired brain. Although part of him felt comforted and reassured that the journey was almost at an end, at the same time he was filled with cold dread and trepidation at the thought of what might be waiting for him in the desolate streets of Northwich.

Everything looked depressingly featureless and similar in the low light of early morning. It took a while before Carl was completely sure that the greenery of the countryside had finally given way to the harsh plastic and concrete of the decaying city. The lack of any illumination surprised and disorientated him. For some stupid reason he had half-expected to find some kind of light in the town. As it was the visibility in the city proved to be exactly the same as it had been out in the country. It was only the shapes of the grey shadows which surrounded him that had changed.

He slowed the bike to the lowest speed he dared travel at and looked desperately from side to side, hoping he would see something he recognised that would point him in the right direction. He knew the city like the back of his hand but tonight he couldn't see anything resembling a familiar landmark. Despite having reduced his speed he still drove past the road signs far too quickly to be able to read any of them. Most were covered with a layer of grime and what appeared to be lichen or moss.

Memory told him that the motorway he had been following bisected the city from east to west and he knew that at some point he would come upon another junction that would lead to the motorway which led to the north and south. He passed a slip road and then cursed under his breath when he realised that had been the exit which would have taken him close to the Whitchurch Community Centre and then out towards the suburb of Hadley where he and his family had lived. Taking care to avoid the wreckage strewn across the carriageway he turned the bike around and doubled-back on himself.

Once off the motorway the roads narrowed and the number of obstacles in Carl's path seemed to increase. Tall city centre offices, apartments and shops lined the sides of the road he followed making him feel claustrophobic and trapped and further exaggerating the nausea and panic with which he already suffered. He turned right towards Hadley and the community centre before being forced to brake suddenly. The road ahead of him was blocked across its full width by a petrol tanker which had jack-knifed and which now lay on its side like the hopeless corpse of a beached whale. The light was so poor that he didn't see the wreck until he was almost on top of it. He slammed on the brakes and pulled and steered the bike as best he could, leaning over to one side with all his weight to desperately try and force the machine to turn in the tightest possible arc. Just at the moment he thought he had succeeded in avoiding a collision the bike kicked out from underneath him, sending him tumbling across the uneven tarmac. He collided with the remains of a burnt out car and lay still for the briefest of moments, stunned and unable to move. Through blurred eyes he watched helplessly as the bike skidded across the ground towards the tanker, sending a shower of sparks shooting up into the cold air as it scraped along the surface of the road. Dazed and unsteady, he forced himself to get up and run over to the bike. Groaning with pain and effort he lifted it up and restarted the stalled engine. With precious seconds to spare he managed to ride away before the closest few bodies of a shuffling crowd were upon him. He had been off the bike and on the ground for less than thirty seconds but already dozens of the creatures were swarming nearby. He escaped by carving a ruthless and bloody path right through the centre of the desperate gathering.

Now that he had an idea of where he actually was the roads gradually became more familiar. Although the relentless darkness and his cloying fear were both cruel and unforgiving, he felt sure that he was infuriatingly close to the community centre that the survivors had used as a base. There was movement in the shadows all around him and he sensed that thousands of bodies were nearby. But then, finally, the light from the bike illuminated the turn into the road he had been looking for. Just that last turning, followed immediately by a sharp right into the car park, and he was there. Momentarily ecstatic, he steered around familiar cars (Stuart Jeffries' car which had been used as a beacon that first night and the high-class car that he himself had arrived in) and screeched to a halt outside the community centre. He banged his fist on the door.

'Open up!' he yelled desperately, fighting to make himself heard over the roar of the bike. 'Open the bloody door!'

He anxiously glanced back over his shoulder and saw that the dark silhouettes of countless stumbling figures were pouring into the car park after him. Despite their forced, laborious movement they were approaching with a frightening speed and determination.

'Open the fucking door!' he screamed.

Stretching his hand out in front of him, Carl grabbed hold of the handle and yanked it downwards. To his surprise the door opened.

Carl rocked the bike back and then accelerated and drove into the hall. Once inside he jumped off the machine and slammed the door shut behind him. As the heavy door fell into place he felt thud after thud after sickening thud as the loathsome creatures outside crashed into the building. Shaking with fear he secured the entrance and leant against the wall. He slid down to the ground exhausted, threw off his helmet and held his head in his hands.

The abandoned bike had fallen diagonally across the width of the entrance hall. The engine had died but the wheels still span furiously and the bright headlamp shone relentlessly, burning into the dense darkness.

There was no movement in the hall. Despite the panic and noise of his arrival, no-one had moved.

With his legs heavy and leaden through a combination of fear and fatigue, he clambered back to his feet, using the wall behind him for support. His mouth was dry and he found himself unable to call out. He stepped over the abandoned bike, stumbled past the dark and silent kitchens and toilets, and walked into the main hall.

Then he stopped moving.

And he stared.

Paralysed with disbelief, devastation and absolute terror, he fell to his knees.

The relentlessly bright headlamp on the front of the bike filled parts of the hall with harsh, artificial light and that cruel and brilliant light revealed a sight so terrible that, at first, Carl was unable to comprehend what he was seeing. Even after everything else that he had seen during the last couple of weeks this new aberration sickened him. He could feel his legs weakening and tasted bile rising in his throat.

The bare wooden floor of the community centre was carpeted with human remains.

Moving without thinking, he stood up and took a few stumbling steps forward. Blood and bone mixed beneath his feet as he picked his way through a macabre maze of cold, grey flesh and crimson red gore. He began to think at speed - searching for explanations which he could neither prove or disprove. Perhaps the corpses were the remains of creatures from outside? Maybe they had somehow found a way into the community centre and the survivors had been forced to leave? There was a body on the ground in front of him. Half-dressed, its exposed skin had been ripped and torn to shreds. Fighting to keep control of his stomach, he reached down and grabbed hold of one exposed shoulder, pulling the body over onto its back. Although it was no-one he recognised, he could see immediately that this had not been one of the sickly, emaciated bastards from outside. What flesh remained on the face was clear and relatively unmarked and, apart from the countless horrific mutilations, the cadaver seemed to have been otherwise healthy and normal. There was no doubt that this was the body of one of the survivors.

Carl began to sob. He stood in the centre of the room and gradually became aware of sounds coming from the darkness in front of him.

'Is anyone there?' he called out hopefully.

No response.

'Hello...' he tried again. 'Is someone there?'

A figure appeared from the shadows, partially illuminated by the light from the motorbike. Suddenly elated, Carl took a few steps forward.

'Thank Christ,' he mumbled. 'What happened? How the hell did they manage to get inside?'

The figure inched closer. Every clumsy step it took forward brought it further into the light from the bike. Two more steps and Carl could see that the body was slumped forward with its head hanging heavily on its shoulders. It slowly looked up and gazed at Carl with familiarly cold, emotionless eyes. A diseased and rotting corpse, without warning it lunged towards him.

'Shit!' he yelled as he moved to one side. The creature lost its already unsteady footing in a puddle of thick, dark blood and slipped down to the ground.

Carl steadied himself and stared at the wretched corpse as it struggled to drag itself back up.

'Shit!' he shouted again in desperation. 'Bastard thing! You fucking bastard thing!'

He took a step closer and kicked the creature in the face, the full force of his boot catching it square on the jaw. It fell back down to the ground and immediately began to right itself again. Carl unleashed his full fury and frustration on the pathetic carcass, kicking and punching at it until it finally lay still and did not move. It was rapidly decomposing. By the time he'd finished with it very little remained.

Crying with pain, exhaustion and anguish, and unable to come to terms with what he had found, Carl walked back towards the bike. He knew that his options were limited - he could stay in the centre or take his chances outside. After travelling for hours he couldn't face going back out there again.

Using the dull light from a torch to guide him, he dragged himself back through the community centre and made his way to the small rooms at the far end of the building. Using the last dregs of energy that he could summon from his tired and aching body, he climbed out of the skylight and out onto the flat roof.

Carl sat on the edge of the roof for hours, being buffeted constantly by a familiar strong, cold wind and watching the dead city decaying around him.

The sun was beginning to rise.

The thought of another day dawning filled him with dread.

38

When Michael woke up Emma wasn't there.

Drugged with sleep, he grabbed a nearby jumper from where
he'd thrown it last night and pulled it over his head before
shuffling through the living room to look for her. It was a cold,
grey morning outside and the house was silent but for the noise
of Emma working in the kitchen. She didn't notice Michael had
come into the room until he dragged a chair across the floor and
away from the table and sat down.

'Hello,' she said quietly. 'Sleep well?'

He nodded but didn't say anything. All things considered, he
had slept well, but he was too tired to engage in conversation
unless he absolutely had to. He knew he'd feel more sociable
when he'd had a few minutes to properly wake up.

'I've been up for ages,' Emma continued. 'There was a storm
a couple of hours ago that woke me. I've just been in here
sorting through the stuff we got while we were out yesterday.'

Yesterday afternoon's priority had been to get Carl safely on
his way back to the city. Although that in itself hadn't taken too
long to organise and arrange, there had subsequently been much
associated thinking, questioning and soul searching which
seemed to have prevented Emma and Michael from doing pretty
much anything else. The supplies which they had collected from
the village had been left in a pile of boxes and bags on the
kitchen floor. Emma had worked hard since she'd got up and had
sorted most of it away.

Michael cleared his throat and rubbed his eyes.

'So how you feeling today?' he asked, his voice quiet, flat
and subdued.

She stopped what she was doing and looked up and briefly smiled.

'I'm okay,' she replied, giving little away. 'What about you?'

'I'm alright.'

Silently and independently they were both still preoccupied with thoughts of Carl, although neither wanted to talk about their missing colleague to the other. Emma found herself wondering what he had found in the city whilst, more pessimistically, Michael was wondering whether he'd got there at all.

'So what are we going to do today?' Emma asked unexpectedly.

Strange question, Michael thought. What is there to do?

'Don't know,' he answered. 'Why, what do you want to do?'

She shrugged her shoulders and returned to her work, wondering what had made her ask such a stupid question in the first place. Perhaps it had just been instinctive? Whatever the reason, the lack of any worthwhile answers was depressing. The complete and utter lack of any positive distraction and interest in their lives, coupled with the constant fear of everything beyond the farmhouse walls, was beginning to grind her down. The relentless boredom, fear and frustration hung over her head like a black storm cloud. And the fact that Carl had left only served to increase her negativity further still.

'Maybe we should make something,' Michael suggested, picking up on Emma's sadness. Not much of a suggestion, granted, but it was all that he could come up with. 'You know, build something...'

'Like what?'

He struggled to answer.

'I don't know. Bloody hell, there must be something we could do. Christ, we could spring clean or decorate a room or bake a fucking cake...I don't know.'

'Maybe we could just sit here and watch the clock until we fall asleep. Then we could get up tomorrow and do the same again...'

Emma's attitude hurt. Michael knew just how she was feeling, but the fact that they had been able to relax a little last night made her apparent anger and disinterest even more frustrating and harder to swallow. Perhaps it was for that very reason that she was like this? Was she now punishing herself for finally allowing herself to drop a few barriers and reveal her true feelings, thoughts and emotions?

Michael wondered if this was how it was always going to be.

39
Carl Henshawe

I slept for about an hour, curled up in a ball on the roof. It was fucking freezing, but it was better to freeze out there than to go back into the hall. I couldn't bring myself to go back inside. I knew I'd have to go through it eventually to get to the bike and get out again, but not yet.

The thing I remember most about the morning was that it was grey. Everything was grey. The sky was grey, the buildings looked grey and the streets and bodies were grey. All the colour had gone, drained and rotted away.

I first looked at my watch just after five, and it took me until just before eight to decide that I was going to do it. The longest three hours of my entire bloody life were spent sitting on the roof of the community centre in the wind and rain thinking about everything I'd left behind in the city and whether I should go back to it. I knew that I had to do something. I couldn't get this close and then just turn around and go back, could I? From the second I'd left my house on the first morning, all I'd thought about was Gemma and Sarah. That was the reason I couldn't see the point of whatever it was that Emma and Michael were trying to achieve. For me there was no point in going on if I didn't have Gemma and Sarah with me.

For a while I even thought about suicide, but I'm such a fucking coward that I couldn't decide how to do it. I didn't have any pills or drink or drugs with me and I couldn't get any without crowds of those fucking things surrounding me. And the prospect of a thousand rotting corpses fighting over me was not worth thinking about. Once or twice I actually stood at the edge of the roof and got ready to jump, but it was nowhere near high enough. I'd probably just break an arm or a leg and end up lying there in agony and waiting for them to get me. Christ, the bloody irony of it all. Millions and millions of people lying dead around me and all I wanted to do was join them but I couldn't. If I'd brought the rifle with me from the farmhouse I reckoned I could have done it that way. Quick and easy. Bloody hell, it had been weeks since anything had been quick and easy.

And in the long lonely minutes that followed even more irony tormented me. I kept thinking about Sarah and Gemma and each time I pictured their precious faces I just wanted to stop and give up. But I knew that Sarah wouldn't have wanted that. If she'd been able to see me up on that roof she would have crucified me. If she'd known that I'd been thinking about giving up and ending it all then she'd probably have done it for me. And if I was honest with myself I'd have felt the same if our positions had been reversed. If she'd survived and I'd been the one that had died, I would have wanted her to be safe and to try and make something from what remained of her life.

So I decided to go home.

I climbed back down into the hall and walked through and started the bike. Without even bothering to think about what might be outside, I just started the engine, pushed the door open and rode out into the cold morning.

I had reached Hadley in a few minutes. As I got to the top of Gresham Hill I cut the engine and let the bike freewheel down towards our estate. I felt scared and I was so fucking nervous that it was hard to think straight. I didn't even stop to think about the bodies. I was too busy looking at everything and thinking how much it had all changed. There probably hadn't been another living soul there since I'd left on the day it had all begun, but everything looked completely different. I went past the pub where we'd been on the last normal Sunday night. The car park was overgrown with weeds and there were rats looking for food around the bins. The doors were hanging open and it was black and cold inside. The last time I'd been there it had been full of sounds and light and people.

Because I wasn't making any noise the bodies didn't seem to take any notice of me. If I moved slowly and took my time they didn't even look up when I passed. I got off the bike and pushed it round into our road. Then I saw our house and I stopped. Part of me wanted to turn round and run but I knew that I had to carry on. But what if I got in and Sarah and Gemma weren't there? Worse still, what if they were there and they'd become like the things which were still dragging themselves around the streets? Whatever I might have found, the thought of leaving and not knowing seemed much worse. I knew that I had to carry on.

I pushed the bike onto the drive and walked up to the front door. There was post in the porch, and like a fucking idiot I picked it up and started to look at it. A gas bill and a credit card bill. I even opened the bloody things to see how much I owed. And I dared to hate the bodies for following their instincts...

I had carried my house keys with me every day since we'd left Northwich. I hadn't ever thought about going back there before, but for some reason I just hadn't been able to let them go. With my hands shaking I unlocked the door and went inside.

I was just like it was when I left it. Everything was where I expected to find it. Gemma's shoes were by the door, my mug was on the kitchen worktop, Sarah's coat was hung over the post at the bottom of the bannister. I took off my crash helmet and just stood there and looked around. It was like the weirdest fucking dream I've ever had. If I half-closed my eyes and ignored the smell I could almost imagine that nothing had ever happened. There was a half-inch layer of dust on everything but other than that it still looked like home.

I stood at the bottom of the stairs and looked up.

This was the real reason I'd come back.

I knew I couldn't do anything for them and that going up to the bedroom wasn't going to bring my girls back, but I had to go up. It took me about ten minutes to climb the stairs. I went up one at a time, forcing myself to climb higher and higher and, at the same time, having to keep control of my emotions and stop myself from running out of the house and getting back on the bike. Eventually I was at the top, standing on the landing, holding onto the bedroom door handle with my hands shaking.

I listened carefully. There was no noise coming from inside the room. I coughed, and still there was no reaction.

My mind was filled with memories of my family.

I pushed the door open and waited.

Nothing happened.

I looked at the bed and saw that they were both still there, still covered up by the duvet I'd draped over them before I'd left. I could just see a few curls of Sarah's hair peeking out from under the covers. Much as I wanted to see them, I didn't want to look at either of them. I wanted to remember them as they were and it was enough just to know that they were still together. I leant across and kissed them both through the bedding before I said goodbye. I shut my eyes and told them that I loved them and that I would always be thinking about them.

And that was all I did. I didn't want to disturb them or move them. I just wanted to know that they were both still there. I just wanted to be sure that they were still together. It was more for Gemma than any other reason. I hadn't been able to get the nightmare thought out of my mind that either one of them might have walked and that my beautiful little girl could have been on her own somewhere.

As it was she was okay. She was lying safe in bed, curled up tightly next to her mum.

And then came the question of what to do next.

The survivors had gone - I hoped they'd moved on, but I knew in my heart that something fucking terrible had happened to them.

My family were safe and were resting peacefully and I knew that I wasn't going to go back home again.

I hadn't expected to be on my own. Getting into the council depot that I'd talked about before suddenly didn't seem like much of an option. Okay, so I could get myself in there, but then what? I'd already discovered that I didn't have the balls to kill myself. So was I going to just sit there and starve or wait to die from dehydration, loneliness, boredom or old age?

The farmhouse I'd just come from was the safest place left.

40

Michael came in from outside.

'We've got a problem,' he said, his face flustered.
Immediately concerned, Emma stopped what she had been doing and rushed out to him in the hall.

'What is it?'

'The van,' he replied. 'It's completely fucked. There's oil and all kinds of stuff leaking out. Looks like something's cracked underneath.'

'So can you fix it?' she asked. A sensible question. Michael shook his head despondently.

'I haven't got a bloody clue,' he admitted. 'I can drive a car, fill it with petrol and change a tyre but that's about all. I wouldn't know where to start with something like this.'

'So what do we do? Can we get by without it?'

'We can, but we'd be taking a hell of a chance. What if the same thing happens to the Landrover?'

'So what do we do?' she asked again.

'We go out and get ourselves another van,' he replied.

And so, less than an hour later, Michael and Emma again found themselves leaving the relative safety of Penn Farm and heading back towards one of the dead villages dotted around the decaying countryside.

For once Michael's usually keen sense of direction let him down. Distracted by a body lurching out at them from out of nowhere at a cross-roads, he took a wrong turn which soon led them out along a long, straight stretch of narrow road. The road climbed for more than a mile before becoming flatter and more level. At the top of the climb the trees and bushes which had surrounded them before and obscured their view disappeared. Everywhere suddenly felt empty, spacious and open. Intrigued, Michael drove through an open gate and into a wide field dotted with a handful of cars. They had arrived in a dusty, cliff-top car park where, from the far side of the field, they could see out over the ocean. Neither of them had thought that they were this close to the coast. In the confusion and disorientation of the last few weeks their whole world felt like it had been pulled and twisted out of shape beyond all recognition. Maps and atlases had been forgotten and put to one side as they had struggled to survive from day to day. Strange as it seemed, the ocean had been the last thing that Michael had expected to see.

A little more relaxed than they had been before (perhaps because for once they couldn't see a single body nearby) they drove to the area of the car park which afforded them the best view of the seemingly endless expanse of water below them and stopped. Michael switched off the engine and slumped back in his chair.

'Screwed that up, didn't I?' he smiled.

'Doesn't matter,' Emma mumbled as she wound down her window slightly. The noise of the wind and the sea was loud and welcome. As well as shattering the otherwise all-consuming silence of the world for a while, it also camouflaged any sound which the two of them might make.

The sight of the ocean filled Michael with an unexpected combination of emotions. He had always loved the sea as a child, and seeing it now made him remember a handful of memories of childhood holidays, when the sky had always been deep blue, the sun huge and hot and the days seemingly endless. The memory of those long-gone innocent days filled him with a now familiar sadness and grief. But those heavy, desperate feelings were also matched by a slight elation because, for once, the two of them were free from the confines of the farmhouse and the barrier and, for a short time at least, away from the millions of bodies which plagued their lives.

'Safest thing to do would be to take one of these cars,' he said, gesturing out across the car park. 'We'll find the one that's in best condition, empty it, and then drive it back.'

Emma nodded and continued to look out over the sea.

'Think it's safe to get out?' she asked.

'Don't know,' he replied. 'There's nothing about. As long as we stay close we should be okay.'

Needing no further encouragement, Emma opened the door and stepped outside. The blustery wind was strong and refreshing and it carried with it the unmistakable smell of the salty water below. She looked out towards the horizon and just dared to imagine for a few seconds that nothing had happened. She had tried to do it many times before but there had always been something in her line of vision to remind her of the limitations of the shattered shell of a world in which she existed. Looking out over the uninterrupted water, however, for a short time at least it was relatively easy to pretend everything was okay. She took a few steps further forward and looked down onto a stretch of sandy beach. Her heart sank as she watched a single staggering body tripping and stumbling through the frothing, splashing surf. Each advancing wave knocked the pathetic creature off-balance. She watched as it struggled to stand, only to be knocked over again when the next wave came. There was a second body in the water wearing only a pair of swimming trunks. Obviously the unfortunate remains of an early morning bather from a couple of weeks ago, the bloated, swollen and discoloured body was gradually being washed ashore.

Michael hadn't seen the bodies. He was still daydreaming as he sat down on the grass next to their vehicle.

'You know,' he began, 'sitting here you could almost convince yourself that nothing had happened.'

Emma said nothing. Having had the same thought just a few seconds earlier, the appearance of the bodies in the surf below had depressed her. She didn't think it was fair to spoil her friend's enjoyment of the moment.

Michael stretched out on the grass, lying back and resting on his elbows. He looked over at Emma and smiled.

'Know what I want?' he asked.

'What?' she wondered, feigning interest.

'A sandwich,' he replied. 'I want a big, thick sandwich on freshly baked, crusty bread. I want salad, sliced ham, grated cheese and mayonnaise. Oh, and I'll have a glass of freshly squeezed orange juice to wash it down with.'

'We've got tinned ham and a little bit of mayo back at the farm,' Emma said, sitting down next to him. 'And we've got orange cordial.'

'Not the same really, is it?'

She shook her head.

'No. Think we'll ever eat like that again?'

Michael thought for a few moments.

'We might do. I bet we could make bread and cheese eventually, and we could have ham if we can catch and kill a pig. And I suppose we could grow fruit and vegetables if we set up a greenhouse...'

'You should get yourself an allotment,' she joked.

'I could do,' Michael said, semiseriously. He sighed sadly and looked up into the sky. 'I don't know, it's fucking stupid, isn't it?'

'What is?'

'Everything we've just said. In a few seconds we've managed to come up with about six month's work. Six months to get a fucking salad sandwich and a glass of orange juice...'

'I know,' she sympathised.

Michael yawned and stretched. He looked across at Emma who suddenly seemed to be deep in thought. He had learnt recently that this was not always a good sign. It was okay to think for a while, but concentrating too deeply on everything that had happened often caused real problems.

'Are you okay?' he asked.

She smiled and nodded and looked down at him.

'I'm okay,' she replied, giving little away.

'But...?' he pressed, sensing that she needed to talk. He stared at her and, once eye-contact had been made, she realised that she couldn't avoid answering him.

'Are we really doing the right thing here?' she asked.

'What, sitting in a car park looking at the sea?' he replied flippantly. Unamused, Emma shook her head.

'No, I'm talking about the house and being out in the countryside.'

Michael sat up attentively, sensing the seriousness in her voice.

'Of course we are,' he answered defensively. 'Why, are you starting to have doubts?'

'What is there to have doubts about?'

'Whether we should ever have left the city? Whether Carl was the one who was right to go back there?'

'I'm not having doubts...'

'So what is it then? Don't you think we can make anything of what's left?'

'I'm not sure. Do you?'

'We might be able to. The bodies are rotting, aren't they? They should disappear over time and if we could...'

'What about disease?'

'There are a thousand hospitals up and down the country full of drugs.'

'But we don't know which drugs to use.'

'We can find out.'

'But if we're sick and we need to get drugs, we'll need to know what disease we've got, won't we? How do we diagnose that? Do you know the difference between malaria, typhoid and gout for God's sake?'

'No, but there are books...'

'So what chance have we got?'

Michael stood up and walked over to Emma. Although she still tried to avoid eye contact, he positioned himself directly in front of her so that she had no choice but to look up into his face.

'We've got a chance,' he said, his voice sounding quiet and strangely hurt. 'Okay, I accept that it might not be much of a chance, but to me it's a fucking chance all the same and I'm going to take it.'

'I know,' she sighed. 'I'm sorry...'

The couple were silent for a few seconds. Both stared into the eyes of the other, their minds full of confused thoughts.

'Look, let's get back,' Michael said eventually. 'It's not safe to be out here.'

With that he turned away and looked around the car park. About a hundred yards away from them was a car. Nothing special - just an ordinary family-sized saloon - but it was the biggest car in the field. With Emma following close by, he walked over to it and opened the door. The remains of the driver and his female passenger sat motionless in their seats. They were both dressed in business clothes and Michael wondered what they had been doing sitting in this exposed and isolated place so early on a Tuesday morning when the catastrophe had first struck. An illicit office affair perhaps, or a married couple passing the time and spending a few precious minutes together before heading off to work? Regardless of the reason, he carefully leant inside the car and undid both seat belts. Cautiously (and with a look of disgust and concentration on his face) he took hold of the driver and dragged his corpse across the grass, leaving it on the ground alongside another car. He then returned and did the same with the passenger. The least he could do for them, he thought, was leave them together.

The keys were still in the ignition. He started the engine and gestured for Emma to get inside.

'Follow me back,' he said, suddenly anxious and feeling uncomfortably vulnerable now that they were making a noise which might alert any nearby bodies to their presence. 'Okay?'

She nodded and sat behind the wheel. Michael ran over to the Landrover, started it up and pulled away.

In convoy the two cars drove out of the car park and back towards the farm.

41

Michael's earlier disorientation worsened as they drove back home. The roads which they'd followed earlier looked even more unfamiliar when he tried to navigate his way back again. The journey was made more difficult by the fact that he kept glancing back in the rear view mirror to check that Emma was still following. He felt surprisingly uncomfortable without her in the seat next to him. He had come to rely on having her around much more than he'd realised. He still felt like he hardly knew her, but the truth of the matter was that he had shared more pain, despair and raw emotion with her than with any other person in the twenty-nine years of his life so far.

He threw the Landrover around a sharp bend in the road and then slammed on the brakes to avoid the back end of a milk float which was jutting out into the road, the front of the float having smashed into a low stone wall. He missed it by inches, and the closeness of a collision shocked him back into concentrating on safely returning to the farm house. Another quick glance in the mirror revealed that Emma was still close behind.

The winding road gradually opened out and became straighter. In the near distance he could see a row of three isolated grey cottages. From one of the buildings (it seemed to be the middle one) a single figure emerged and staggered into the middle of the road. It stopped and turned to face him.

'Fucking hell,' Michael said under his breath to himself as he stared at the pathetic body in front of him. 'Just look at that stupid fucking thing.'

He pushed his foot down harder on the accelerator, the Landrover quickly gaining more and more speed. At that precise moment Michael focussed all his pent up anger, fears and frustrations on that one pitiful creature. For a few seconds he felt that destroying it would somehow make amends for the loss of just about everything and anything that had ever mattered to him.

As Michael raced ahead the distance between the two cars increased. Concerned and confused and certain that something was wrong, Emma accelerated to try and keep up with him.

The body in the middle of the road lifted its tired arms into the air above its head and began to wave Michael down.

'Jesus Christ,' he muttered. It took a full few seconds for the true importance of what he was seeing to sink in, and by that time he was almost upon the body. It was moving with more direction, purpose and intent than he'd seen from any of the corpses before. Instinctively he slammed his foot down on the brake and brought the Landrover to a sudden juddering halt. He knew before he'd stopped that it was a survivor that stood in the road ahead of him. Even from a few meters away he could tell from the expression on the man's face and by the way he carried himself and reacted that he was still alive.

'Thank God,' the diminutive man gasped as he approached Michael. He looked up as Emma stopped the car a short distance behind the Landrover. 'Thank God,' he said again, 'you're the first people I've seen in weeks...'

'Are you alright?' Emma asked. She was already out of her car and walking towards the man.

'I'm okay,' he replied quickly, chattering like a nervous child. 'I'm better now I've seen you two. I thought I was the only one left around here. I was going to...'

'What's your name?' Michael asked abruptly, cutting across him.

'Philip, Philip Evans,' he answered.

'And where do you live?'

The little man gestured towards his house.

'Here,' he said, simply.

'Then let's get inside,' Michael suggested. 'It's not a good idea for us to be standing out here like this.'

Philip obediently turned and led the others back towards his cottage. Emma looked him up and down as she followed him indoors. He was short and shabbily dressed. A noticeable stoop made him appear much shorter than he actually was and his grubby clothes were worn and had obviously not been cleaned or even changed for several days, maybe a week. His tired face was ruddy, pockmarked and unshaven and his hair greasy, ruffled and unkempt. Philip itched and scratched at himself continually.

They stepped through the low front door and found that inside the house was as vile, odious and squalid as its owner. Dark, dank and musty, it was the perfect breeding ground for countless deadly germs and diseases. Michael immediately wanted to turn around and leave but he knew that he couldn't. No matter what his first impressions of Philip Evans were he was a survivor and, as such, he felt duty bound to try and do something for him. He was the first survivor they had seen since they'd left the city. More to the point, he was the first survivor they'd found since that first night in the community centre back in Northwich.

'Sit down,' Philip said as he closed the door behind them and ushered them both into the living room. 'Please sit down and make yourselves comfortable.'

Emma glanced down at the sofa next to her and decided to remain standing. It was covered with crumpled food wrappers, crumbs and other, less easily identifiable rubbish.

'Can I get you a drink?' he asked politely. 'I'm sorry, I'm just so surprised to see you both. When I heard the noise of your engines I thought that...'

His words faded in volume as he disappeared into the kitchen to fetch drinks (despite neither of the survivors having taken him up on his offer). Glad to be alone for a moment, Michael seized the opportunity to speak privately to Emma.

'So what do you think?' he whispered.

'About what?' she replied.

'About him,' he hissed. 'What do you think we should do?'

She thought for a moment. She knew what she had to say but didn't particularly want to say it.

'He's a survivor and we should offer to take him with us,' she said with obvious reluctance.

'But...?' he pressed, sensing that she wasn't telling him everything.

'But look at the state of this place,' she continued, gesturing at their cold and stale surroundings. 'Christ, this house is disgusting. It's making me feel sick just standing here, and by the look of him he's bound to be contagious, isn't he?'

'We don't know that for certain, do we?' Michael argued despite the fact that he agreed with her completely. 'We've got to try and do something for him, haven't we?'

She nodded dejectedly and then changed the sour expression on her face as Philip returned to the room, still talking.

'...and after that when we couldn't find him we decided that something was definitely wrong,' he babbled, his voice tired. The little man paused and stood still to cough. It was a violent, hacking noise, like a smoker's rasping early morning cough, and he struggled to catch his breath.

'You alright?' Michael asked.

Philip looked up and nodded, his face flushed and red.

'Fine,' he wheezed. 'Just picked up a bit of an infection I think.'

He carried a circular metal tray which he put down on the table after brushing a layer of rubbish down onto the dirty carpet with a single sweep of his arm. He handed Emma a chipped mug and then passed one to Michael. Emma peered into her cup and sniffed it. It was undiluted lemon cordial. She glanced across at Michael who discreetly shook his head and gestured for her to put the mug down.

'Do you know what's happened?' Philip asked.

'Haven't got a clue,' Michael replied.

'I searched the village but I couldn't find anyone else alive. I can't drive so I haven't been able to get into town. I've just been stuck here waiting for someone to come,' he stopped talking for a second and looked at Michael again. 'Are you two from town? Are there many of you there?'

Emma answered.

'We came here from Northwich just over a week ago,' she replied. 'And there are just the two of us now. We left a few people there but other than that we hadn't seen anyone until we found you.'

Philip sank down into an armchair with an expression of bitter disappointment on his face.

'That's not good news,' he muttered. 'I've been stuck here waiting and I haven't been able to do anything. My telephone's not working and the electricity's been cut off and...'

'Philip,' Michael interrupted, 'just listen to me for a minute. Whatever happened here has happened right across the country as far as we know. Just about everyone is dead...'

'I've seen some people,' the little man whittered, not listening, 'but they're not right. They come when they hear me, but they're sick. They bang on the door for hours trying to get inside but I just lock it and sit in the back room until they go.'

'We think you should come with us,' Michael continued. 'We're living in a farm house a few miles from here and we both think it would be better for you if you were to...'

Philip still wasn't listening.

'Do you know what makes them act like that? I really don't like it. Mother's not well and it upsets her when I tell her that...'

'Your mother's here as well?' Emma asked.

'Of course she is,' he replied.

'She can come with us,' Michael offered. 'We should get your things together and get out of here as quickly as we can.'

'She won't like leaving,' Philip mumbled, 'she's lived here since she and Dad got married.'

'Maybe you'll be able to come back,' Emma said, sensing that Michael was keen to get moving and doing her best to sensitively persuade Philip to leave.

Philip thought for a moment and then nodded.

'You're right,' he finally said. 'It's probably for the best if we all stick together. I'll go and tell Mum.'

With that he turned and walked towards a door in the corner of the room. Beyond the door was a narrow, twisting staircase which he began to climb. Emma instinctively followed but Michael stopped her.

'What's the matter?' she asked.

'Let me go first.'

Philip was already at the top of the stairs waiting breathlessly. As Michael approached he lifted a single finger to his chapped lips.

'Be quiet please,' he whispered. 'Mum's found all of this a little hard to deal with and I don't want to frighten her. She's very old and she's not been well these last few months.'

Michael nodded and managed a half-smile despite the fact that the air at the top of the stairs was rancid and he could clearly hear the ominous humming of germ-carrying flies close nearby.

Philip pushed the door open slightly and stuck his head into his mother's room. He stopped and turned back to face the other two.

'Give me a minute with her, will you?' he asked.

He disappeared into the room and pushed the door shut behind him but Michael followed immediately. Philip didn't notice.

'Mum,' he said softly as he crouched down at the side of the bed. 'Mum, there are some people here who can help us. We're going to go back with them for a few days until things settle down again.'

Michael stood a short distance behind Philip. Emma cautiously entered the room and walked over to stand next to him. He leant down and grabbed hold of her arm. With tension and fear obvious in his voice he hissed at her to quickly go back downstairs.

'Why?' she quietly asked. She took a single step forward to get a better view of Philip's mother and then covered her mouth with horror and disgust. Mrs Evans' skin was discoloured and decayed, her hair lank and greasy. Flies buzzed around her decomposing flesh and were feeding on her constantly writhing body. Michael walked up to the bed and pulled back the soiled sheets which covered the old lady. Ignoring Philip's protestations he stared down at her emaciated body. She was tied to the bed with strong ropes which were stretched tight across her stained night-dress. She'd been dead since the first morning.

'I had to tie her down,' Philip stammered anxiously. 'She wouldn't stay in bed. When the doctor saw her last he said she had to stay in bed until she was better...'

'Philip,' he sighed, 'your mum's dead.'

'Don't be stupid,' the little man scoffed, laughing with disbelief. 'How can she be dead? She's not well, that's all. Bloody hell, how can she be dead you daft bugger?'

'This has happened to millions of people, Philip,' Emma said, fighting to keep control of her nerves and her stomach. 'I know it sounds crazy, but most of the people who...'

'Dead people can't move,' he shouted, resting his hand on his mother's shoulder. 'How can she be dead if she's moving? Answer me that?'

'Living people don't rot,' Michael replied. 'Now your choice is simple, either come with us now and leave her here, or you both stay.'

'I can't go without Mum,' he wailed. 'I can't leave her here on her own, can I?'

Michael took hold of Emma's arm and gently pushed her back towards the stairs.

'Wait for me by the front door,' he said quickly. 'I'll be down in a couple of seconds.'

He turned back to try and reason with Philip.

'Come on, just accept it will you?' he began. 'Your mother is dead. She might still be moving, but she's as good as dead. She's the same as those other people you've seen outside.'

Emma listened anxiously as she crept back down the stairs. She waited on the bottom step for Michael.

'What are you going to do if you stay here?' he continued. 'You probably haven't got much food or drink and your health is suffering. We're your best chance, Philip. Get your stuff together and come with us.'

'Not without Mum. I can't leave without her.'

Michael shook his head dejectedly.

'No,' he said simply.

Without any warning something inside Philip snapped. In a fraction of a second the meek little man became an uncontrolled animal. His fears and frustrations bottled up since the nightmare had begun, he suddenly exploded with fury and savage emotion, lunging at Michael and sending him flying across the bedroom. Surprised by the force and the violence of the unexpected attack, Michael lost his balance and tripped backwards through the doorway. With Philip desperately holding onto him, the two men tumbled down the stairs and came to rest in a heap at Emma's feet.

'Get back to the car!' Michael yelled as he struggled to hold the other man down. 'Get the fucking engine started!'

Despite having the speed and intentions of a man possessed, Philip was weak and slight of stature and it didn't take much effort on Michael's part to overpower him. He wrenched him around and grasped his scrawny neck in a dangerously tight headlock. He dragged Philip towards the front door of the cottage, ignoring his pitiful, wheezing cries.

There were three bodies in the road between the car and the van. Emma ran past them and climbed into the car and started the engine. The corpses - joined by more from the shadows nearby - began to crowd around her. She struggled to see between them and waited anxiously for Michael to appear.

More bodies were reacting to the sounds of the struggle inside the building and were heading towards the cottage. Emma accelerated, hoping that the sound of the car's engine would distract them and give Michael and Philip a chance to get out. A couple of stumbling figures turned around awkwardly and staggered towards the car. An equal number continued to move closer to the house.

Michael looked up and saw that there were corpses in the doorway. Philip, sensing that he had been distracted momentarily, managed to squirm free. He took a few steps away from Michael and wiped tears from his eyes, oblivious to the danger of the approaching cadavers.

'Why can't I bring her with me?' he pleaded, still refusing to accept the bitter truth.

Michael grabbed hold of his arm to pull him out of the house but he recoiled and managed to twist himself free again. A body reached out and grabbed hold of Philip's shoulders. Another caught hold of one of his legs. Terrified, he began to kick and scream.

'Get them off me!' he yelled. 'Please, get them off!'

Michael tore the creatures away from him and pushed them back out into the street. He looked up and saw that there were about twenty figures around Emma's car and he could see her panicked face staring back at him through the glass. He knew that he had to make a choice and he had to make it immediately. Keep trying to persuade Philip to leave without his mother or just leave without either of them. He glanced back at the pathetic shell of a man who stood in the middle of his living room, whimpering and snivelling.

The decision was made.

Michael ran out through the doorway, pushing bodies to the side, and pausing only to pull the door shut behind him hoping to give Philip something of a chance. He fought his way through the ragged crowd and climbed into the Landrover and started the engine. From where he sat all that he could see was a mass of grotesque, decaying faces staring back at him. He gave a couple of short blasts on the horn and, when Emma did the same in reply, he pushed down on the accelerator and moved away. The decomposing bodies offered hardly any resistance.

He watched in the mirror until he was sure that Emma was following and then put his foot down.

42

Seven miles to Penn Farm.

The maze of twisting country lanes which surrounded the farm and connected it to the numerous villages and small towns nearby was confusing and disorientating. Michael found it hard to keep concentrating because he was preoccupied with other thoughts. Had he done the right thing in leaving Philip behind or should he have made more of an effort to drag him away from his home? He knew that the poor confused soul wouldn't have abandoned his dead mother without a lot more persuasion, and he also knew that they hadn't had the luxury of having time to argue. When it came to it the decision had been a pretty clear cut choice between Emma and Philip. He couldn't stand the thought of risking Emma's safety for even a second, but at the same time he felt wracked with guilt when he remembered the pathetic, frightened little man he'd left quivering alone in the stagnant surroundings of his dead mother's house.

A short while earlier in the car park, in those few precious seconds when he had stood out in the open next to Emma, he had allowed himself to feel a faint flicker of optimism. Momentarily they seemed to have been miles away from the close confines of the farmhouse and the wandering bodies. He had felt strong and safe as he had breathed in deep gulps of cold, sea air. But reality had returned with a vengeance. Now an all too common feeling of claustrophobic despair had returned.

A T-junction in the road appeared. It looked familiar and Michael sensed that they were finally heading in the right direction. Then a signpost he had seen before, soon followed by the rusting wreck of a blue estate car which he remembered having seen crashed into the base of an old oak tree. Without a doubt they were at last on the road that would lead them back to the farmhouse.

Driving back along the same road towards the farm but approaching it from the opposite direction was Carl. Feeling numb and weak with nerves and with every muscle in his body aching with heavy tiredness and a deadly fatigue, he glanced down at the motorbike's controls. He was still travelling at a reckless speed, but he didn't dare slow down as the needle on the fuel gauge had dropped to the lowest possible level. He hadn't planned on making two long trips on the same tank of petrol. Now little more than fumes remained in the tank.

Forcing himself to keep going, he swerved around another one of the wandering bodies and increased his speed still further. The body span around and grabbed at the carbon monoxide-filled air where the bike had just been.

With less than three miles to go Michael's nervousness increased. He felt a constant and very real fear in the back of his mind whenever they were away that something might have happened to the farmhouse. If the gate or any other part of the barrier had collapsed then their home could well be surrounded by scores of relentless, decomposing corpses. Although there was still a way to go, he began instinctively to search for the turning which led to the track running from the road to the house. It was on their left somewhere, but he knew it would be difficult to see from the angle they would be approaching at.

They rushed past the trees, bushes and buildings lining the sides of the roads at a dangerous speed but neither Michael or Emma cared. Both were individually content to risk a degree of safety to get back home in the shortest possible time.

Carl was almost there.

Just a couple of hundred yards remained between him and the turning onto the track to the farm. He too searched constantly for the elusive junction. There were bodies all around him, stumbling onto the road in whichever direction he looked. Yet again the silence of the rest of the world seemed to have amplified out of all proportion every sound the motorbike made. Like a perverse Pied Piper a growing crowd of restless corpses followed him, attracted by the throaty roar of the powerful engine.

Carl's heart sank as that same roar suddenly spluttered and died.

He was out of fuel. Damn close to the farmhouse, but not close enough.

As the bike freewheeled to a standstill he frantically tried to decide what to do. He quickly took off his helmet and threw it at the closest few bodies before dumping the bike and beginning to run. Exhausted, hot and tired he sprinted down the road and towards the track with what seemed like hundreds of corpses in close (but slow) pursuit and with more swarming around him from the trees and shadows surrounding. He was faintly aware of a low mechanical sound in the distance but he was too scared to stop. He had to keep moving. He reached the turning onto the track and began to sprint up the hill in the direction of the farmhouse.

At that moment the Landrover and car appeared, both still in close convoy and both out of sight of Carl. Disorientated and surprised by the unexpected appearance of so many bodies, Michael missed the turning. The sound of their vehicles had attracted plenty of cadavers along the way, but why were so many of them here now? Had their collective interest been aroused by the noise from the Landrover when they'd first left Penn Farm earlier that morning?

Emma flashed her headlamps at Michael and gave a blast on the horn, not sure if he knew he'd passed the turning onto the track. Furious for allowing himself to be distracted by the crowds, he braked hard and tried to turn around. The road was infuriatingly narrow and his frantic three point turn took many more turns than it should have done. Each time he reversed or drove forward more and more of the shambling creatures were dragged under the wheels of the Landrover.

Emma smashed through the rotting crowd and accelerated up the hill back towards the house. The rough track seemed worse than ever - the wheels of the car were smaller and less forgiving than the larger wheels of the van and Landrover. Each dip and trough of the uneven ground caused her to lurch forward in her seat and rattled her to the core. Weak and defenceless bodies were thrown to the side but there seemed to be still more and more of them further ahead. She accelerated again and managed a momentary glance into the rear view mirror. Michael was on his way up the track close behind her.

Carl was managing to outrun the bodies. Now that he had ditched the motorbike the sound he made was greatly reduced, and in turn that reduced his attraction to the ragged corpses all around him. But he was tiring fast. The air was dry and he had a painful stitch which he tried unsuccessfully to breathe through. He knew that he could not afford to stop but at the same time he was beginning to have real difficulty in keeping going. For a second he could hear the noise he'd heard at the bottom of the track again, and this time he realised that its volume was steadily increasing. The corpses dragging themselves up the hill towards him gradually broke off their pursuit and began to stumble back down again, distracted by this new sound. Carl looked over his shoulder and then turned back to look ahead again. In the near distance he could see the gate and the barrier and, just beyond that, Penn Farm.

Without warning Emma's car appeared with Michael in the Landrover close behind. Carl span around and could hardly believe what he was seeing. He stood in the middle of the track waving his arms and yelling out loud, desperately hoping to attract the attention of one of the survivors. Emma noticed him, but at the same time three close shadowy figures also heard his anxious cries and threw themselves at him. They dragged him down to the ground where he kicked and punched and struggled to pick himself up. With an instinctive venom and anger, the creatures ripped at his flesh with vicious, twisted fingers.

Emma slammed on the brakes and jumped out of the car. Michael pulled up close behind (the track was too narrow to pull up alongside Emma) and ran to Carl's side.

'Fucking hell, it's Carl,' he shouted as he grabbed hold of the first of the three bodies and threw it to one side. 'Where did he appear from?'

Emma took hold of another cadaver's shoulders and wrenched it away from the man on the ground. Michael kicked the last one away and then helped Emma to get Carl into the car. Already they were being surrounded by hundreds of diseased figures.

'Get back to the house,' he screamed as he bundled Carl into the back of the car and pushed Emma into the front. Before he had even closed the door she had accelerated away again and was careering down the final incline towards the gate spanning the stone bridge.

Michael shoulder charged his way back through the sickly throng to the Landrover and managed to force his way back into the driver's seat. He slammed and locked the door and then looked up and down the track. More and more bodies were converging on the road ahead. The frequent noise from the house over the last day or two must have attracted them. Perhaps their brains were beginning to function with more clarity and reason than before? Maybe these hundreds of corpses had actually stayed close to the farm and laid in wait because they knew that the survivors had been hiding in there? And now the combined noise from the bike, the Landrover and the car that Emma was driving seemed to have brought every last one of them out into the open.

He put the Landrover into gear and drove forwards, obliterating any of the corpses that foolishly remained in his way. But there were literally hundreds of them now, maybe even more than a thousand. He noticed that Emma had stopped a little way short of the gate and already her car was being swamped by ragged figures. Why didn't she open the gate and go through? Cruel realisation suddenly dawned. He had the keys.

Like a man possessed he sped down the track. There were just too many of the damn creatures around. There was no way he could get out of the car and unlock the single padlock which they used to secure the gate when they left the farm. There were too many bodies around for him to risk being out in the open. There was only one option. He drove on and smashed through the wooden gate, sending splinters of wood flying in all directions. He drove across the dusty yard and skidded to a sudden halt right outside the steps leading up to the front door of the house. He anxiously looked back to make sure that Emma was following. She careered into the yard with a body clinging onto the bonnet of the car, trying desperately to smash the windscreen with a tired and wizened hand.

Knowing that he literally had just seconds to spare, Michael grabbed the keys to the Landrover from the ignition and took the house keys out of his jacket pocket. He jumped out of the car and ran up the steps and tried to unlock the door. His hands were shaking with nerves.

'Open the bloody door,' Emma screamed.

The lock clicked and they were inside. Michael gestured for Emma to get in while he went back for Carl. The other survivor could hardly move. He was physically and emotionally destroyed.

A few seconds longer and the three of them were back inside the farmhouse with the front door locked and secure.

'Get him into the kitchen,' Emma ordered. Michael dragged Carl through and lay him on the cold and hard tiled floor.

'Think he's going to be alright?' he asked breathlessly.

She shrugged her shoulders.

'Don't know,' she mumbled as she checked his injuries. Nothing too deep. Nothing obviously serious. Just flesh wounds.

They were distracted by a dull thumping sound from the other side of the room. Michael looked up to see that a crowd of bodies had gathered at the kitchen window. With heavy, uncoordinated hands they began to bang relentlessly on the glass.

'Upstairs,' he shouted. 'Move!'

Emma didn't argue. Between the two of them they grabbed hold of Carl and hauled him up to the bedrooms.

Once they had laid him down on Emma's bed Michael left the room and slowly walked around the top floor of the house. He looked out through virtually every window and stared out at in horror at the nightmarish sight which greeted him. His worst fears had been realised.

The house was completely surrounded.

43

'Jesus,' Michael hissed as he stared down from the window in Emma's room. 'There are more and more of those fucking things coming in by the second. There are bloody thousands of them down there.'

Emma had been sitting with Carl who lay motionless on the bed. She got up and walked over to where Michael stood and glanced down over his shoulder into the farmyard below. He was right - there was already a dense crowd of hundreds of detestable figures surrounding the house and their numbers were increasing constantly. They continually poured in through the gap where the gate on the bridge had been.

'Why do they keep coming?' she asked under her breath. 'We came here because we thought there would be fewer of them, so why do they keep coming here?' She knew that Michael couldn't give her any definite answers to her questions, but she felt a need to ask anyway.

'I don't know,' he replied. 'I still think it's got to be the noise.'

'But we've not been making any noise.'

'We have compared to the rest of the world. Christ, how many times have we been through this? The whole planet is bloody silent. Every time one of us moves you must be able to hear it for miles around.'

'So the sound of the car engines...'

'Keeps attracting them. And even when the sound dies down, I think they're staying close because they know we're nearby.'

'Do you really think so?'

He nodded sadly.

'It would explain why there are so many of them around here now, wouldn't it?'

'So if we stay indoors and keep quiet and out of sight for a while then they should...'

He shook his head with a resigned sadness.

'I don't think that's going to work anymore,' he sighed.

'Why not?'

Rather than answer her, Michael instead just opened the bedroom window slightly. The sudden forcing noise as he pushed the sticking window open caused a ripple of excitement to quickly spread through the rotting crowd below.

'Just listen to that,' he whispered.

Emma did as she was told, and was soon aware of a cold, alien sound coming from the diseased hordes below. The shuffling of weary, leaden feet, the occasional guttural groan, the sound of clumsy bodies tripping and falling - each individually insignificant noise combined to create a constant, chilling soundtrack.

'It's too late for us to just sit still and play dead now,' Michael explained. 'It's got to the stage where they're making enough noise by themselves to keep attracting more and more of them here. And with a crowd of this size, it doesn't matter how quiet we are, the bastard things are going to keep coming regardless.'

As realisation dawned, Emma stepped back from the window, sat down on a chair and rested her head in her hands.

'So what do we do now?' she asked anxiously.

Michael didn't answer.

A heavy and ominous quiet descended on the room, disturbed only by the noise from outside and by Carl who groaned in pain.

'How you doing?' Michael asked, his voice still a hushed whisper.

Carl didn't respond. Emma stood up and leant over the injured man. She looked him up and down, thought for a second or two and then walked back over to Michael.

261

'It's difficult to say how he is,' she sighed, whispering so that Carl couldn't hear her. 'He's exhausted and he's still in shock. He doesn't look too badly injured physically, but he's really suffering.'

'Has he said anything to you?'

'What about?'

Michael closed the window and moved away from the glass.

'About what he found in the city if he ever got there? And why he came back if he did?'

She shook her head.

'He hasn't said anything. I think we should...'

Michael wasn't listening. He walked over to the side of the bed and knelt down next to Carl. Carl didn't respond. He lay there motionless, staring up at the ceiling.

'Mate,' Michael began cautiously. 'Carl, can you hear me?'

He swallowed painfully and nodded.

'You okay?'

'No,' he answered, his voice tired and little more than a whisper.

Carl's eyes flickered shut and then opened again. Without moving his head he looked over towards Michael, then back to Emma, and then back to Michael again.

'Did you get to Northwich?' Michael asked. 'Did you get...'

'I got there.'

Michael glanced over at Emma.

'So what happened? Why did you come back?'

He looked up at the ceiling again, licked his dry lips and swallowed hard.

'There was no-one there,' he mumbled.

'Where, at the community centre? Did you manage to get back to the community centre...'

'They've gone. There was no-one there.'

'So where did they go?'

Carl slowly lifted himself up onto his elbows, paused for a second, took a deep breath and then swallowed again.

'I don't think they went anywhere. When I got there the door was open. Inside the place was full of bodies.'

'What bodies? The ones from outside or...?'

He shook his head.

'Survivors. I don't think they'd been dead that long.'

'What happened?' asked Emma.

'The bodies must have got inside. There's so many of them that the survivors didn't have a chance. There's only one way into that building so there was no way out...'

He slumped back onto the bed, tired by the effort of talking.

'Fucking hell,' Michael spat, standing up quickly and walking across the room. He kicked the bedroom door and it slammed shut, sending a sudden noise like a gunshot echoing through the house and causing the creatures outside to stir again. For the first time since he'd watched the world die around him weeks ago he couldn't think straight. He didn't know what to do. They had reached a dead end and there didn't seem to be any options. The farmhouse was under siege, and the only other place of refuge that they knew of was gone.

Emma sensed his fear and walked over to stand close to him.

'What are you thinking?' she asked cautiously, although she didn't really want to know. Her mind was also filled with hopeless thoughts.

Michael didn't answer. He turned to face the wall, not wanting her to see the frightened tears welling up in his eyes.

'We've got to do something,' she insisted. 'Do we just sit here and wait or do we...?'

'We don't have much of a fucking choice, do we?' he snapped. 'We can take our chances outside or we can sit in this room and wait until it's safe again. And that's going to take bloody ages...'

'The house is still secure...'

'I know it is, but what use is that to us anymore? Go into any room downstairs and there will be a hundred of those fucking things staring in at you through the window. Once they see you they'll go fucking wild and before you know it we're back to square one...'

'What do you mean?'

'I mean that it's only going to take a little bit of careless noise or for a few of those things to catch sight of one of us and we'll be right back to where we started. We could sit in this fucking house in silence for six months until all but a handful of them have disappeared and we'd still have a problem. All it needs is for one of them to see us and start hammering on the door and then more would hear that, then more, then more...'

'So what are you saying?'

He shrugged his shoulders and wiped his eyes.

'I don't know...' he muttered, taking care to avoid letting Emma know what he was really thinking. But she was intelligent and persistent and she'd already worked it out for herself.

'I think you're saying that we have to leave. I don't think we can stay here any longer.'

He nodded.

'Don't know where we're going to go or how we're going to get out of here...'

'But we don't have any option, do we?'

Michael didn't respond. He wiped his eyes again and looked around the room. For almost a minute he said nothing.

'We've got to keep out of sight and out of earshot of those bloody things,' he eventually announced, 'and we've got to get as much stuff together as we can. We'll just have to fight our way through.'

'But how? How are we going to get to the cars...?'

'We'll wait for a couple of hours until it's dark,' he interrupted, 'and we'll see if a few of them disappear. I'll try and get the generator started and...'

'Why?'

'Because it will distract them, won't it? If there's a louder sound round the back of the house they're more likely to go looking for us there, aren't they? Anyway, we'll wait and give

Carl a chance to come round and pull himself together, then we'll just have to go for it.'

With that he walked out of the bedroom to start collecting their things from the upstairs rooms of the house. Emma stayed where she was, leaning against the bedroom wall. Now that the conversation had ended an uneasy silence had descended upon the building. The deceptive peace, however, was short-lived. She quickly became aware of the bodies outside again. She stood there in absolute hopeless terror and listened as the dragging footsteps of hundreds upon hundreds of rotting corpses advanced closer and closer towards them.

44

Although the nights were beginning to quickly draw in, it seemed to take an eternity for darkness to finally arrive. Each nervous, painful minute dragged unbearably, almost to the point that every last second seemed to take a protracted eternity to pass. In the time that it took the low grey light to fade completely to black, Carl did not move. He lay motionless on the bed, still staring up at the ceiling. Emma wondered if he was even aware of what was happening around him, or whether he had become completely withdrawn and catatonic. Whatever, she decided that she didn't want to disturb him. She didn't dare take the risk, at least like this he was quiet. She was frightened that if she tried to help him or even get him to try and move he might suddenly turn and crack, and that any reaction from him might provoke another unwanted and terrifying response from the vast crowds outside the house.

Both Emma and Michael had managed to pack their few belongings. Between them they had done the same with Carl's gear which had been bagged up in black plastic refuse sacks. They stockpiled their luggage in the shadows at the top of the staircase, not daring to get any closer to the front of the house for fear of being seen. They had no way of easily reaching the more important supplies downstairs. As much as they needed their clothes, they both knew that taking the food and other items left in the kitchen could well be crucial to their continued survival.

Michael and Emma passed each other on the landing close to the bedroom door. They stopped there for a few seconds and spoke to each other in hushed, anxious whispers.

'You okay?' he asked. Emma's eyes looked tired and frightened in the half-light.

'I'm alright.'

'Carl okay?'

'No change.'

'Is he going to be alright?'

'Don't know.'

'Christ, you were the one studying to be a doctor.'

'Fuck off, this is way beyond anything I studied. I don't even know if I'm going to be alright anymore, never mind anyone else.'

'Sorry.'

'Forget it.'

'Got much stuff together?'

'Got my clothes and a few odds and ends. What about you?'

'The same. We're going to have to get downstairs though and try and get some of the stuff in the kitchen packed.'

'So how are we going to do that? There are bloody huge windows in every room. We can't go anywhere without being seen from outside.'

'I know.'

'We're going to have to leave with what we've got, aren't we?'

'I think we'll be lucky to get that much out.'

'So what are we going to do?'

Michael shrugged his shoulders.

'Get out with nothing and start again somewhere else, I suppose,' he sighed. 'Do what we did when we arrived here. Find somewhere that looks half-decent, get ourselves settled and then get out and get supplies.'

'But won't the same thing happen again?'

'Probably.'

That wasn't the answer Emma had wanted to hear. It was what she'd expected him to say, but she had still been hoping for a little more encouragement.

'So how do we get out? Have you thought about that?'

Michael shrugged his shoulders again.

'We'll just have to make a run for it. Get Carl up and about, get loaded up with stuff and then go for it. We'll have to fight our way through.'

'Think we can do it?'

A third nonchalant shrug. A few moments of awkward silence followed.

'Are there still as many outside?' Emma wondered.

'Can't tell,' he replied. 'Probably. I've seen a few of them walking away, but there are just as many still coming in over the bridge.'

'They can't get inside, can they?'

'We'd have to be unlucky. It's locked tight down there but...'

'But what? They can't get in, can they?' she interrupted, again looking for reassurance from Michael..

'But there are thousands of them,' he continued. 'Their sheer mass could do some damage.'

'I don't think they'll be able to force their way in.'

'Neither do I. But then again this time yesterday I never thought they'd get through the barrier...'

'But they didn't get through, we let them in.'

'Doesn't matter, does it? Fact is they're through. And it wouldn't matter how they got inside if they managed to get in here. Wouldn't matter if they put a window through or if we let them in through the front door. Fact is we'd be completely fucked whatever.'

'When are we going to do this, Mike?'

'As soon as we can. We're kidding ourselves if we think it's going to get any better for us tonight. We're not going to gain anything by waiting.'

45
Carl Henshawe

It's half past nine and I'm feeling much better.

I know there's no way out of here, but I still feel better because I know that something's going to happen. We're not going to sit here like fucking prisoners for the rest of our days. Something's going to happen tonight.

When I was running back to the house I was faster than the lot of them. I could outrun them. They're nothing, just bags of skin and bone. They don't have any strength and there isn't a single one of them that can hurt me.

I keep seeing Sarah and Gemma's faces and I can hear Sarah telling me what to do. She's telling me that she wants me to make a go of this. She's telling me that she wants me to get off my backside and make a stand.

I can hear Emma and Michael talking about getting away again.

The only way we can do it is if we fight.

When I'm ready I'm going to show every last one of those bastards outside who's in charge. They're weak and they're sick and I'm strong.

I'm going to take them out.

One at a time.

46

Quarter to ten.

Michael was sitting in a chair in the corner of the bedroom with his eyes closed. He was tired and he needed to rest but there was no way he could sleep, not even for a second.

Emma sat on the edge of the bed where Carl still lay. She had taken care to position herself so that even though it was dark, she could still clearly see both men. She watched them anxiously in the dull light, waiting either for Michael to open his eyes and decide that they should move or for Carl to return to full consciousness. She was a little less worried about Carl now. He seemed much calmer. He was generally still and quiet, but his face now seemed relatively untroubled, almost to the point of appearing relaxed.

Taking care not to make any more noise than was absolutely necessary, she stood up and walked over to the window. Peering down cautiously into the yard below she saw that the seething mass of dark, heaving bodies remained. An apparently endless sea of bobbing, rotting heads. Hundreds and hundreds of them clamoured to get closer to the house and their sheer number was still the overriding concern because, individually, the corpses were slow and dumb. While she watched she saw five or six of them lose their footing on the muddy bank and tumble helplessly into the stream, unable to get up and get out again. She saw another one of them become caught on the jagged remains of one of the gateposts on the bridge, trapped and unable to move. The remnants of its ragged clothing had become snagged on a large wooden splinter but it couldn't see how to pull itself free.

There was another reason why the bodies terrified her.

It was more than just their horrific appearance and the fact that their rotting flesh was host to many unknown and deadly diseases. Emma was morbidly fascinated and repulsed by the creatures because, less than a month ago, each one of them had been like herself. An individual. A person. A human being with a clear and identifiable personality and individual tastes, skills and beliefs. What scared Emma - what chilled her to the core in fact - was what these once ordinary, normal people had become. Chances were many of her friends and family had gone the same way. And who was to say that when she died, she too wouldn't spend the rest of eternity dragging her decomposing body aimlessly around their dead world?

One or two of the bodies weren't a threat. A group of between, say, ten and fifteen was a concern, but nothing they couldn't deal with. But in the cold darkness outside the farmhouse tonight there she could see hundreds upon fucking hundreds of them.

'No better?' an unexpected voice asked from the shadows behind her, startling her momentarily. She span around quickly. It was Michael. He was up and out of his seat.

'They're still here,' she replied with her heart thumping anxiously in her chest. 'They're still coming.'

'I'm sorry,' he said, his voice low, sensing that he'd startled her. 'I didn't mean to make you jump.'

She nodded and turned back to look out of the window again.

'Do you think they know we're in here?' she asked.

'I don't know,' he answered. 'I think they sense that there's something different about us. It might just be because of the noise we make, it might be because of the way we move...'

'But what do they want from us?'

'I don't think they want anything.'

'So why are they here?'

'Instinct.'

'Instinct?'

'Yes. Like I said, we're different, that's all. Whatever's left of their brains is telling them we're not the same as they are and

271

they're drawn to us. I don't think they mean us any harm, they just want to know what we are. If they react towards one of us, it's because they're looking out for their own safety.'

'They think we're a threat?'

'I think so, yes.'

Michael took another few steps closer to Emma and gently put his arms around her. For a second she involuntarily recoiled at his touch. She meant nothing by her response. She wanted to be close to him but, at the same time, she wanted to be alone. Truth was she didn't know what she wanted anymore.

'Are you alright?' he asked, concerned.

'I'm okay,' she replied, turning round to face him but not quite managing to make eye contact. 'I'm just tired,' she mumbled, 'that's all.'

'Sure?' he pressed, not convinced.

She shook her head and her eyes filled with stinging tears.

'No,' she finally admitted, reaching out and grabbing tight hold of him. She pulled him closer and buried her face in his chest. 'I don't think we're ever going to get away from this house.'

'It's going to be okay,' he said instinctively and without any degree of conviction in his words.

'You keep saying that,' she sobbed. 'You keep saying that but you don't know if it's true, do you?'

She was right. Michael knew as much and decided that it was better to say nothing. Still holding onto Emma tightly, he shuffled closer to the window and peered outside. As she'd already suggested, nothing out there seemed to have changed.

'Come on, we've got to go,' he announced suddenly.

'What?' Emma protested, pushing herself away from him. 'What the hell are you talking about. We're not ready to go yet...'

'It's not going to get any better,' he said, his voice surprisingly calm and unemotional. 'We could wait here for months but we'd be fooling ourselves if we think it's ever going to get easier.'

'But what about Carl?' she nervously snapped. 'We can't leave here until he's...'

'You're making excuses,' Michael sighed. 'We've both been making fucking excuses all night. We've just got to do it.'

She knew he was right and didn't bother to argue. Truth was they had both been avoiding the inevitable. But suddenly Michael seemed determined to make a move, and she watched him with quickly mounting trepidation. There was a new found concentration and direction in his voice which she understood but which also frightened and disturbed her. She knew that this really was it. She knew Michael was right and that leaving was their only chance, but that didn't make it any easier to accept or to deal with. She watched as he pulled a thick jumper over his head and tightened the laces on his boots.

Michael looked up and noticed the concern on her face.

'You okay?' he asked.

She nodded quickly but it was impossible to hide her fear. Her legs were heavy with nerves. She could hardly breathe.

'Look, I'm going to try and start the generator,' he continued. 'There are fewer of them out the back and...'

'What, only five hundred instead of a thousand?'

'There are fewer of them,' he continued. 'I'll see if the noise will distract them.'

With admirable strength Michael seemed to have switched off his emotions and was concentrating all his attention and effort on the task immediately to hand. He walked towards the door and then stopped and turned back to face Emma. He looked ready to say something to her but didn't.

'Are you sure about this?' she asked.

He shrugged his shoulders.

'No,' he replied with brutal honesty, 'but I can't think of any other option. Now do me a favour will you and try and get Carl to wake up. Get him ready to leave. As soon as I'm back inside we'll have to go for it.'

With that he turned and disappeared into the darkness leaving Emma alone, staring into the space where he had just been, trying desperately to make sense of the sudden confusion all around her.

Michael crept down the staircase, frightened that even the slightest noise might have a devastating effect on the vast crowd outside the house. Perhaps even something as insignificant as stepping on a loose, creaking floorboard would be the final straw that might whip the rotting masses into the frenzy that could see them forcing their way into the house.

With his heart pounding in his chest with cold, dark fear and with his entire body drenched with a sticky, clammy sweat, Michael lowered himself down onto his hands and knees and crawled along the hallway, keeping out of sight of every window and every door. He had reached the back of the house in just a few seconds, and he carefully lifted himself back up onto his feet, hiding in the shadows and keeping his body tight and flat against the nearest wall.

Once upright he had a clear view of the back lawn through a small square pane of dirty glass. There were still many, many bodies outside, but on this side of the house their numbers seemed fewer and much more diffuse. He watched as the shadowy silhouette of one of the pathetic creatures stumbled past. As soon as it had gone by he silently turned the key in the lock and pushed the door open. Holding his breath he slipped through the narrowest gap he could and then pushed the door shut behind him. He was outside.

He had seen thousands of the lamentable corpses over the last few days and yet, at this most dangerous time, he still found himself unable to tear his eyes away from them. Standing perfectly still he watched them move. They lurched and staggered, their legs heavy and uncoordinated. For the most part their heads were bowed and it seemed to take more effort than any of them could muster for them to look up.

The shed which housed the generator was some twenty meters away from where he stood. He knew that to run towards it would attract more attention. It made sense to try and walk slowly to match the laboured pace of the cadavers around him.

But moving slowly seemed to infinitely increase the mental effort and strain involved with every single step. He was now inches away from the first few bodies and he knew that one false move would be all it would take to set off a deadly chain reaction throughout the enormous crowd.

Step by painful, dragging step he moved across the back lawn. Bodies stumbled past him, some even collided with him, and yet he forced himself to remain focussed and not to panic. He wanted to run. He wanted to kick and punch at the bloody corpses all around him and smash his way through to the generator. This was like playing with fire. The mental pain was like being forced to lie down in scalding hot water and not move. Each second was agony, but every alternative was worse.

Another cadaver lurched into his path. For a fraction of a second he allowed himself to look into its cold and clouded eyes before quickly looking down at the ground. He winced with repulsion as the body crashed into him, and he instinctively lifted his hands to protect himself. The body's torso was weak and rotten. His hands pushed effortlessly through the creature's decayed flesh and into the chest cavity. Biting down on his lip to stop himself from shouting out in disgust, he carefully pulled himself free and carried on towards the generator.

Four meters to go. The wind was cold and the air damp with spitting rain but Michael didn't care. Three meters, then two meters. Almost there. With numb, trembling hands he reached out for the door handle. Resisting the temptation to increase his speed by even a fraction, he pulled open the door and disappeared inside. The gusting wind caught the door and slammed it shut behind him and he cursed the noise which rang out through the silence like a gunshot.

There was a torch in the shed which they had purposely left there for emergencies. Using the dull light from its dying bulb he scanned the machine's control panel. It had been days since they had used the generator, and he prayed that it would work tonight. He remembered Carl's instructions (he'd taught both Michael and Emma to operate the system) and began to prime the machine. He looked up and saw through the flapping door (which constantly opened and shut in the wind) that there were bodies all around. He flicked the switch to start the generator and, as it coughed and spluttered and failed, every last one of the bodies he could see immediately turned and began to walk towards the shed. He tried the generator again and, again, it died. Once more and the same response. Terrified and unable to think straight, he tried the machine for a forth time. It finally burst into life and began to chug and thump reassuringly. Clouds of dirty fumes billowed up into the swirling night air.

All around the house and throughout the surrounding countryside, approximately one and a half thousand bodies began to move towards the mechanical noise. Over fifteen hundred bodies staggered towards Michael.

There was no time to think. He kicked open the door and ran back towards the house, fighting his way through a thick sea of clumsy bodies. He kicked and punched and powered through to the back door which he lunged towards. As he tugged and pulled at the handle more than a dozen pairs of twisted, rotting hands grabbed at him, catching hold of his hair, his clothes, his shoulders and his legs and arms. He screamed and writhed to free himself but it was useless. He could struggle free from the grip of one corpse, only to be caught by countless others. He began to feel himself being pulled back into the disease-ridden crowd.

'Michael!' he heard Emma scream. He looked up and saw that she was on the other side of the back door. She was pushing at the door, struggling to open it against the sheer volume of sickly cadavers outside. Michael managed to shuffle a couple of steps to his right and get one arm back inside the building. With a strength and determination that she had never before possessed, Emma grabbed hold of him and dragged him back into the house. A body was pulled inside with him and, while Michael kicked and punched at the wretched thing, Emma slammed the door shut, severing an emaciated arm in the process.

The body on the floor stopped moving momentarily and Michael crouched down, struggling to catch his breath.

'Okay?' Emma asked, shouting to make herself heard over the noise coming from the frenzied crowd outside.

He nodded.

'Think so,' he gasped.

She turned to look out of the window in the door. The small pane of glass was filled with a mass of dark, dangerous shadows, every last one of them clamouring to get inside.

'We need to...' Michael began before being interrupted by another noise, this time from the front of the house. He looked at Emma for a split-second before standing up and running down the hallway.

It was Carl.

'Shit!' Michael yelled to Emma. 'What's he doing?'

The two survivors watched helplessly as their friend unlocked the front door. He lifted his hand to the latch and then stopped and turned to look over his shoulder when he heard the others approaching.

'Ready?' Carl asked, grinning with excitement and misguided anticipation. His face was grotesque and almost unrecognisable. Already scratched, bloodied and bruised, his features were distorted further by the dark shadows of the besieged house. He seemed blissfully unaware of what was waiting for him on the other side of the door.

'Fucking hell,' Michael gasped, 'he's going to open it! He's lost it. He's completely fucking lost it!'

Emma was rooted to the spot with fear. She couldn't move or even think. Her lips formed silent words of desperation and terror.

Carl lifted up the rusty rifle they had found and smiled again at Michael.

'Come on, Mike,' he yelled. 'We'll have them. You and me'll have the fucking lot of them!'

Michael could hear the bodies fighting to get into the house with a new found purpose and ferocity. He was about to try and talk to Carl and make him understand when he opened the door.

'Get upstairs now!' he screamed at Emma. He grabbed hold of her arm and half-dragged, half-threw her up the staircase. He followed close behind but stopped and turned back when he was only a couple of steps up.

Blissfully unaware, Carl opened the door fully and, for a single second which seemed to last longer than ten, nothing happened. A moment of stillness and unexpected calm which was suddenly shattered by a tidal wave of rotting flesh and bone which powered into the house. The force of the surge was such that Carl was lifted clean off his feet and smashed against the nearest wall. In seconds the hallway was filled and Carl had completely disappeared from view, swallowed up and destroyed by the vast and unstoppable crowd.

Turning quickly, Michael ran up the stairs after Emma. She was hiding in Carl's attic bedroom. He slammed the door shut behind him.

'Get the fucking bed!' he screamed. 'Help me push it in front of the door.'

Taking one end each, the two of them shunted the heavy wooden bed down the length of the room and turned it sideways so that it completely blocked the door.

'Where's Carl?' Emma asked, although she already knew the answer. Michael didn't bother to reply. He ran over to the window and looked out. The bedroom was at the front of the house. It was dark but he could make out their Landrover and car in the yard below.

'We've got to get out,' he said, his voice trembling with emotion. 'I've still got the keys to the Landrover...'

'But what about our stuff? Christ, all our stuff's...'

'Forget it,' he snapped.

'But how are we going to get out? We can't just...'

Michael ignored Emma's questions. He opened the window and leant outside. A few of the bodies below caught sight of him and their ferocity seemed to increase when he stepped out onto the roof.

'Follow me,' he said, turning back momentarily to face Emma.

She walked over to the window and looked down.

'I can't...' she whined.

'You've got to. You haven't got any choice.'

Fighting to stay calm and in control of her body and emotions, she watched as Michael carefully shuffled around and lowered himself down along the slanted roof until his feet were resting in the guttering. Lying flat with his stomach pressed against the tiles, he shuffled sideways until he was directly above the porch. Once there he stopped and looked up at the bedroom window again.

'Come on,' he hissed. Emma looked at him and then looked down at the mass of bodies in the yard. More and more of them were reacting to Michael's voice. Unsure, she climbed up onto the windowsill and tentatively put one foot outside. Moving painfully slowly, she then lowered herself down until she was hanging out of the window. She stopped again, paralysed with fear.

'You can do it!' Michael yelled, sensing her unease. He prayed that she couldn't sense his.

He lowered himself down the last few feet onto the roof of the porch and then stood still for a moment to regain his balance. He glanced down at the shifting sea of figures below and saw that he was now close enough to be able to see the faces of the hundreds of corpses gathered around the house. Just meters away from his feet an endless column of creatures struggled to force themselves into the building.

Emma still clung tightly onto the windowsill for dear life, too afraid to move. A sound from inside the house distracted her and she looked back through the open bedroom window to see that the bed blocking the door was being shoved out of the way. The volume of bodies that had entered the house was astonishing. It was the sheer mass of cadavers that was forcing the door open.

As she watched a thick and constant stream of featureless figures began to pour into the room.

'Move!' Michael screamed, distracting her. She looked down and watched as he dropped from the roof of the porch onto the yard below. It was a drop of some ten feet and he landed awkwardly amongst the bodies, twisting his ankle. Ignoring the pain and the clumsy, grabbing hands which reached out for him, he forced his way over to the Landrover and unlocked the door. Kicking and punching at the corpses holding onto him, he fought his way inside and started the engine.

Another new sound meant another surge of bodies, this time all heading towards Michael.

Emma looked up. The bodies in the bedroom were close. She had to move. She stretched her legs out behind and lay on the sloping roof, moving her toes constantly, hoping to feel the guttering and use it for support. She followed Michael's route across the roof and then stopped when she was above the porch. Distracted by the light in the yard coming from the Landrover's headlamps which Michael had just switched on, she watched in horror and disbelief as he began to drive away.

'Michael!' she screamed.

She watched the Landrover as it moved away from the house. Michael slowly steered it back round in a wide arc, finally stopping when he was as close as he could get to the front of the house and the porch. For a fraction of a second Emma thought that he was going to leave her behind.

She dropped down onto the roof of the porch and caught her foot on a loose slate which crashed to the ground beneath her. Unsteadied, she struggled to regain her balance and lurched forward. As she desperately fought to grab hold of something solid to hang onto, more slates worked free under her weight and she fell down to the yard, the mass of bodies breaking her fall. Within seconds she was completely engulfed.

Michael jumped out of the Landrover and dived into the crowd surrounding Emma. He grabbed her by the scruff of her neck and yanked her free, pushing her towards the Landrover which she dived into. She slid across to the passenger seat and then reached out for him. She took hold of his right hand which he held out and pulled him towards her. But the collective strength of the creatures was too much and they took him from her, dragging him down onto the ground.

Michael sensed that he was about to die.

But fucking hell, he thought, he'd survived so much, why the hell should he give up now? And even more importantly perhaps, he knew that he couldn't leave Emma to suffer alone. With the very last dregs of energy that he could summon from his frightened and exhausted body, he scrambled to his feet and kicked and punched at the figures around him. He reached inside the van, grabbed hold of the steering wheel and pulled himself in. He yanked the door shut behind him, leaving countless carcasses to smash their decaying fists against the metal and glass.

'Ready?' he asked breathlessly.

Emma nodded and swallowed hard.

Michael forced the van into gear and lifted his foot off the clutch. For one desperate moment it seemed that the volume of bodies surrounding the Landrover might prove too much for it to overcome. The engine roared but it did not move. He accelerated again, this time increasing the power steadily until the engine screamed to be released. With one sudden, juddering movement they began to edge forward, carving a bloody passage away from their home and out through the rotting masses.

Emma glanced back over her shoulder at what remained of Penn Farm. Through her tears she could already see that the farmhouse was now little more than an empty shell. There were dark, shadowy figures moving at every window.

Epilogue
Michael Collins

We drove for hours, only stopping once in all that time to siphon more fuel from a crashed car on a deserted stretch of road.

We gave up for the night when I couldn't keep awake to drive any longer. We'd been following a twisting road which led along one exposed edge of a high mountain valley when I spotted an empty car park. Emma didn't want to drive. We decided to rest.

I parked the car, stopped the engine and got out. A stupid thing to do, perhaps, but it didn't seem to matter anymore. If any bodies were near by (and I couldn't see any) then what could they do to us? What could they take from us? We had nothing and we could lock ourselves into the Landrover if we needed to.

We were in a beautiful place, and for a short time nothing seemed to matter. The moon was high and proud in the sky and the night was still. Across the valley a steep, jagged mountain-face climbed away from us. It was as remote and inhospitable a place as we could have hoped to find.

'You alright?' Emma asked as she walked round to stand next to me. I nodded and instinctively pulled her close. The warmth of her body was comforting.

'Want to keep going?' she asked me suddenly.

'Don't know,' I answered truthfully. 'Do you?'

She shrugged her shoulders.

'Is there any point?'

'There's got to be somewhere we can go,' I said. 'Somewhere they can't get to. Another Penn Farm...'

I looked down into her face and stopped talking. She was half-smiling, and her expression seemed to be telling me that although she really did want to believe me, she didn't. Tears of pain and frustration began to roll down her delicate cheeks from her tired eyes.

In silence we clambered into the back of the Landrover together and lay there on the floor, holding each other tightly.

'We'll be okay,' I heard myself say.

She smiled briefly and then buried her head in my chest.

We had nothing left to lose but our lives. We lay there in the darkness and waited for morning.

FOLLOW THE COMPLETE AUTUMN STORY IN THE BEST-SELLING NOVELS

AUTUMN: THE CITY

AUTUMN: PURIFICATION

AUTUMN: THE HUMAN CONDITION

ALSO AVAILABLE FROM DAVID MOODY

STRAIGHT TO YOU
and
TRUST

All books available in paperback and a wide range of ebook formats from Infected Books

For more information visit:

www.djmoody.co.uk

www.theinfected.co.uk

www.infectedbooks.co.uk

Printed in the United States
87819LV00001B/4-39/A

9 780955 005107